SEDUCED BY DARKNESS

Also by Delilah Devlin

Fiction
INTO THE DARKNESS

SEDUCED BY DARKNESS

Delilah Devlin

AVON

An Imprint of HarperCollinsPublishers

HarperCollins books may be purchased for educational, business, or sales
promotional use. For information please write: Special Markets Department,
HarperCollins Publishers, 10 East 53rd Street, New York, NY 10022.

FIRST EDITION

Designed by Diahann Sturge

Library of Congress Cataloging-in-Publication Data

Devlin, Delilah.
    Seduced by darkness / Delilah Devlin. —1st ed.
      p. cm.
    ISBN: 978-0-06-116124-7 (pbk.)
    1. Vampires—Fiction. 2. New Orleans (La.)—Fiction. I. Title.
    PS3604.E88645S43 2008
    813'.6—dc22   2007043161

08 09 10 11 12   OV/RRD   10 9 8 7 6 5 4 3 2 1

This book is for Connor and Kelly,
whom I love unconditionally
and who love me despite my obsession.

ACKNOWLEDGMENTS

Special thanks to my friend Layla Chase who taught me "the rules" but only sighs now when I break them!

Thanks to my critique partners and dear friends for adding polish to this story and supporting me: Megan Kerans, Jo-Ann Power, and Mary Fechter.

More thanks to "Team Delilah," my friends and readers who root for me even when I'm stepping off the ledge: Patti, Erin, Heather, Sharon, Jenn, Rocky, and Serena.

And kisses for my biggest fan: I love you, Mom!

CHAPTER

I

His brother had thought Hell a fiery abyss, but Nicolas Montfaucon knew better. It was wet, smelled like a sewer, and sounded like the rush of collective hopes draining toward the sea.

With a heartbeat as leaden as his footfalls, he followed the sound of flowing water. His rubber boots sank in the rain-soaked grass as he stepped off the cemetery's entrance road to head toward the water's edge. Bayou St. John's previous sluggish ambience had given way to a torrent in the aftermath of the storm. Just as the security team had reported, the waters that breached the levee in the early morning hours spilled into the bayou, raising it well above any thousand-year flood plain.

They couldn't have planned for a worse scenario. The mausoleum lay in the center of a newly etched basin.

A cold, tight knot of horror settled in his gut, numbing him to the elements, while a soft rain fell like God's kiss of benediction before the coming battle. The prickling unease lifting the hair on the back of his neck was familiar, but one he hadn't experienced to this degree since the searing heat and biting sand of Palestine over seven hundred years ago.

Quiet, muffled voices drew him deeper into the cemetery. He followed the blurred edges of a once pristine graveled path, now strewn with long tangled strands of Spanish moss and broken tree branches, around sturdy stone crypts— ones untouched by the raging storm that had drenched New Orleans and changed its landscape irrevocably.

He glanced toward the dark gray clouds giving his team cover for what they must do. At least God hadn't added one more insurmountable burden to overcome this day.

"Erika, Pasqual?" he called softly as he approached.

They turned with dread tightening their pale faces.

He noted their quick sideways glances and knew their loyalties might be tested. Just the night before one quarry had escaped their net. Did they know his role in the deception that had allowed the newest Born female to flee?

"The crypt is submerged," Pasqual said, nodding ahead toward the swollen bayou.

Nicolas followed his gaze and found the winged angel that graced the top of the Morel mausoleum, the bottom edge of her robe licked by foaming, lapping waves of dark water.

"We brought a pirogue," Erika said, shivering despite the humid heat, "but the water's so swift . . ."

Nicolas nodded. "I'll go. We'll have to tie off the boat on both sides of the bayou to keep it from being swept away."

"The crypt was solid. The doors were chained," Pasqual said, his voice strained. "Do you really think he could have escaped?"

Nicolas's lips curved and tightened. "His sarcophagus was in the center of the cemetery. The bayou jumped its banks and carved a new path—straight through his prison. Do you think that's coincidental?"

Erika's brown eyes looked overlarge in her slender face. "How will we contain him?"

"If the doors are still locked, we'll wait for the waters to subside to discover whether his coffin remains intact."

"If they aren't locked?" she continued.

He shrugged. "Then we prepare ourselves."

"How do we do that?" she asked, a note of hysteria in her brittle voice. "No one's got a standard operating procedure for the end of the fucking world."

"Someone has to go into the water," Pasqual said quietly, his expression dark and troubled.

"I said I'll go," Nicolas said, straightening his shoulders. "I placed him there. It's my duty to make sure he stays."

"Not alone, you won't."

Nicolas turned at the sound of another voice, one familiar and welcome.

A tall dark-clad figure stepped from behind a large oak.

Nicolas wondered if he'd just arrived or had chosen the most dramatic moment to appear. Simon Jameson's long brown hair was plastered against his skull and touched the tops of broad shoulders clothed in a rain slicker.

"Simon, bad news travels fast," Nicolas said, his tone dry.

Despite the dire circumstance that brought him here, Simon smiled. "A little bird told me we had trouble."

Nicolas raised a single brow at the thought of the mage's familiar braving the remnants of the storm. "Her wings must be sodden."

Simon's lips crimped in the semblance of a smile. "She's tired and drying off." Then his gaze turned to the sunken crypt. "I'll go with you. You may have need of me."

"I'll be glad for the company." Whatever the reason for the falling out between the powerful mage and the leader of the vampire *sabat*, Nicolas held no grudge against Simon. Their acquaintance was older, forged in blood and battle. "I'd appreciate any help you can provide."

Sloshing footsteps sounded behind them as more of the security team arrived, carrying a long, slender flat-bottomed boat and poles.

Using ropes suspended between the trees, Simon and Nicolas fought the swift current to drag the boat toward the stone angel. Once the boat scraped the spikes atop the iron fence surrounding the crypt, Nicolas stripped, dropping his clothing to the bottom of the boat. Then he tied a rope around his waist and said a quick prayer.

"Hold this in your mouth," Simon said, slipping a carved, polished red stone from his pocket. "You'll need your hands free."

Nicolas didn't question why he should keep a rock in his mouth. If his friend thought it necessary, that was enough for him to know. Likely a protective amulet, anyway. He could use all the help he could get.

Urgency and dread filled him. He had to see the damage below the surface of the black water for himself. He set the cold stone on top of his tongue and clamped his mouth closed. Then he lowered himself over the side of the boat, gripping it hard, shocked by the force of the water dragging at his body. Nicolas clutched the edge of the pirogue and shot Simon a glance.

The mage stood in the bottom of the boat, coiling the rope around his brawny fists and arms, and nodded. "Catch hold of the iron bars, and I'll let out the rope."

Out of instinct, rather than need, Nicolas drew in a deep breath through his nostrils and submerged. The dark water roiled around him, battering him with stones and debris. He forced open his eyes against the current and grimy sediments, but could see only a few inches in front of his face.

For long seconds he held his breath then made himself relax against the urge to gasp. He didn't really need the air to live.

The current slammed him against the iron bars surrounding the crypt. He held tight then circled the fence, handhold by handhold, until he felt the gate's hinges. With his feet against the gate, he bent his legs and made a powerful thrust, which propelled him forward in the eddying waters, toward the door of the crypt.

He reached out, grabbing for the carved edge of the stone door frame and followed it downward to the latch. Where a heavy chain should have wrapped around the mechanism, he found only a drooping handle, bobbing with the current.

Still, the door was closed.

He braced his feet against it and pulled with all his strength to bend the handle upward and lock it closed until he could return with another chain.

At that moment, a dull pounding came from inside, then a powerful thrust slammed open the door, tossing him backward into the current, which swept him toward the gate.

Despite the murky water, he saw a pale, ghostly apparition appear in the entrance of the crypt.

Sweet Mother of God! Nicolas bit down around the stone that threatened to lodge at the back of his throat.

The monster swam in the doorway, his mouth opening in a hideous grin.

Nicolas ground his heels against the iron bars and pushed forward again, launching himself toward the demon to drive him back inside. If he had to hold him there for an eternity, he'd never let him out. He'd uphold his oath—one given over the grisly remains of his wife.

When he barreled into the demon, the creature's body felt . . . less than solid . . . gelatinous. The pale flesh gave way beneath Nicolas's grasping hands. His torso disintegrated in rotten bits of flesh, tugged apart by the rapid current.

Nicolas screamed around the stone while his hand reached through the disintegrating body to grasp the demon's spinal cord.

The beast's face remained solid for only a moment longer

while his grin turned triumphant, mocking Nicolas, before the skin stripped away to reveal a skeletal grimace.

Nicolas squeezed his eyes shut as he let go his fierce grip on what remained of the demon's prison, his body, trying to forget the familiar face the monster had stolen and worn for centuries—his brother's.

1307
Poitiers, France

The heavy wooden door splintered beneath the force of a short log wielded like a battering ram. Once they breached the door, the soldiers dropped it to the floor and flooded into the small cell, surrounding Nicolas and his brother Armand before they had a chance to reach for their swords.

"Haut les mains! Raise your hands!" The shout was shrill. The soldiers looked ready for battle, hands gripping their swords so tight their knuckles gleamed white in the pale morning light sifting through the narrow cell window.

Nicolas almost smiled. These soldiers were green as saplings if two sleeping, unarmed men could frighten them so. Perhaps they believed the rumors.

Nicolas swallowed and gave his brother a quick nod, raising his hands slowly above his head. They'd been warned a plot was afoot to arrest the brethren from The Order.

Days earlier, Armand had scoffed at the idea. Who would dare touch God's Knights?

"Why are you doing this?" his brother asked, his voice strong and calm.

Nicolas knew Armand's faith led him to believe God would intervene, but Nicolas had heard the rumblings. The Templars' wealth was incentive enough for those who coveted and feared their power. King Philip had long whispered in the ear of the Pope, raising specters of demon worshipers and heresy to foment hatred for the warrior monks.

"In the name of the king, you are under arrest for the crimes of heresy, devil worship, and sexual perversions."

Nicolas snorted, earning a savage kick from the sapling nearest him. Stubbornly, he refused to bend to the pain and aimed a narrowed glance at his attacker.

"Brother, do not test their will," Armand said. "All will be sorted out. This is a mistake."

Only the mistake landed them in another sort of cell for months—a dungeon cellblock inhabited by a dozen of their brother knights. Subjected to vicious tortures that left their bodies permanently purple with bruises, sleeping in their own feces, and near starvation, most of the knights despaired of ever being set free. One had taken his own life.

"Think you now that God will intervene?" Nicolas asked his brother. Past despair, past all hope, he knew they were both doomed to die—burned at the stake for their refusal to confess. Armand because his faith would not allow him; Nicolas because he could not allow his brother to die alone.

"This is a test. We must remain strong. Didn't the Lord answer us at Damiette?"

That Damiette had been taken and lost repeatedly during a Crusade nearly fifty years ago didn't seem to diminish

Armand's faith. He'd been raised on the stories of the exploits of the Templars.

Unwilling to tear the curtain of belief from his brother's eyes, Nicolas rolled his head against the damp, mossy stone of the cell wall. "If this is a test, then I have failed," he muttered. "I promised our father I would keep you safe."

"Father trusted our devotion would lead us to glory. By our steadfastness, we have already earned our passage through St. Peter's gates."

Nicolas held grave doubts that this was true. In the name of God, they'd been exhorted to commit gruesome retributions against the heathen Saracens. He kept his thoughts to himself so as not to upset his brother or give fodder to their inquisitors. How easy it would be to end their torment—a simple confession of crimes, however ludicrous, would earn him peace.

"You're cold. Share my blanket." Armand huddled closer and lifted his flea-ridden blanket to drape it around both their shoulders.

For this alone, Nicolas remained. For his brother, whom he loved more than his own life. They'd never been apart.

"I'm not a fool, you know," Armand whispered. "I do know there is little hope we will live, Nic."

"Then why not give them the words they want? Confess!" Nicolas leaned close and curved his fingers into Armand's thigh. "Let them punish us to cleanse our souls," he pleaded. "Then we will be free."

His brother's tired smile gleamed brightly in the torchlight. "Perhaps you should do it, Nic."

Nicolas's throat closed, and he gave a violent shake of his head. "Not without you. I will never abandon you," he said, his voice hoarse.

"Then we will be together always, brother."

Present Day

Fresh from her shower, Chessa heard the heavy knock and glanced at her clock on the bedside stand. Still an hour before she had to be at work.

Not the super. She'd paid her rent. Besides, he'd fled with the rest of the building's inhabitants when the Mayor ordered evacuation.

And not her partner seeing whether she wanted to get a cup of coffee before reporting to duty. Her partner wasn't coming today.

Or ever again.

Curious, she threaded through piles of discarded clothing to her front door and peered through the peephole into a hallway lit only by grayish, pre-dusk light from the landing window. The power had gone out sometime during the night. Just one more annoyance on top of the last hellish twenty-four hours.

A familiar man stood on her threshold. Broad shoulders, long dark hair—her body clenched. "Nic?" What was he doing in the city again so soon? How the hell had he gotten in? She'd heard most of the roads around the city were closed due to flooding.

"Chessa, open the door."

Something in his voice had her gripping the doorknob tight. Her chest tightened. She didn't want to know what brought him here.

"Please," he said, weariness and raw, aching need flavoring the rich timbre of his voice.

Although they'd sated their appetite for sex a few hours ago, Chessa's body softened instantly, heat tightening her womb. She hated the way her body betrayed her.

They'd said their farewells, she reminded herself. "We had a deal, Nic. You stick to your turf—I'll stick to mine."

"Chessa, open the goddamn door."

The "or else" he left unspoken in his lightly accented voice. She got the message and turned the knob, stepping aside to let him in as she wrapped her towel tightly around her body.

A quick, sweeping glance told her there was trouble. Big, fat vampire trouble. Nicolas looked a mess.

His long black-brown hair hung in damp, curling tendrils around his lean face. His exposed skin was grimy-looking, and he smelled of sewage and sour swamp water.

His hands reached for her.

Without time to sidestep, she found herself smashed against his chest, his strong hands clutching her close.

She leaned back in the circle of his arms and stared into his face. What she saw troubled her. His jaw was clenched tight, and his face was unnaturally pale—even by a vampire's standards. "What's happened?"

His throat tightened, but he shook his head and lowered it.

Only she'd just had a shower, and he stunk to high heaven. Besides, she needed space to calm the riot of feelings he aroused.

Ones she was still uncomfortable acknowledging even existed. She pressed her palms against his chest to halt him.

She loved Rene. Although he'd chosen to enter a mage's sanctuary with another Born vampire, Chessa wasn't over him yet.

Her feelings for Nicolas were strictly carnal—and she needed to get her libido back under control. Unbridled passion had been unleashed by proximity to Natalie Lambert's coming into season, as only a transforming Born could inspire. That arousal had spilled over onto Chessa and Nicolas—it was the only explanation Chessa would allow for the strength of the desire that even now made her body yearn toward his.

Nicolas's chest heaved, and his eyes narrowed to feral slits. "Don't deny me. Not now."

She wrinkled her nose. "You stink."

"Then *we'll* shower," he said, a dangerous edge to his voice.

As always, his first terse words had her melting. "Tell me why you're here," she said, searching for a way to put him off while she shored up her fading resistance.

Another shake of his head, this time sharp and violent. "Later," he ground out.

Then she noted the wildness in his eyes. Something had rattled his cage. Nicolas was never anything but completely in control. Chessa felt the last bit of solid ground crumble beneath her. "All right," she said softly and held up a hand to ward off a kiss. "But shower first." He'd have to let her go to follow her.

However, Nicolas wasn't giving her the space she needed to regroup. He grabbed the top of her towel and ripped it away, then slammed his mouth on hers, backing her toward the bed-room.

Chessa's bare feet skidded on her wood floor as she dug in her heels, but he swept her along, through her bedroom into the bathroom, all the while punishing her lips with a brutal kiss.

When the edge of the tub brought them up short, he reached behind her and yanked aside the shower curtain. "Turn it on."

Dumbly, she reached behind her, fumbling to turn the knob, finally sending a spray of water that misted around them before he lifted her above the rim of her tub to set her inside.

Nicolas tore at his clothes, dropping them at his feet, then stepped beside her in the stall, crowding her against the cool tile walls. "Any more objections?" he asked, in his oddly rasp-ing voice.

She shook her head, overwhelmed and mute with rising desire. Her body already strained toward his. Her breasts swelled, her nipples beading tight and hard. Her legs trem-bled, and her sex released a trickle of fragrant moisture she couldn't deny.

His hands reached around her and grasped her bottom, lift-ing her off her feet, crushing her breasts to his chest, her mons against the base of his rigid cock.

With his erection pressing into her belly, any objection was obliterated. She flung out her arms and gripped his shoulders, aiding him as he angled her body toward his and thrust his cock between her legs.

Chessa groaned as he slid inside her. "Bastard, we had a deal."

His response was a flex of his hips to thrust hard inside her, tunneling deep, pressing higher until the strength of his hips and cock had her feet dangling above the porcelain bottom of the tub.

When he'd reached inside her as far as he could, he wrapped his arms around her, squeezing away her breath and laid his cheek alongside hers, his chest heaving.

She shivered from arousal so strong it nearly choked her and from fear of whatever had shaken Nicolas to his core. She'd never seen him like this. "What is it? What's happened?"

His head drew away, and his gaze burned as it slid to her lips. "Later," he groaned.

Again, the wildness in his gaze and the tension that gripped his broad shoulders and arms as he held her unsettled her. This wasn't Nicolas with his sardonic quips and ever-watchful gaze. Accustomed of late to him showing up at unexpected times to tempt her, this was different.

He was frightened.

Although tempted to argue, to chide him and try to drive him away, she wound her arms around his neck, her legs around his waist, and pulled him close, dragging his head down to bury against her shoulder.

If she were honest with herself, she was glad he'd come.

Not that she was ready to be anybody's rock. She had problems of her own. A life to sort out. One far away from the vampire enclave at *Ardeal*.

Nicolas was entrenched in that life, but she had broken free decades ago and vowed she'd never go back. Whatever was bothering him now wasn't her problem.

But she could hold him and let his warmth and strength provide her comfort as well. She had her own needs and a desolate loneliness that had filled her when she'd shut her apartment door hours earlier and realized the only friend she had in the world was lost to her forever.

"Stop thinking," he growled.

"Just fuck me," she bit out, meeting his hard gaze with a glare of her own.

Their hips churned against each other in a desperate coupling. Not at all the sexy, teasing pummeling she'd come to expect—that in itself was an indication of his upset. His movements lacked finesse. He gave no thought for her pleasure, which he was always so careful to draw out—torturing her with her own desire.

Instead, his hands gripped her ass hard, pushing her up and down his cock, grinding her back against the cool tiles as he powered into her.

When he came, his eyes squeezed tight, his body grew rigid, and he held his breath for one endless moment. After his pulsing release waned, he dropped his forehead against the tiles. "Get out."

Surprised at the harshness of his voice, she didn't question him, just unwound her legs from his waist and slid down his body. She stepped out of the tub to dry herself with a towel while he remained inside, drawing the curtain closed behind him.

She couldn't think of a thing to say. Despite the steamy air inside the room, she shivered.

Damn. It sure as hell felt like she cared about the fact he'd tossed her out of her own shower.

CHAPTER

2

Nicolas pressed his hands flat on the cool tiles and knocked his forehead on the wall.

He'd screwed up. He'd come for comfort when he knew she was only capable of giving sex. If she wasn't already running for the door, she'd be ready to throw him out on his ass.

One look at her wary, green eyes and he'd lost it. Her black hair still dripped where the ends lay on top of her shoulders, rivulets trickling down her pale chest. Naked, except for the lush towel that encircled her lithe, trim body, and freshly fragrant from her shower, he'd pressed relentlessly inside.

His sly, carefully orchestrated plan to seduce her lay in tatters. He'd watched and waited for her for so long, finally stepping in when she was at low ebb and needful of his particular brand of kink. When her partner had succumbed to Natalie's sweet first bite, the handwriting had been on the wall, but stubborn little Chessa was nothing if not pig-headed. She'd held out the hope of Rene resisting the allure of the virgin vamp. Even resorting to seducing them both rather than abandon her carefully laid plans.

Chessa thought herself in love with Rene Broussard and grieved for his loss. Nicolas had made himself convenient, but had been careful never to let her see his need for her, treating their loving with a nonchalance he was far from feeling. He'd discovered her need for submission, sensing it the first time he'd let his anger over her obsession with Rene get the best of him. Chessa had melted like warm chocolate when he'd striped her ass that first time, begging him for release until her voice had grown hoarse.

Tonight, he'd managed to fuck everything up. He'd bared his emotions, letting her see past the carefully constructed mask.

The smell of the murky bayou choked him. He swallowed bile that rose up to scald the back of his bruised throat. *Dieu!* He'd fucked her with sewage still clinging to his skin.

Nicolas reached for a bottle of bath gel and tipped it over his chest and shoulders—better to smell like gardenias than death. First, he'd clean up, and then he'd see whether he was back at square one with Chessa.

Beyond his need to slake himself on her body and make things as right as they could be between them, he needed her on his team.

*   *   *

Her body still humming, Chessa roamed her bedroom, the question of whether to dress or not revolving in her mind. Yesterday, she would have dressed and snuck out the door, giving him the unmistakable message she was no one's doormat.

However, the room was stuffy and hot without air-conditioning or a fan to stir a breeze, and she still ached with unfulfilled lust. She stretched on top of her bed and shoved a pillow under her head to raise it and watch the door for when Nicolas left the bathroom. He'd brought her this far, he'd damn well finish the job.

She bent her knees and let one drop lazily to the mattress, then raised it again—an indolent wag that kept her mind from racing around the possibilities that had brought him here.

Not that she was ready to be sucked into whatever hellish quest he was on at the moment. Chessa was just curious.

And horny.

Smoothing a hand over her knees, she scraped over the scabs of the rug burns he'd left on her knees the previous night when he'd taken her ruthlessly on a hotel room floor. Right after Rene had followed Natalie through a time portal.

She thought about Rene and Nat again. A subject she'd been avoiding. That last moment when the couple had stepped through the glowing vertical pool, their hands clasped, their expressions had been happy—at peace with their decision to leave this world behind.

However tonight, the hollow ache in her chest didn't seem quite as empty as before.

The bathroom door creaked, and Nicolas strode out, droplets of water gleaming on his naked skin.

Did he have to be so damn beautiful? He was a walking, breathing sex god from the tops of his broad shoulders to his ripped abs and muscled thighs. She'd wanted to make Rene her fuck buddy—her love puppy—and keep him on a short leash. Nicolas wanted to hold the lead with her. Didn't he realize she was Born?

"You could have used a towel," she groused, trying to tamp down her instant reaction to his body. No use letting him know just the sight of him was enough to soak her panties—if she'd been wearing any. "You're dripping all over my floor."

One dark eyebrow rose, mocking her in his usual fashion—and raising her blood pressure. "I think it hardly matters, Princess. This place is a mess."

Relieved he'd regained his composure, she gave him a slow grin and let her knee drop to the mattress, exposing her pussy fully to his interested gaze. She trailed a finger along the inner curve of her thigh, stopping just short of the curls covering her sex.

His chest rose. His jaw tightened.

When his gaze settled between her legs, Chessa teased him with a swirl of her fingertips, dipping just inside her cunt.

His cock jerked, rousing at the juncture of his thighs.

Chessa pulled back the hood guarding her clitoris and gave the little knot a scrape with her thumbnail. Just enough to make her breath catch—just enough to draw him closer.

He crawled onto the end of the bed and gripped her ankles, then roughly jerked her legs wide apart.

Chessa gasped and her nipples ripened, drawing into exquisitely tight little points. This was the Nicolas who made her burn. The one whose attentions she found impossible to deflect.

He bent and kissed her knees. "You're healing nicely," he murmured. "I'll have to keep you off them for a while." His gaze burned a trail up her legs, following the curve of her thigh to stare at her sex. "Have I ever told you that you have a pretty pussy, Chessa?"

She gave him a narrowed glance. He never gave her compliments.

"Next time, shave it."

Her breath huffed and she played at trying to close her legs, but he held them firm in his strong grasp. His head descended, and his breath swept her moist sex, heating her up, causing more liquid excitement to trickle from her cunt.

When his mouth opened wide and drew on her lips, her hips rolled, pressing closer, urging him deeper.

However, he seemed content to nibble and lick—sexy little forays that did little more than tease and raise her temperature. His tongue stroked over her outer labia, wetting her curls, then lapped the tender flesh between the dual lips, tasting her, seeming to savor her flavor since he came back for more.

Chessa gripped his hair in both hands and tried to center him, aiming his head over her opening.

He resisted, turning his head to nip her inner thigh. "When *I've* had enough, Chessa."

But she couldn't take any more. He'd primed her in the shower, left her aching and empty.

Her fingers released their grip on his hair and swept over her breasts, squeezing them, pinching her nipples as her belly tightened and trembled. Her hips ground up and down, seeking penetration, but when he didn't deliver, she decided to take it for herself and thrust her fingers between her legs, tangling them with his foraging lips and tongue.

He bit her index finger, then stroked it, tip to knuckle.

Encouragement enough. She slid it farther down and thrust it inside herself while his mouth coaxed her palm aside to suckle on her clit.

God, that was it. Just a little more. Her hips slowed, savoring the rise. Her breaths deepened, her sighs turning into moans.

Then his hand closed around hers and pushed it up her belly. His mouth left her, and he lifted his head. His face was tight, cheekbones honed with passion, his lush lips blurred and moist from her juices.

But his gaze frightened her, taking her beyond mere sensual thrill. This was why she'd stayed. Only he could reach inside to draw out her deepest fantasies, push every one of her sexual buttons to ignite a burst of super-heated lust.

Chessa held her breath, knowing her whole body shook in anticipation—something he couldn't miss.

She hated when she surrendered power. The harsh, drawn intensity of his expression told her he'd accept nothing less than total capitulation. Her eyelids fluttered down to close out the sight of him. *Coward!* "Please," she moaned.

His hands closed around her legs in a bruising grip and pushed them up and wider. "Hold them," he ground out.

With her breasts mashed beneath her thighs, her breaths came in short gusts, but she obeyed, gripping them tight, opening her eyes to watch his fierce expression.

His hands lifted her ass from the mattress, and he centered his thick cock at her entrance, staring down at her pussy for a long moment as he dipped inside. Then he glanced up to hold her gaze captive as he plunged forward, burying his cock in her cunt.

On his knees, he flexed his hips forward and back, thrusting hard, stroking her inner walls, cramming deep and swirling his hips to touch on the bundle of nerves inside her channel. Her G-whiz spot crackled and burned with electric excitement.

Chessa moaned, a thin, feminine sound she couldn't hold back. Moisture gushed from her inner walls, coating his shaft, easing his entry as he withdrew and stroked back inside.

He leaned over her, bracing his weight on the backs of her thighs, using her resistance to keep him upright but off-balance to slam into her again and again.

Liquid seeped from inside her, soaking her sex. Each harsh stroke slapped noisily, wetly. Faster, harder, until he drove the breath from her lungs with the force.

When her orgasm slammed through her, her thighs stiffened, pressing him back. She let go of her legs and wrapped her ankles around his neck, clasping him tight.

His hands left her ass and caressed her legs, wide sweeps up and down as he continued to stroke inside, slowing as the pulsing spasms along her channel faded.

Finally, he reached around his neck and unhooked her ankles, urging her legs to the mattress. He stretched over her, a hand curving behind her neck to lift her head. His eyes glinted in the shadowy light.

Then he tilted his head, offering his blood.

Something she'd never shared with him. Something he'd noticed and commented on. Because to Chessa, drinking from someone who mattered was more intimate than sex.

"Drink from me," he whispered.

She'd resisted the temptation before, knowing the intimacy of the act would only tighten their bond. They lived worlds apart. A good thing, when she sensed he intended to breach every one of her walls. She wasn't ready to surrender too much of herself ever again.

"Drink," he rasped.

Her incisors slid down at his command. Their bodies still joined, she shivered, knowing he was asking her to cross a threshold in their relationship.

She murmured, nuzzled his neck, then opened wide to sink her teeth into the jugular vein pounding just under his skin. His salt and copper flavors filled her mouth, flooding her tongue, and she swallowed.

Better than cum, better than the musky flavor of his sweat-slick skin. He smelled of almonds, tasted of *Revenant—minion*. That's how Inanna, the leader of the coven, treated him—how she saw all of his kind.

But Chessa knew better because of the force of his personality, his intelligence, and strength of will.

Nicolas smelled and tasted like heaven.

He tasted like hers.

That thought jarred her back to reality. Her eyes slammed open and she disengaged her teeth, licking to close the twin wounds she'd made. He wasn't hers. He was just a convenient fuck.

She licked droplets of his blood from her lips and settled her head on the pillow to look up at him, trying to pretend he hadn't shaken her. "You didn't come."

His lips stretched slowly in a wicked grin. His eyes narrowed. "You know missionary isn't my thing."

She sucked in a deep breath. Nicolas liked it nasty.

Her vagina tightened around his cock as she realized he was far from through. He'd trained her better than Pavlov's dogs.

The trembling started again as her whole body tightened in anticipation. "I'm late for work." She tried to inject resentment in her voice, but even to her own ears, she sounded breathless, eager.

Nicolas leaned down, and his mouth opened over hers. Their tongues met first and dueled. Then Nicolas drew hers into his mouth and bit it, slicing deep with a razor-sharp fang. Blood seeped into their mouths. Only then did he seal his lips over hers, showing her this coupling wouldn't be gentle.

Their lips circled and ate. His tongue stabbed into her mouth, licking, scraping the tips of her sharp fangs, drawing his own blood to pool with hers.

Still supported by his large hand, Chessa's head rocked and her body undulated beneath his where she lay trapped, blanketed from chest to toes. His height and breadth thrilled her, overwhelmed her.

At last, he lifted his head and gave her lips a quick hard kiss. "Get on your belly," he said, dragging himself up and to the side.

"I thought you wanted me off my knees," she said, but turned and lay down on her stomach.

"I have another plan."

The mattress rose beside her and his bare feet padded on the wooden floor. Not far, to her dresser. Something scraped the dresser, then he was coming back.

She squealed when he gripped her legs and tugged her sharply toward the end of the bed, draping her hips over the edge.

She planted her feet on the floor. So this was how he'd take her.

"We'll need a pillow." He reached beyond her gaze to the top of the bed, snagged a pillow and stuffed it under her hips.

Forced onto her tiptoes, she felt less sure of his intent.

When the first sharp slap landed on her up-tilted bottom, she gasped, and then she released a deep sigh, curling her fingers into the bedding. He'd found her hairbrush. The flat side made a very satisfying crack.

He warmed the backs of her thighs and the fleshy globes of her ass with successive slaps.

At the beginning, she waited in breathless anticipation of each stroke. Gradually, she was squirming, groaning, lifting toward him. Finally, begging him out loud. Juiced, swollen, her pussy leaked fluids into the bedding beneath her. "Nic, my cunt. *Please, slap my cunt.*"

His hand rested on her bottom between strikes. Testing her warmth? But never glancing against the part of her weeping for attention.

A finger slid between her pussy lips. He brought it to her mouth and she licked it clean, tasting herself, tasting him. She tried to suck it into her mouth but he drew away.

Sharp, natural bristles swept her bottom. He parted her buttocks and scraped the bristles down the crease, raking over her asshole.

She jerked, her breath catching. She held her breath when he brushed the moist hairs covering her pussy, sweeping up, then down.

The brush landed on the bed beside her and then his lips pressed kisses to her ass, his tongue licked along the crevice, sliding over her sensitive little hole, then lower, to tuck inside her vagina.

Chessa's toes curved painfully as she pressed into the floor, trying to raise her buttocks higher.

His tongue flickered and stabbed until her pussy opened and closed, trying to pull him deeper.

His thumb traced the path upward and circled her hole. Reflexively, she tightened.

He made a tsking sound, telling her resistance would do her no good.

"Nic! God, please." But what did she want? For him to stop his torture? For him to take her cunt again?

Or did she crave it in the ass? He'd trained her to take his girth. Forced her past any inhibitions. He'd have her however he wished, and she'd love it.

One thick thumb pressed inward, easing past the circle of muscle that gripped him tight.

A ragged inhalation and she was poised, waiting for him to stretch her farther—well past comfortable, dipping into pain.

His tongue stroked over her clit, caressing the hood

stretched tight over the burgeoning knot. Still, he worked his thumb into her ass, circling his wrist to loosen the muscle.

Chessa sobbed and rubbed her nipples on the comforter. She needed more, needed him plunging inside her. "Jesus, Nic. Fuck me!"

He withdrew, rising behind her. His hands spread her buttocks, his thumbs pressing on either side of her asshole. Then the thick, blunt head of his cock nudged her there, pushing into her, stretching her. The tight ring of muscle held fast, resisting his entry. Spittle dropped into her crease and he rubbed his crown in it, and then pressed into her again.

"Breathe," he growled. "Let me in."

Chessa didn't realize she'd been holding her breath and let it out slowly, moaning when his cock pushed past the tight ring and entered her.

His hands bracketed her hips and lifted her higher and he angled his hips to deliver short glides forward and back, easing deeper into her until she was taking all of him.

Beyond thought, she was a trembling well of sensation. Almost every erogenous zone she had was stroked and caressed.

As he fucked in and out of her ass, her legs dangled, her bottom cushioned the slap of his lower belly, adding heat to the flesh he'd already warmed. He didn't just hold her still, he moved her forward and back, so that her breasts scraped the comforter. His balls banged against her pussy. Only her clit remained inviolate—but it swelled and ached.

His strokes sharpened, his hands gripped her ass hard. He was close. *God, so was she.*

"Not enough!" he rasped. "I need to touch you."

"Jesus, don't stop now."

"Come with me." He leaned over her, maintaining the connection, and pushed her toward the center of the bed. Then an arm hooked beneath her belly, raising her.

"What about my knees?"

"I'll get you pads," he growled. "Have to touch." Then his hands slid around her belly, smoothed down to reach between her legs, and he resumed his strokes.

Chessa drew a hissing breath. She didn't know how much more she could take. Then his fingers thrust inside her, his thumb scraped her clit, and her cunt convulsed.

The orgasm swept over her and her back arched, her bottom pressing deeper on his cock. His hand closed around her shoulder and pulled her up and she leaned her head on his shoulder as he bit deep.

His release was quieter than hers. His strokes shortened, quickened, and then he groaned against her neck.

Chessa heard it as darkness swept over, and she screamed.

Only Nicolas had ever made her scream.

Shadows lengthened in the room as Chessa slept. Nicolas checked his watch and set it on the nightstand. Time to wake her. Time to talk.

He knew what she'd say. It wasn't her problem.

How could he convince her that this was bigger than either of their histories? A monster was on the loose. She would think he'd primed her, using sex to get her to agree to join him. Chessa didn't trust anyone and would doubt his motives most.

Because she wanted a reason to send him away.

He rolled to his side and scooted closer to her back, tucking his knees behind hers, placing his arm around her stomach to pull her closer. "Chessa, wake up," he whispered into her ear.

"Mmmm . . ." She stirred and snuggled her butt closer, rubbing against his cock. She relaxed for a few moments longer, then jerked against him. "Shit! I fell asleep."

When she tried to bolt from the bed, he held her back. "We have to talk."

"Not now, Nic," she said pushing at his arm. "Don't you know we have a city under water? I only came home for a quick shower and a change of clothes."

"We've got bigger problems."

"What could possibly be bigger? We have thousands of people crowding into the Quarter, including rogue scum looking for prey. I have to be out there."

"The crypt was compromised."

Chessa sucked in a deep breath, her body going still. "Sounds like you're going to be busy," she said quietly.

Nicolas gritted his teeth. It was that or shake her. "I need you with me."

"You have a security team at your command. You don't need me."

"I need you on the council."

"Never." She bit the word out like a bullet.

"Inanna's too powerful. No one will stand up to her. She won't react well when she finds out."

She wriggled against him, trying to free herself. "Not . . . my . . . problem."

"That's what I thought you'd say," he said, sliding his thigh over hers to hold her still.

"Is this why you're here?" she asked, her voice rising.

"I need you."

She snorted. Her entire body lay stiff and resistant beneath his. "Obviously. Let me up."

"Chessa—" He stopped. She was too angry to listen. Perhaps he should give her a little time. "All right. I won't ask again." Nicolas squeezed her, and then kissed her shoulder. As soon as he removed his arm from her belly, she rolled from the bed to her feet in one fluid movement.

When she faced him, her expression was devoid of emotion. Her eyes glittered. "You got yours tonight. I got mine. Now, we keep to our own turf. *Like we agreed.*"

Rising on one elbow, he nodded. Give her space. Let her think. When all hell broke loose, she'd have to listen.

"I have to shower again. Lock the door behind you." She turned on her heel and strode to the bathroom, closing the door quietly behind her.

He wished she'd slammed it. If she blew hot, she'd come around sooner.

At a slow simmer, she'd give new meaning to stubborn.

CHAPTER
3

Chessa slammed a palm against the vending machine, jostling it, but not loosening the Coke hung up in the mechanism.

She cursed and gave it another slam, then heard a throat clear behind her.

"Go easy, Cheech. That's public property." Police Lieutenant Byron Williams stood behind her wearing a lopsided grin.

Chessa aimed a killing glare his way, but Byron didn't scare easily.

His smile widened in his dark face. "Wake up on the wrong side of the bed?"

Chessa let his comment slide, wincing inwardly at how close he'd nailed it. She'd mentored him when he was a rookie cop. She never commented on her private life—something he knew all too well. "Did May and the kids get out okay?"

Byron's smile dimmed, and he nodded. "They're staying with her parents in Baton Rouge."

"That has to be rough. Your house?"

Byron grimaced and shook his head. "Can't get out there. Word is the whole block's underwater. Guess I'll just have to wait and see." He fed the machine another dollar and his Coke pushed hers down. "Meantime, we gotta keep busy. The streets are gettin' meaner by the minute, and we're short-handed." He bent and pulled out two cans.

Chessa grabbed hers and held it away, popping the top and cursing again when foam spat over her hand. She ignored his chuckle and drank down the soda in several gulps.

His eyebrows rose. "A little thirsty?"

"This'll do for now."

"Why don't you cut through the Quarter and check out the blood bars? Kill two birds. Reba has reports from hotels complainin' about guests stackin' up in the rooms. You know what that means."

Chessa grimaced. Only a vamp on a binge could add a little carnage to the chaos.

Byron held up his Coke and started to turn. The wicked glint in his eyes had her stiffening. "Oh, and just to make your life a little easier, you got a new partner."

Surprised, since she'd only reported Rene's desertion that morning, she called after him, "Wait a damn second! Who the hell did you find in the middle of all this shit to take Rene's place? You know I need a little time to take care of his desk—"

Byron just shook his head. "Came from higher up. Not a thing you can do. Just suck it up, Tomas. Seemed like they knew it was gonna happen."

Chessa drew in a deep breath, trying to calm the sparks setting off a blaze of red-hot anger. How could the brass drop this on her now? Every cop deserved downtime after losing a partner. "Where is he?" she blurted, barely holding back the list of expletives she'd rather let loose.

Byron winked. "Checkin' out his new digs. Almost wish I had time to make the introductions." He chuckled as he left.

"Dammit!" Chessa stalked toward the cubicle she'd shared with Rene for four years. "The bastard had better keep his paws off Rene's things," she muttered.

She rounded the corner, drawing up short at the sight of a broad pair of shoulders stretching a dark T-shirt and a round, tight ass nicely displayed in many-times-washed blue jeans. That great ass was bent over a desk drawer. "Those aren't your things," she bit out.

Her new partner straightened and glanced over his shoulder, giving her a slow, delicious once-over that left her hot and confused.

How could you meet somebody and be immediately aroused and pissed off at the same time? She'd had handsome before—Nicolas was on par with this one's rugged good looks. Dark, wavy brown hair worn a little long, wide, muscled shoulders, a taut trim waist and flanks shouldn't leave her salivating.

Must have been the smile. A slight amused curl of firm lips. Or maybe the steady stare of his gorgeous blue eyes that seemed to note every detail of her appearance, but didn't ogle or hold a hint of any judgment. His gaze was appreciative, assessing—as though gauging her for game.

She'd worn a T-shirt and leather pants despite the muggy heat outside. She'd been feeling a little Goth—no makeup, but she'd ringed her eyes in black. She felt like a ghoul, planning a hunt—the scarier she looked, the better.

But she hadn't planned on having to drag a partner around behind her. Even one who ignited every red corpuscle of her being into a sensual frenzy. He'd be a major distraction.

How could she get rid of this guy? She lifted her chin.

She'd let out The Bitch.

"This isn't a good time," she snarled. "Let's do this another day—like say, never?"

His firm jaw eased, and his smile deepened. "Um . . . actually, orders are I'm to stick to you like glue."

"That order couldn't have come from Chief Esterhazi, he knows better."

"Nope, not anyone you can rattle. Name's Alex, by the way." He held out his hand.

Chessa ignored it—not wanting to touch him. She wondered if he'd been warned what she was, or if the brass were amusing themselves finding out how the new guy fared when he realized his partner wasn't human.

Alex glanced around the cubicle, his gaze touching on the disorder.

Chessa picked up documents from Rene's tray and put them down—ignoring the way Alex took over Rene's space.

When he sat in Rene's chair causing it to squeak, she spun

and stared down at her own desk. Yesterday, Rene had pulled her across his lap and fucked her in that same noisy chair.

She dragged in a deep breath and reminded herself Rene wasn't coming back. So she had a new partner. For now. How the hell could she get rid of him?

Well, if she had to endure him dogging her steps tonight, then maybe she'd throw a few surprises his way. If she was lucky, she'd send him running home. "It's chaos out there. If you're coming with me, you're gonna have to move quick. We're going on foot. Most of the roads are bumper to bumper where they aren't covered in water. Besides most of the places we're heading are all here in the Quarter."

Alex sat back in the rolling chair, leaning as far as the old metal and vinyl chair would allow. He raised his arms and put his hands behind his head, which stretched his dark T-shirt across a drool-worthy chest.

Chessa forced her glance away.

God, he pissed her off. Probably knew exactly what he was doing, too. How had he gotten under her skin so quickly?

"So, what are we looking for?" he asked, lazy amusement in his voice.

"Nests." She turned away and picked up the stack of reports Reba had left on her desk.

A metal whine told her he was poking around Rene's desk—the top drawer where he'd kept his stash of butterscotch candies. The crinkle of the bag indicated Alex had decided to help himself to one.

She hoped he choked on it.

"Where'd your partner go in such a rush?" he asked, his

voice a delightful blend of whiskey and growling male. "Did he evacuate? Doesn't sound like much of a cop, if he'd abandon his job at a time like this."

Her back stiffened and she shot him a glare over her shoulder. "The circumstances were beyond his control," she ground out. "That's all you need to know." Besides, what would he say if she told him Rene had followed a Born vampire through a time portal opened by an ancient mage to aid her escape from rogue *Revenants* intent on making sure she never bore Rene's child? He'd probably say, "Yeah sure. Tell me another one."

His dark eyebrows rose, and his lips pursed in a silent whistle. "You two close?"

Annoyed with herself for taking his bait, she tossed one uninspiring report after another onto the bulging heap in her top drawer and slammed it closed.

"You two were covering that murder suspect, Natalie Lambert."

Chessa tamped down anger that rose to burn the back of her throat. "She was a person of interest."

"Is there a difference?"

"She wasn't the killer." She glanced down the list of addresses left in her hand and ripped out the page with the likeliest ones. Grabbing her leather jacket where she'd left it slung over the back of her chair, she shrugged into it, pulling it over her holster.

"I take it we're ready to roll."

"Just don't get in my way." She stalked out of the cubicle, heading through the drab hallway to the steps that led down to the station floor and onto the street. She walked fast, hoping he'd get the message and keep the hell away.

Exiting the station, she was struck again by the sights that assailed her.

Water, water everywhere . . .

People in varying degrees of dress and oddly matched clothes, as though they'd scavenged along the way to cover themselves, milling on street corners, eyeing the few uniformed cops with suspicion and calculation in their gazes.

Unless one of them pulled a gun, she'd leave any trouble to the fellas on the beat. Stolen appliances and baby milk weren't high on her list of sins. Since lockup was already overfilled, she wasn't willing to babysit until they could move a prisoner.

Luckily, she wouldn't be taking any.

Her first stop was the Dupres hotel. As she drew near the tiled steps, a heavy footstep crunched directly behind her.

She let loose a low, filthy curse. She should have scented her new partner before she heard him, but the stench of backed-up sewer water overpowered her keen sense of smell.

Not that she thought moving fast would really shake the bastard off her tail. After all, she hadn't turned on the vampire warp speed.

The revolving door whooshed silently, and she stepped into the lobby, Alex close on her heels. She passed a security guard she recognized who gave her a nod and didn't challenge her as they passed.

Good. The staff was keeping the riffraff out of the hotel. Only paying guests would be passing through the doors.

The interior of the hotel sweltered. The smell of the street strengthened in the stagnant air. Small tea candles burned on low tables and a candelabrum burnished on the counter of the reception desk. People lounged around the tables, playing cards, talking smack.

Where light didn't quite reach, shadows grew—ominous, pregnant with menace.

Her hackles rose. Her "spider sense" alerted to something preternatural in the putrid air. She strode to the counter and slapped her hand on the polished wood to get the staff's attention. "Someone made a report?" she asked, flashing her badge.

"Room four-o-five," one tall, lanky black man said. "We heard screams. They wouldn't open the door. Sounds like a really bad party goin' down in there."

She glanced down at the name tag on his rumpled uniform coat. "Marcus, you keep out of the way, you hear? We'll take care of it."

Marcus's nod was quick, his expression relieved. If he'd been here very long, he likely had a good idea what was happening in that room. The hotel was notorious for high-rolling blood parties.

She skipped the elevator and headed toward the stairs, wondering how many times Alex would stumble in the dark as he tried to follow the sound of her footsteps.

A beam of light flashed over her shoulder, and she glanced back.

He held his flashlight shoulder high, his expression impossible to read in the dark. "Wouldn't want you to trip on the stairs, *partner.*"

She heard his silent gloat and narrowed her gaze. All right, he'd embarrassed her. Made her feel small. Even if she was trying for bitch of the year. "Glad you thought of it," she muttered.

"Police issue."

She slammed her palm against the door to the stairwell, and they entered the darkness. Up four flights of stairs that didn't wind him a bit.

In front of room 405, she laid a hand on his arm. "Once we're in, you stay behind me. Follow my lead."

"This is your turf," he said agreeably.

Tucking her hand into a pocket inside her jacket, she started to have second thoughts about bringing him along to a bloodfest. Anything could happen. She really should have warned him.

She wrapped her fingers around wood, sanded smooth, and withdrew a stake.

His eyebrows rose. "Planning on camping out, are we? Got a tent in there, too?" he asked, leaning close to look down at her chest, only to draw up short, when the pointed end poked at his belly. Raising his hands in surrender, he backed up a step. "Not much of a sense of humor. I'll remember that."

"Do that," she said, turning the stake and handing it to him. "Anything comes at you with fangs, put this through its heart."

Maybe he did know a little something. He tucked it in the front pocket of his cuddle-soft blue jeans.

Must have been a really deep pocket.

The door swung open, and they both fell back a step.

Alex swung his flashlight toward the woman in the doorway. She squinted at the bright light, a bottle of rum dangling from her fingers. Her clothes were awry, the buttons on her shirt mismatched. "You here for the party?" she slurred.

A red rivulet of blood slid down her neck, and she pitched forward toward the floor.

Alex caught her easily and lay her down in the hallway, next to the wall.

Chessa sighed and knelt beside her, bending close to lap at the wounds on her neck, closing them. When she'd finished, she stood and wiped the back of her hand across her mouth, grimacing with disgust. "Fuck me! She's soused." Not bothering to see how her partner reacted to her actions, she shoved past him and entered the vampire's den.

Stars glittered in the clearing sky, shimmering through the water where he waited, still clinging to the skeletal remains of the brother. Wide swaths of light crisscrossed the surface above him, sending greenish darts of light into the depths. Voices, distorted by water and distance, sounded thick and muffled in the distance.

After his bones were released by The Guardian, he'd been swept away on a giddy, frightening ride, afraid he'd be carried to the sea and forever confined to its depths.

Instead, he'd been washed up against the bank of a river, snagged by the fallen branch of a tree. His fate once again aided by the mystery of the Great God.

One voice neared. A male.

The wait felt interminable, laden with lush anticipation. After an eternity waiting in the darkness, soon, he'd be free. All the unsuspecting fool had to do was enter the water and reach down to examine the bones lying just beneath the surface.

Such a human need—to honor the dead. A weakness he would exploit.

When the large hand hovered above him, gleeful lustful power swirled inside.

Contact—the hand to his naked skull, even through a glove—was all he needed to complete his journey. He slipped upward and wrapped around flesh—warm, thrumming with life—and crept up a thickly muscled arm.

His new host dropped the skull back into the water and shook his hand, his expression wrinkling.

He couldn't see him! Didn't know what crawled up his arm, along his shoulder, and then slid around his face to enter his moist, warm mouth as it opened around a scream. The moment must have crept as slowly as a tiger crouched on his belly, inching toward its quivering prey.

The man choked, clasping his hands to his throat, sinking to his knees. Breath stopped on an inward wheeze. Inside him, the flicker of his life doused. His heartbeat slowed to a sluggish halt. His body slumped upright.

The heart still quivering inside the deep chest of his victim, the creature commanded it to beat again, forcing the muscle to remember its purpose, squeezing rhythmically—a slow steady throb that pushed blood through his veins.

Awareness of his new body encouraged him to drag in a deep breath, testing the taste and smell of the fouled air around him. After the close confines of a stifling crypt, the rich odors were ambrosia.

He opened his new eyes and slashed his gaze around him, noting men gathering at the river's edge, peering into debris, calling softly to one another as though walking among the gravesites of the dead.

He drew another breath, drawing strength into his being and savoring again the scents of this new place. The humid air felt thick in his lungs and redolent with the putrid smell of the swirling water, the scent of stale sweat rising from his new body—and the smell of the humans nearby.

"Hey, we got an officer down!" The shout sounded from behind him. A heavy hand landed on his shoulder. "Bernie, you okay?"

A smile stretched his new lips and "Bernie" looked up from where he knelt in the muddy grass. Thanks to the memories of his new host, he understood the words that filled his ears.

He curved his long, thick fingers like a shovel, smiling still as he drove them beneath the rib cage of the man leaning over him—straight inside his chest to wrap his fingers around his pulsing heart.

He liked this new world. As he gripped the quivering mass of muscle, he licked his lips. Nothing and no one would ever close him away again.

CHAPTER

4

Cigarette smoke rose like a thick cloud to burn her eyes as Chessa stepped through the suite's living room area. The windows, open due to the heat in the unventilated room, admitted only a lank breeze that barely stirred the flames of the burning candles dotting empty surfaces of tables and the mantel of a fake fireplace.

Beneath the smoke wafted the odor of sex—spent cum, sweating bodies—along with the acrid aroma of spilled whiskey and the musty smell of blood. The orgy was still in full swing.

Chessa barely spared a glance for the dusky-skinned woman straddling a man on one sofa while she bounced energetically on his lap. She stepped over the calves of a man bent over the spread-eagled legs of a blonde as he tongued and fisted her, sweat gleaming on his shoulders and flexing triceps. The woman arched her back from the floor and gave a guttural groan. She was hurting so good, but not bleeding.

Next.

A hand cupped her ass and Chessa aimed a glare at Alex, who gave her an unrepentant grin. "Just trying to blend in, sweetheart."

Her nipples pricked into full alert, and she wished like hell she'd worn a sports bra to smash them back into obedience.

His hand touched her elbow, and she followed his glance to a corner where a woman knelt between two men. The men suckled her breasts, their hands roaming her generous curves.

When one drew away from her breast, she saw blood, a thin dark stream pulsing from her nipple. Both men followed its trail, lapping up the rich liquid from her belly.

Alex touched her elbow.

Chessa shook her head. "They're just fucking. As long as they play nice, drink blood only for mutual pleasure—"

A scream ripped the air, coming from a bedroom deeper in the apartment.

Chessa tensed and pulled out another stake from an inner pocket.

Alex dug his hand into his jeans and drew out his stake, cupping its length along his arm to hide it.

She gave him a nod and strode toward the open door of the bedroom.

Inside, three people lay naked across a bare mattress. A woman lay draped over one man, her pussy engulfing his cock. Another man knelt behind her, riding her ass, his mouth opened and clamping hard on the back of her neck. The wound was deep. Blood streaked down her back. Her body trembled, her mouth gasped as she reached behind her to claw at the man, her arms flailing wildly.

His deep groan held a note of triumph as he shared a conspiratorial glance with the man beneath the woman who lifted his head and bit the front of her throat.

While blood burbled from the fatal wound painting all three in deep crimson, Chessa leapt onto the bed and drove her stake into the back of the man at the top of the doomed threesome.

His back arched, his mouth gaped wide in horror before his whole body burst into a flash of flame, muting to dust in an instant.

The woman collapsed like a rag doll against the second vampire.

He thrust her body upward, slamming it into Chessa who toppled from the bed beneath the leaden weight.

From the corner of her eye, she saw Alex dive for the bed, pinning the vamp with an elbow to his throat while he shoved the stake through his sternum and straight into the bastard's heart.

A billowing cloud of ash choked the air a moment later, and Alex rolled off the bed, stripping away his T-shirt.

Chessa dumped the girl's body to the side and leapt to her feet in one lithe movement. "How'd you hold him down?" she asked.

"I had surprise on my side," he said easily, shaking vamp dust from his T-shirt. "He was busy watching you."

She couldn't take her eyes off him. His chest was lightly furred and heavily muscled. A polished red stone hung from a thin black cord just below the base of his neck. She had the odd urge to curl her tongue around it. His arms flexed in interesting ways that sparked a curl of heat deep in her womb. All that power in his human frame . . .

Her nipples spiked tighter, and she plucked her T-shirt from her chest, realizing immediately it was soaked in blood. "Shit!" She stripped off her jacket and headed to the bathroom, grabbing bath towels from the rack above the toilet to wipe it clean.

"Here, put this on," Alex said, standing behind her in the mirror. He dangled a clean shirt, a man's white button-down dress shirt, at the end of his index finger.

Despite the deep shadows, his gaze met hers in the glass. A challenge was laid down in the arch of one dark brow.

Chessa never backed down from a dare. She recognized it as a weakness in her makeup. Still, it didn't stop her from setting her jacket on the counter, and unbuckling her shoulder holster.

With a stubborn tilt of her chin, she tugged the hem of her soiled T-shirt from her leather pants and stripped it off in one fluid movement. Her gaze locked with his again, daring him to look lower at her bared breasts.

His nostrils flared, his jaw hardened with a ripple of tensing muscle. Then his eyelids dipped as he took in the sight of her small, rounded breasts and bare midriff.

"You should see whether anyone noticed we dusted off a couple of their friends." She shrugged on the white shirt.

His glance followed her movements as she rolled up the sleeves to her wrists. She didn't know why she didn't start on the buttons at the front first. Maybe she didn't want him to know she trembled a little inside.

Okay, she did know why she did it, but just wasn't ready to admit she liked the sexy way his gaze clung to her pebbled nipples.

"No one cares," he rasped. "They're too busy fucking."

That word on his lips . . .

The crisp cotton fabric scratched the tips of her sensitive breasts as she tugged closed her purloined shirt. She suppressed a shiver.

God, she was hungry. The scent of blood still filled her nostrils, the aroma of sex roused another deepening hunger.

She gave Alex a sideways glance. He'd be a meal and half—and she hadn't seen his cock yet.

But she didn't do partners. At least, not until she was sure she trusted them. Nothing worse than looking a guy in the face every day if he's had you and heard you beg.

"Then let's make sure they know we mean business. Maybe they'll keep playing nice for a while." She clutched her stake in her hand and turned away from his hot stare in the mirror. The sooner they moved on, the sooner she could quench at least one of her hungers.

After making their point with the other occupants of the suite, they started down the list of hotels with infestations. Twice more, they interrupted bloodfests gone too far—with three rogue vampires eating dust on their way to hell.

Alex had surprised her with his cunning and strength. And

especially with his coolheaded reactions. He had experience. Lots of it. She could see why he'd been assigned as her partner.

Not that she was ready to concede she needed a new one. He was still too distracting—too much sexy male stuffed into blue jeans that hugged his ass and his glorious package.

God, she had to get off that one-rail track. Nodding to the bouncer at one of the last bars still open in the Quarter, she jostled roughly past patrons looking for a place to ride out the chaos outside.

The bar was one of her favorite haunts, one she'd used to introduce Natalie to the glories of a casual feeding.

She headed down a narrow corridor at the back to the secret room—the blood bar. She'd worked up a raging thirst. To hell with what her partner thought. He'd see the real her in a minute, and maybe, he'd ask for that transfer before she had to pitch a fit with the brass.

Inside, only acoustic guitars played. The air was stifling hot and stunk of too many bodies standing too close together. It suited her fine. The heat intensified the aroma of the blood. Muted voices and laughter didn't mask the sound of dozens of beating hearts.

A slightly built man with long dreadlocks brushing the tops of his bony shoulders sat on a stool with his elbows resting on the bar behind him.

Her choice made in an instant, she walked up to him. "Fed anyone tonight?"

His chocolate gaze slid over her, and his eyes widened. "Been waiting for you, babe."

She gave him a feral, heated look—all the warning she'd give him, this wouldn't be a gentle feeding.

His sex stirred in the front of his loose pants as he stared. "Gonna need a dark corner?" he said, his voice purring.

"Suits me fine," she bit out.

He canted his head to the corner of his choice and slid off the stool, wending his way through the bodies blending erotically together on the dance floor.

Chessa followed, all her attention on the man leading her into the darkness. She hadn't had enough of Nicolas's blood earlier to blunt her appetite. Now, her thirst ruled her, knotting her belly. Dread-man might be just an appetizer. She needed to feast, to fill one hunger to the exclusion of the other that had been steadily growing with every hour spent with Alex.

Dread-man stopped in a corner behind a large silk potted plant. "How do you want me?" he asked, his tongue sliding over his full lips.

"Our clothes stay on," she growled.

Looking only mildly disappointed—after all the man knew he was going to get a mind-blowing release—he shrugged. "Whatever the lady says." His gaze cut away, and he nodded to someone behind her. "He going to feed, too? Not that I have any objections."

She whipped around to find Alex standing behind her, his legs braced apart, his arms crossed over his chest.

His expression was watchful, tense. "Just keeping your back."

"Get lost," she snarled.

"Don't think so. You look ready to explode. Don't want to have to pull you off your meal."

"I've been doing this before you first sucked a tit."

Eyes narrowed, he stepped close and leaned down, his lips hovering above hers. "He'll feed your thirst. Let me feed your lust," he whispered. "We're partners, remember?"

Jesus H. Christ! Trembling now with need, Chessa could barely get her mind around what he offered. A thin, mewling moan clawed its way out of her tight throat.

"Shhhh," he crooned, slipping an arm around her back, pulling her hips flush with his. "You can have this," he said, caressing her with his thick cock through their clothes. "But you can't ever bite me, hear?"

She nodded, drugged by the rolling motion of his hips and the movement of his lips as he spoke.

His body drew away and she started to follow, but he dragged apart the lapels of her leather jacket and reached for the buttons of her shirt, plucking them apart to bare her breasts. Then he reached for the button at the top of her leather pants and opened it, dragging down the zipper just far enough to fit his hand inside. He smoothed his palm down her lower abdomen, his fingers combing through her pubic hair, until he dipped between her lips and toggled the hard little knot burgeoning at the top of her sex.

Snuggling her face into the corner of his neck, she sighed, licking her lips, letting her fangs descend and scraping them lightly over his throat.

He drew back sharply. "Uh-uh. That's what he's for," he said, nodding to Dread-man standing right behind them.

Dread-man fitted his body to her backside and slipped an arm around her belly, his hand sliding up to cup a naked breast.

"Kinky, much?" he asked, a smile in his voice. Then he lifted his other hand and turned his wrist, offering it to her mouth.

Chessa licked his clean, salty skin once. With her gaze on Alex, she sank her fangs deep into a vein, moaning when warm, viscous blood filled her mouth. God, he was delicious! Rich, alcohol-free.

Dread-man's gasp was as harsh as the cock grinding into her ass.

Sandwiched between the two men, she let herself go, trembling uncontrollably as blood slid a sinuous path down her throat to fill her belly, and Alex began rubbing her aching clit.

His thick fingers circled, his nail scraped the tender hood, lifting it, baring the tiny kernel to the exquisite motion of his fingertip, swirling harder.

Chessa moaned and shook, then undulated her hips between them, grinding backward to take the thrust of her host's cock and forward to tempt Alex into penetrating her clasping pussy.

"Want more?" His voice was a sexy slide of bass tones and sugar.

Her teeth still gum-deep in flesh, she could only murmur hungrily.

Alex's lips curved with smug approval, and he shoved her pants down her hips.

Dread-man squeezed her tit hard, fitting the ridge of his cock between her naked cheeks. His thrusts grew harsher, stronger, pausing at the top of each upward stroke, pretending he buried himself in her ass. He came quick, hurried along with a long hard draw of blood that left him cursing as he ground against her.

Alex cupped her pussy and thrust fingers inside her cunt.

Desperate to be filled, she circled on his two fingers, clasping her inner muscles, welcoming the wet surge of desire as it coated his hand.

Dread-man, still acting amorous after his release, came into play, palming a bare cheek and sliding long slender fingers into her crevice.

When he fingered her asshole, Chessa jerked.

"Easy, lady. Let me in," he rasped in her ear.

She quivered then backed onto his finger, wriggling side to side to ease his entry then riding up and down to take him deeper.

Only Nicolas had ever breached her there. All the more reason to let this stranger take her now. She couldn't let Nicolas be special.

Alex thumbed her clit and stroked three fingers inside her. "Let go of his wrist, sweetheart."

Barely understanding, she murmured and kept on riding the many fingers thrusting hard inside her body.

A rich, deep chuckle tickled her ear. "Let me kiss you."

A kiss. Alex's mouth on hers. His tongue . . .

She opened her jaw and disengaged her fangs from her host's arm, lapping quickly to close the wounds. She tilted her chin to lock lips with Alex.

His tongue stroked into her mouth, tasting of butterscotch, and something else wild and unknown.

His mouth came off hers and she moaned, clutching at him as he slid down her body. She grabbed at his shoulders when her trembling legs threatened to give way.

When his tongue lapped at her clitoris, she bit back a deepening groan and stopped all movement. Concentrating instead on just holding herself erect while he plied her pussy and throbbing clit with wicked glancing caresses.

When his fingers entered her again, she screamed, rocking back and forth, fucking both their hands, surrounded by male heat and scent.

Her orgasm stole her breath, leaving her lungs emptied of air, her heart pounding fiercely. Her head felt as though it exploded, blown away with the strength of her release.

When she roused, she found herself squatting between them, held tight, her forehead pressed to Alex's chest.

"We should stand her up. Get her clothes back on," Dreadman said quietly.

"Leave us," Alex said.

"Sure, man." He patted her shoulder, giving her a quick squeeze.

"Thanks for the gift," she murmured, feeling drained and too tired to act tough.

"Anytime, lady. You just ask for Leo."

"Think you can move?" Alex asked.

"Of course," she huffed, embarrassed to find her pants trapping her ankles, her body draped like a drunk's with her ass hanging out. "What the fuck just happened?"

"I'd say you left it a little too long. You should have had a bite before you came out."

She stirred, turning her head to look up at his lazy smile. "How do you know so much?"

"Been around a while."

"That's no damn answer." Chessa shook her head. "How do you know so much about vampires?"

"I'll tell you all about it, someday soon."

She pulled back, a nasty suspicion forming. "Are you a *Revenant?*"

Alex's lips twisted. "I'm no walking corpse."

Nicolas would love to hear himself described like that! She pushed away the thought. Alex might not be a turned vampire, but he was something—and she was just the girl to figure out what.

"Ready to stand?" he asked, quirking an eyebrow.

"Oh!" She'd forgotten she was only half dressed, and the interesting half was completely naked. She scrambled up, reaching down for her pants.

Alex was already gliding them upward, his hands smoothing up her naked thighs as he "helped."

Chessa slapped his hands away, feeling her cheeks heat. In all her years visiting this bar, she'd never given in like that. She liked being the one in charge. She straddled the bastards she chose and kept them tethered until she was done. They were the ones left weak-kneed and smiling.

Not that she was smiling now.

Alex stood beside her, and she realized he'd blocked anyone's view of what had happened in their dark corner all the while with his broad shoulders. Had he known how out of control a vampire's feasting could get—how close to the edge of desperation she'd been?

"This isn't happening again," she said, with the sinking feeling he knew she was all bluster. Someday, probably sooner than later, she'd put off feeding just a little too long, and he'd be there, waiting to oblige her. Likely choosing her next blood donor.

She hoped it would be someone as tasty as Leo.

"Where to next?" he asked, hands shoved in his pockets, emphasizing the bulge of his cock at the front of his pants.

She realized with a start, he could have had her, but didn't even try. Instead, he'd seen to her pleasure.

Now, he was back to business, like nothing had happened between them. She liked that. Appreciated the fact he didn't get maudlin over a little sex and expect it to lead to anything.

Damn, she was finding it hard to hold on to her resentment.

"Back to the station," she replied, her tone curt. "We've exhausted our list. With communications out, we'll have to check in with Reba for any new reports of trouble." She left her shirt hanging out of her pants and tucked her sleeves back under the cuffs of her jacket.

When she finally lifted her gaze, she noted warm approval in his expression. "Don't start getting sentimental."

"Wouldn't dream of it, partner."

"Yeah well, time to roll."

His hand on her arm stopped her. "You always so grumpy?"

Not always. Once, she'd actually been content. But that time was long ago. "If it's a problem, you know what you can do about it." The huskiness in her voice wasn't due to the sudden onslaught of memories—of a soft baby's cheeks or the sweet, warm glow in her husband's eyes.

Those memories were shut away along with the manila file that burned a hole at the bottom of her locked file cabinet. Rene had found it only yesterday, exposed it and her.

Only Rene had touched the one soft spot she still had buried deep inside her heart. She'd wept in his arms, let him love away the pain—at least for the moment.

The room shimmered and she didn't know she cried until Alex swept away a lone tear from her cheek with the pad of his thumb. "Sure," he said softly. "I know what I can do. Meantime, we have a city to keep safe."

Grateful he didn't pass a comment or try to soothe her with an embrace, she turned and strode away, tamping down the pain and the memories until the next time they surfaced. What the hell was it with partners, anyway?

They headed out through the throng of close-pressed bodies. When they reached the street, they spotted Lieutenant Williams who waited, his face set in a grim mask.

Christ! Had he been inside? Did he know just how chummy they'd gotten? She cleared her throat. "You waiting for me?"

He nodded and looked up and down the street, a furtive look that wasn't part of his nature. "I need you to see something. Think it's right up your alley, Cheech."

She stiffened. "What's happened?"

"Bodies down by the river," he said, his voice tight. "Uniform cops. Their hearts ripped out."

Sick and twisted—something only *kin* would do. Her blood chilled.

CHAPTER
5

Nicolas stuck to the shadows, standing beneath the long fronds of Spanish moss trailing from an ancient oak. He watched as the cops combed the bayou bank with their flashlights, looking for clues, photographing the victims, and grieving over their friends' bodies.

He waited patiently, knowing Chessa would be here sooner or later. Since the night was burning away fast, he hoped for sooner.

The carnage had begun. The Devourer had fed and would grow stronger and more frighteningly cunning as he cut a swath through New Orleans.

A squad car pulled up and Chessa climbed out, looking rumpled and wearing a man's wrinkled white shirt beneath her leather jacket.

Nicolas stiffened, his gaze darting to the tall man climbing out to stand beside her in the glare of headlights. As though the gesture was an old habit, the man's hand settled at the small of her back.

Chessa didn't deliver him a blistering glare, just a quick worried glance.

Merde! Bitch! Nicolas drew a deep breath, stunned by what he saw. Only hours ago, she'd begged him to fuck her, but here she was with another man—one she seemed to know rather well.

His hands fisted at his sides, readying to drive them through the handsome face of the human standing beside her.

Nicolas forced himself to think, drawing a deep cleansing breath.

He'd never been a jealous lover—knew all vampires craved sex almost as much as they did blood. A blood fuck with a host wasn't considered an infidelity. But vampires left their hosts behind. They didn't consort with them afterward. Courtesy among lovers meant seeking strangers to feed the two hungers. Comfort and affection were drawn from those you loved.

Only Chessa didn't love him. Regret washed through him. Maybe she never would.

But who the hell was this man?

He stepped out of the shadows and strode toward the cozy couple as they conferred with several officers beside a long yellow stripe of crime scene tape.

"Halt! Get your hands above your head or I swear I'll pull this damn trigger."

Nicolas rolled his eyes, tempted to flash by the young officer faster than he could blink.

Chessa's gaze landed on him, and her eyes widened for a moment. She gave him a subtle shake of her head.

He paused, then raised his hands obediently.

"It's okay, Len," she said, her voice husky. "Let him through."

Len gave him a narrowed glance that swept him up and down. A warning not to cause any trouble because he'd be watching. Then he holstered his weapon and stepped back.

Nicolas gave him a mirthless smile and ducked beneath the tape to join Chessa and her "friend."

"I'm Nicolas Montfaucon," he said, ignoring everyone else as he leveled a glare at the man standing beside Chessa.

The man's lips curved in a slight smile, his expression slyly amused, and he held out his hand. "I'm Alex, Chessa's new partner."

Another bloody partner! Although he would have preferred to ignore the hand held in his direction, Nicolas gripped it hard, gauging the other man's strength.

"Good grief, Nic," Chessa muttered. "If you wrestle him to the ground, I'll fucking clout you."

Nicolas flushed, realizing he had been squeezing a little too long and hard, not that the human showed any signs of conceding the silent battle. He was strong. A cocky young bastard.

"Who's he to you?" Alex asked.

"Family," she bit out. Then giving Nicolas a searing glance, she lifted her chin toward the river's edge. "I take it you've already seen the damage."

Nicolas gave a sharp nod.

"Damn," Chess said. "It's your guy, isn't it, Nic?"

"I warned you we would need to work together."

"What's this all about?" A barrel-chested black man in a dark suit asked.

Chessa sighed. "Lieutenant Byron Williams, meet Nic. He's a . . . well, you know . . ."

A grim smile stretched his broad mouth. "Another blood-sucker? I guessed," he said, his voice pitched low. His gaze narrowed on Nicolas. "I s'pose we could use a specialist's help with this one."

Chessa's eyebrows lowered, and her hands fisted at her sides. "We aren't teaming up!"

The lieutenant's gaze whipped to Chessa. "Can I trust him?"

Chessa's lips thinned, but she gave a sharp nod.

When he looked at Nicolas again, his expression turned thoughtful. Seeming to come to a decision, he pulled a tissue from his pocket and wiped at the sweat gleaming on his fore-head. "Look, I don't know you. Any other time, I'd tell you to butt out and let us do our jobs, but I gotta city in chaos and half my officers are gone."

"This is not a good idea," Chessa gritted out.

The tall black man gave her a lopsided smile. "Cheech, normally I'd let you handle whatever it is you do alone and give you backup only when you ask. I can't do that right now. You're gonna have to work with your people on this one."

"He's not one of mine." This time her rejection was softer, but no less agitated.

Nicolas felt a ripple of satisfaction at Chessa's anger. Although he hadn't planned on joining the police investigation, it made sense. They could keep tabs on the victims and try to find a pattern, a direction the demon was heading.

The lieutenant ignored Chessa's tight-lipped rejection. "You got knowledge of what this thing is?" he asked, directing the question to Nicolas.

Nicolas grimaced. "I know what, just not who he is at the moment."

The burly black man sighed. "Sounds like this is gonna get complicated."

The lieutenant didn't have a clue just how complicated it already was. Not that he had a need to know. "It's going to get bloodier before we're done," he conceded.

"Just so you know, there are only a few of us on the force who know about you guys—know there's scarier things out there than human killers."

Nicolas bowed his head, understanding the unspoken stipulation. This arrangement would be strictly confidential. "We'd like to keep it that way, too."

"I need to know what we're facing."

Nicolas glanced around, making sure no one listened beyond their select circle, then pitched his voice low. "It's a demon we seek. An ancient one. Our coven kept him imprisoned in a sarcophagus for eight hundred years. Yesterday when the water rose, a river ripped through the cemetery, flooding the mausoleum, and allowing him to escape."

"A demon? Shouldn't be hard to spot. What's it look like?"

Nicolas leveled his steady gaze on Byron. "You have anyone missing from the patrol?"

"Bernie Watson." The lieutenant's dark eyes widened. "He looks like us? Like Bernie?"

He nodded, his mouth tightening. "For the moment. Until Bernie's body dies. Then he'll crawl into someone else."

"Fuck me!" His lips pursed around a low whistle. "What's with the hearts?"

"His favorite meal."

"And he's been on a diet for a long damn time." The lieutenant scrubbed a hand across the top of his close-cropped hair. "Fuck me!" he repeated.

"Precisely." Nicolas slid a glance at Chessa who'd folded her arms across her chest. Defiance bristled in her stiff posture.

"So, we look for a trail of bodies with missing hearts," Alex said, his expression grim. "What's that gonna tell us? How do we catch him?"

Nicolas would have liked to ignore the other man, but knew he had to work with him if he was going to team with Chessa. "That's the tricky part. After he's finished his feeding frenzy, he might lay low for a while, but he's going to remember things. He'll want revenge."

"Against whom?"

"Against me," Nicolas said quietly. "For one."

"You two got a history?" This from the lieutenant whose eyebrows lowered in a suspicious scowl.

"I was the one who imprisoned him. I was his guardian."

Those thick brows pressed ominously closer. "You thinkin' to be the bait?"

Chessa jerked, her wide-eyed glance settling on his face.

Nicolas locked his gaze with hers. She cared. She might not admit it even to herself, but she did have feelings for him.

"Not my preference," Nicolas said, tightening his jaw. "I'd like to catch him first."

"If he comes for you, then what?" Chessa whispered.

"We give him another body to inhabit." He hoped she didn't ask whose, because he hadn't thought that far ahead. Someone would have to be sacrificed. "An immortal one. Something he can't kill to escape."

"Can't the bastard die?" Lieutenant Williams asked.

"We tried centuries ago. If there's a weapon that can kill him, we haven't found it."

Chessa looked at the employee file picture of Bernie Watson. She'd known him by name, but couldn't remember much more. His file said he had family here. A wife, two children.

If his family spotted him on the streets now, they'd be defenseless.

She handed the photo to Nicolas who glanced at it quickly and passed it to Alex.

They sat in an empty interrogation room. By her choice. She didn't want Nicolas standing in her space. Leaving his scent behind, burnishing the sight of his broad shoulders and lean body in the place she spent more time than her home.

Alex sat in the circle, seemingly oblivious to the anger rolling off those broad shoulders. But she felt the searing heat each time Nicolas's steady gaze landed on her—and passed to Alex.

He knew.

Could likely smell the lingering scent of arousal that had enveloped them both back in the blood bar. Chessa licked her lips, nervous now because sensual heat was rising again to choke her.

Damn Natalie and her virgin pheromones. Chessa had always kept a tight lid on her desires, letting them out at will when she needed to feed, closing the dark bottle with a vicious twist when she'd satisfied her hungers.

That ability was gone. Seated beside two of the men she'd had sex with in the last twenty-four hours was testing her control.

She squirmed on her seat, fighting the clenching of inner muscles that remembered the stretch and burn of Nicolas's big cock and the fierce lash of Alex's tongue on her swollen clit.

They had more important things to worry about. A demon to capture—and the sooner the better. Maybe then she'd get her life back on an even keel.

Alex tossed the photo in the middle of the employee file. "So, what's next?"

"Dawn will be breaking in a little while," Chessa said, not wanting to start this conversation. "We can't scour the city for him."

"Maybe your partner can follow leads on any sightings."

"I had a busy night, too," Alex replied. "I need shut-eye same as you."

"Then we meet back here after dark?" Chessa said, rising from her chair, trying to make a quick getaway.

"Why don't you head home, Alex?" Nicolas said, his voice a dangerous, low rumble.

Chessa's nipples peaked hard against her borrowed shirt.

That tone was one he used when he commanded her obedience—in bed. Shit!

"Think I might just do that," Alex said, his tone cheerful. "Chessa, want me to drive you home?"

His expression was so innocent, she narrowed her eyes. What was he trying to start? She'd only known him for a night, but she already read the sly amusement beneath the guileless look.

Nicolas's hand closed over hers, holding her in place. "I'll see her home. We have coven matters to discuss." His cutting tone was clear. Alex wasn't welcome to join that particular conversation.

"You sure, Chessa?" Alex asked softly.

She nodded, unable to cram a denial past her straining vocal cords. As soon as Alex left she was gonna kill Nicolas.

"All right." He nodded to Nicolas, an unspoken warning in his eyes.

Gawd, they were acting like two pit bulls facing off over a bone! Only she wasn't gonna just lie there in the bowl. "See you tonight, *partner*," she said, her tone silky-smooth.

Alex's grin stretched wide, and he lifted one wicked eyebrow as he left, a throaty chuckle echoing in his wake.

When the door clicked closed, she leapt to her feet, dumping her chair on the floor. "What the hell do you think you're doing?"

Nicolas rose just as fast, his upper lip drawn back in a snarl as he faced off from the other side of the table. "I should be asking you the same thing. That bastard's scent's all over you. Did you fuck him as soon you met him? Breaking in a new partner?"

"It wasn't like that—and it's none of your damn business anyway!"

"Like hell it isn't."

"You don't own me."

"You're mine. You will come to admit it if I have to remind you every time we meet."

"Whatcha gonna do? Brand my forehead?"

"Maybe I'll brand your sweet ass so every time you sit, you'll know whose ass it is!"

His comment, delivered in his slightly inflected French accent, struck her at once as comical—and just about the sexiest thing he'd ever said to her. *I'm one sick puppy.*

"I want to go home," she said, her body trembling with sweet, aching desire.

"I'm coming with you."

"I was counting on that."

They left the file on the table and departed the station, walking side by side past the people still roaming aimlessly on the street like shell-shocked refugees.

She noted their presence, but ignored them, not able to think beyond the anticipation sizzling through her body. What would he do once he had her alone? His stark, feral expression excited her beyond common sense.

They didn't touch. He didn't glance her way even once. He stalked like a rangy cat, his long strides eating up the concrete as dawn crept between the huddled buildings in the Quarter.

At her apartment building, he held open the door, daring her to pass close to his body.

Heat simmered on his skin, scorching her, building a liquid, melting passion that had her thighs so tense she had to concentrate to put one step in front of the other.

Then they were at her door, and her hand shook as she stuck the key in the lock and turned it.

Nicolas came up behind her, pushing her over the threshold with his body, his hands already stripping away her jacket before she'd kicked the door closed behind them. Buttons popped as he skimmed the shirt off her shoulders, but he twisted the fabric, somehow binding her hands behind her.

His hands came up within her sight, cupping her breasts, squeezing hard. His cock pushed hard against her ass.

God, she needed him now. Inside her. Stretching her. Cramming deep. She didn't care which particular portal he chose, so long as he did it quick.

"Nic! Oh God!"

Her whole body quivered as he jerked her pants open and skimmed them down her thighs, trapping her knees, then he turned and lifted her in his arms, striding toward the sofa.

He dropped her over a plush upholstered arm, facedown, her bottom raised.

Chessa struggled to toe off her boots, but his hands were everywhere, rushing up the backs of her thighs, parting her buttocks.

Fingers thrust hard inside her vagina, gliding deep, swirling to capture the wetness spilling from her inner walls.

"He touched you here, didn't he?"

"Yes!" she gasped.

He thumbed her clit, a sharp jab that shot a bolt of electricity straight to her womb.

Then his fingers slid up, and he circled her asshole. "Did he take you here?"

"No. Not him."

His breath choked. "You had someone else, too?"

"Leo," she groaned, resenting the fact he demanded the details. Who she fucked wasn't any of his damn business.

"Leo," he growled. "Did he fuck your ass?"

"Just his fingers," she said, nearly sobbing now. Her pussy already weeping with creamy passion.

"Maybe I'll let him keep them." He plunged two fingers in her ass, not waiting for the tender flesh to ease around him. "Did you like it?" he asked, his whisper harsh and ragged.

"Yes! I fucking loved it! I came so hard I crumpled like a dirty Kleenex."

"Bitch! This is my ass."

Chessa was too far gone to care how thin the ice was beneath her at the moment. She sensed his rage close to the surface— savage, hot anger ready to erupt all over her. "It's whose ever ass I choose, you bastard!"

"We'll see about that."

The first slap landed low, between her legs, cracking against her swelling cunt.

"God. Jesus. Fuck!" She bit her lip to keep from telling him to do it again.

"Does Alex know you like this?" he purred, his hand caressing one fleshy globe.

She bit harder on her lip, piercing the skin.

Another slap landed in exactly the same spot. This time, sounding wetter.

Christ, she'd come like this! One more time and she was done.

But the next open-palmed swat landed on her ass, one cheek then the other, over and over until her skin burned and she squirmed again, rubbing her bared breasts against the thick corduroy, abrading her swollen nipples, trying to get off on just the sweet hot pain.

When a noisy sob escaped her lips, he stopped. He pulled away, leaving her dangling over the sofa, her skin cooling.

For a moment, she feared that was all he'd give her—revenge for what he saw as her betrayal.

The soft rustle of clothing sliding over skin soothed her.

She wished he'd say something, even if only to rage at her more. His sudden silence yawned like a dark chasm, one misstep on her part and he'd leave her there. Empty, unfulfilled. Her ass in the air.

She stayed silent. Obedient. Knowing that was what he demanded.

She was Born. Born to lead. Born to rule over him.

That he didn't accept this role—with her—only fed her desire. Only Nicolas had ever mastered her.

His hands gripped the notches of her hips.

She squeezed her pussy, a futile effort to deny him entrance, proving her *dis*-obedience as he pushed the thick crown of his cock inside her.

His rich chuckle washed over her, licking at her nerve endings, pulsing through her channel where her body readied itself for his invasion. "Why fight me, when this is what you want? All you want from me."

She closed her eyes, turning her face into the rough material. Wrong! He had it so wrong. She wanted more, but didn't dare seek it.

Then his hips lunged forward, and he impaled her on his strong, thick cock.

Chessa sobbed again, tears wetting the sofa beneath her. "More!" she gasped.

He tunneled in, cramming harshly past her throbbing inner tissues, working his way inside with quick, sharp jabs that pushed the air from her lungs.

Her hands clenched behind her, her back arched, scraping her nipples against the rough cloth.

Mindless, unable to move against him, she quivered in the thrall of his hard loving. Her pussy caressed his shaft with moist ripples, giving him proof of her pleasure.

Wicked, clever Nic kept her on the edge of orgasm, stroking hard, then halting until the ripples faded, then forcing her back up the steep cliff with sweet, sharp thrusts that shook her whole frame.

"Beg me, Chessa. Beg me for release."

"Never, bastard," she whimpered, knowing she'd scream for it. *Soon.*

But she didn't want it to end. The connection they shared, forged over tears and blood four decades ago, was one she didn't want to break.

As long as he fought for her surrender, she'd withhold it.

Abruptly, he withdrew.

She moaned a protest, muffling it against the sofa.

When he spread her cheeks, she nearly gave him the screams.

His cock bumped her tiny hole then circled, pressing hard. Impossibly thick and blunt, he burned her, pain tightening the little ring of muscle.

Fingers thrust into her cunt, capturing moisture then rubbed her asshole, lubing her with her own desire. This time when he pushed his cock against her, he gained entry.

The shock of it, the intrusion of the thick column straight up her ass, had her sucking air between clenched teeth.

"Beg me, Chess."

"I won't," she whimpered again. "Never," she lied, goading him to prove him wrong.

He pumped inside her, several sexy glides that dragged at the tight, sensitive ring.

Chessa mewled and gasped with the exquisite pain, feeling as though he pierced her all the way to her heart.

"I'm your master, Chessa," he said, his voice roughening. "Admit it. I'll give you what you crave."

"Nic! Oh please."

"Tell me." He ground deep then came to a dead halt, leaning over her, squeezing out what little air she'd dragged into her starving lungs.

All right! she silently screamed. "Fuck me . . . hard. Please, please, please."

"That's what I wanted before. You begging. Not enough now." He swirled his hips. "Tell me."

On fire, her whole body quivering like a scared dog, she clamped her chattering teeth. "You're my master," she whispered and closed her eyes. God, he'd never let her take that back.

Nicolas kissed the back of her neck, crushing her fists

against the back of her hips, then leaned away and stroked his hands down her shoulders and sides, soothing her, relaxing her—lulling her into blind submission.

She knew he wouldn't be easy despite his gentle, smoothing hands. With a quick upward jerk, he lifted her off the sofa and held her there, the pressure in her ass increased tenfold and she couldn't hold back a second longer. "OhGodOhGodOhGod!"

With powerful surges of his hips and straining thighs, he thrust upward, slamming her body down on his cock, fucking her mercilessly over and over until a shriek of painful ecstasy washed over, leaving her hanging limply, suspended in his hard hands while he milked every last rhythmic convulsion that tightened her pussy and her ass.

His shout followed, and his legs shook, making them both tremble.

Chessa had never known the like of what he gave her. Mastery with a capital "M."

He pulled out and turned her, reaching behind her to tug off the shirt binding her arms.

As soon as she was freed, she wrapped her arms around his neck and snuggled close to his sweat-slick chest, letting the tears spill down her face.

Nicolas understood her. Knew she wasn't capable of offering love—he had to demand it. While she wasn't yet ready to admit how deep her feelings were, soon she'd have to put to rest the ghosts of her past.

With Nicolas holding onto her tight, she thought she might be ready to let go.

CHAPTER
6

The air sifted softly through the window, a hot flicker that teased the sweat glistening on his chest. Nicolas held Chessa while she slept, her head resting on his shoulder, her soft hand cupping the muscle above his heart.

He'd been harsh. Angrier than he'd ever been with anyone—ever—letting loose in a way that had him pulling back inside himself, wanting to distance himself from *that man*.

He'd never wanted to cause her true pain. Sexy spankings were one thing, but he'd damn near raped her.

The sight of her so relaxed and cozy with her new partner had incited the beast inside. Had Alex been a blood host looking to trade for the privilege of fucking her, he wouldn't have minded—much.

However, she'd see him every day. Work beside him, share time with him. Nicolas could never experience that with her. Not as long as she clung stubbornly to her vow never to return to *Ardeal*. The old plantation with its inbred coven of vampires was a political cesspool, but he and his team had a purpose. A higher calling that pulled them above the petty wars of the others.

Chessa was a gifted warrior. She had a seat on the *sabat* that she refused to take. And she was Born!

Frustration built inside him at the thought she wasted herself here. Chessa had an advantage he would never have. He'd been turned, raised from the dead, like every other male vampire he knew. Made a *Revenant* by his bride to serve her and breed her.

That he'd been offered the duty of guardian to the "*Griza-shiat*," the One Who Devours, had been the central reason he'd agreed to give up his humanity all those centuries ago.

However, Chessa had been born a vampire. She was truly immortal. Not a reanimated corpse.

He'd felt the difference between those who ruled and those who served every day of his afterlife. Inanna commanded them, ruled their thoughts when she chose, bedded them at her convenience and pleasure.

His position as commander of the coven's Security Force, even over Born females already serving in the unit, was testament to his triumph of will. Of late, he suspected she'd groomed him for another purpose.

Knowing the wily bitch, she'd planned it from the day they'd first met.

1308
Poitiers, France

The guards had taunted them for days of their coming execution. Of how the fire stacks had already been prepared and covered with hay to protect them from the rains so they'd burn hot with little smoke—until they singed flesh. How the previous prisoners who'd burned had screamed and begged for God's mercy at the last.

Armand prayed daily for their souls, for he had given up on regaining an earthly freedom.

Nicolas grew more morose and angry at Armand for his intransigence—and for his foolish faith.

Still, Nicolas wouldn't recant. He refused to leave Armand. Besides, it was already too late to consider it. Those who'd stubbornly withheld their confessions, hoping for the Pope's intervention, were offered only absolution now before facing their deaths.

They'd both die here. There was no hope left.

"You have visitors."

Nicolas looked around, unsure to whom the guard spoke. Only five remained in the small cell. One had died with a hacking cough weeks earlier; another had committed suicide, fearing death by fire more than eternal damnation for his sin.

Armand suffered with the hacking cough now, and his eyes burned brightly with fever. Perhaps he'd be spared an excruciating execution after all.

"You and your brother, get up!" The guard struck the bars with a stick. "You have visitors."

For the first time in months, the key turned in the lock and they were let out of their squalid cell. They shuffled slowly through a dim corridor lit with torchlight toward a doorway from which light spilled onto the dirty floor. Just beyond the doorway lay the stone steps that led up toward freedom.

Fresh clean air swept down the steps, and Nicolas paused to savor it.

"Move!"

Shoved from behind, he stumbled toward the doorway.

"They're in there. Don't try to escape."

Nicolas shared a quick curious glance with his brother, then stepped into the room.

Two people waited inside.

Nicolas's gaze landed first on a woman swathed from head to foot in a dark cloak. She held a thin veil over her face. Only her almond-shaped brown eyes were visible. He was put to mind of the Saracens' women. Beautiful, mysterious creatures who smelled of sandalwood and exotic perfumes. As this one did. His sex stirred, and he shifted his stance.

Wide-eyed and curious, her gaze swept over him, pausing on the wayward flesh that strained against the threadbare cloth covering his groin.

His chin lifted at her immodest stare.

Amusement glinted in her eyes, and she turned to his brother. A quick sweep of her dark lashes, and then she turned to glance back at the man standing behind her. She nodded slowly.

Only then did Nicolas recognize the man behind her. "Simon!" he gasped.

Simon Jameson strode toward Nicolas, opening his arms to

give him a strong hug. He pulled back and kissed both his cheeks, seemingly impervious to the stench.

He offered the same to Armand, but his embrace wasn't quite as warm. Nicolas and Simon had forged a bond deep as any two who've fought with their backs to each other in a pitched battle.

"You are looking well." Nicolas murmured, not mentioning that Simon must have recanted early in the Inquisition.

Simon's cheeks were tanned, his brown hair sun-streaked, his scent fresh and healthy. "I am well and just returned from Palestine."

"You went back? Why? I thought you'd enough of sand and heat."

"I returned for something more important than my comfort."

Nicolas held his gaze, knowing there was more to what he said, but aware of the ears pressed to the door outside the small room.

For the first time in months, his senses sharpened, his mind settling on something . . . intriguing. "Why are you here?"

"I would like to offer you and your brother a chance to escape this hell."

Nicolas sighed, trying to dampen the hope starting to knot his stomach. He'd had so many disappointments. "We will not recant."

"You will not be required to."

"But how? Father Guillaume will never agree to free us."

"He is willing to turn a blind eye if you are willing to undertake a solemn duty—one approved by Pope Clement."

Nicolas's interest was piqued. "I take it this will be a dangerous undertaking?"

"Perilous to your lives and your souls," Simon whispered.

While Armand and Nicolas stood in stunned silence, Simon told them of a sarcophagus he'd retrieved from Palestine that imprisoned a demon.

Nicolas silently scoffed, no longer believing in heaven or hell—or creatures more cruel and deadly than kings and Popes who betrayed men for power and wealth. But he listened, recognizing a chance for freedom—one his zealot of a brother would embrace.

"You will be guardians of a monster who can never be released."

"His jailers?" Nicolas asked. "Does he really need that when he's sealed inside a coffin?"

"He's devious. Not easily confined. And immortal."

Immortal? Another myth. Nicolas could see the jaws of their trap yawning wide. How simple just to agree. "Why us?" he had to ask.

"Because I trust you."

Nicolas shook his head. There had to be more. "Why choose Templars? Why my brother and I?"

"Because you are loyal to each other. Loyal to your Order. Willing to sacrifice." Simon's gaze seemed to reach inside him. "I know you don't believe me, Nic, but I can save you. We were friends, and I know enough about you to trust that if you say yes," he said, his gaze sliding to Armand, "you will never abandon your oath."

Armand nodded. "For a just cause, I would agree—and so long as I do not have to recant my vows to my Order."

"I will not ask that, but there is one stipulation." Simon looked to the woman.

Her black eyelashes lowered, and her head canted. A dark, slyness entered her gaze.

Nicolas stiffened. Would the price be too high after all?

"You will not have to recant," she said, her soft musical tones rang with a steely authority, "but you will have to give up your life . . . as you know it now. This will be the least of the trials you will face."

Simon drew a deep breath, his lips tightening. "Nicolas, may I introduce you to Ina—"

"You must give up your vow of celibacy," the woman interrupted. "Will you do that?"

Her voice wrapped around him, cloying, enslaving. Nicolas felt a moment's alarm at her unusual allure. His body tightened as it had not in years. "As long as my brother does not have to, I'm willing."

"Her name is Inanna," Simon said, a hint of warning giving an edge to his voice.

Nicolas swept away his concern, so enraptured was he becoming to the sensual promise glittering in her dark eyes.

Inanna let go of the veil, allowing it to fall away from her face.

His breath caught and held, so stunned was he by her beauty. His body stilled; his cock filled fast.

He'd been right about her origins. Dusky, creamy skin, full red-brown lips that stretched wide as he stared. Her face was a perfect, delicate oval.

Her amusement was matched by the flare of arousal he sensed in her deepening breaths and flaring nostrils.

They became lovers before she gave him to Anaïs.

*   *   *

Present Day

Chessa stirred, wakening slowly as fingers softly glided up her belly and cupped a bare breast.

Nic. She rolled, trying to snuggle closer despite the muggy heat in the apartment, but he slipped away. Not willing to open her eyes and lose the lazy lassitude that gripped her, she drew up her knees, determined to sleep a few minutes longer.

However, strong hands gripped her thighs, tugging them down, pulling her body to lie on her back. Then his heavy body came over her, settling softly on top of her.

She squinted and wrinkled her nose, pretending an annoyance she didn't feel. "I was sleeping."

"Now you're not." His face, shadowed by the deepening darkness of the room, hovered just above hers.

"I ache. You were a little rough." Not that she truly minded. She just didn't want him to know how much she'd liked the way he'd taken her—roughly, possessively. Already her body blossomed with a fragrant heat he couldn't miss.

One of his large, slightly roughened palms cupped her cheek. "If I tell you I'll be gentle this time . . ."

"I won't believe you. Gentle isn't in your repertoire."

"You think I'm incapable of gentleness?"

"Where I'm concerned, yes." And she was glad of it.

"Shall I prove you wrong?" His voice slid as softly over her as the caress of his palm to her cheek.

Something new? A wicked torture she'd endure before he unleashed his passion? Chessa turned to press a kiss into that wide palm. "I'm ready to be surprised," she whispered.

"This isn't a game. I'm not playing." His thumb brushed lightly over her lip.

Faint alarm rang inside her. He sounded so serious, but she wasn't ready for the next "stage" of their relationship, whatever that might be. "Just fuck me," she said, surprised by the tremor in her voice.

"You play at being so tough. Why?"

"Who's playing? It's who I am."

"Liar," he whispered. Then his mouth came down on hers. But instead of a deep, demanding kiss, his lips glided once, then lifted.

She raised her head off the pillow, unwilling to let go. Her mouth pressed hard to his, trying to incite his desire. His cock stirred against her belly and triumph filled her.

But he lifted away, leaving the invitation of her lips and moved down her body, his mouth landing on her chin and following the deep curve of her neck down her chest to the slope of her breast. He nuzzled her nipple before tracing a slow, wet circle around its circumference.

Confused and growing angry, Chessa gripped his hair hard and pulled. Tenderness wasn't what she wanted—wasn't something she'd accept from him.

A growl erupted, vibrating on her breast and she gasped, clasping her thighs together at the answering ache. "Dammit, Nic! Suck it hard."

The tip of his tongue lapped around the tip of her nipple, just a soft, teasing caress—nothing like the biting, animal frenzy she'd come to expect.

She pulled his hair again. "I never expected you'd bore me," she groused.

His hands shot up and grabbed her thumbs in his hair, pulling them back until she winced and let go. Then he raised his head.

His expression was dark as the thunderclouds had been a day ago.

Inwardly she sighed. She had him now.

His cock jerked against her tummy. "Think you can manipulate me so easily?"

"Of course not," she lied, breathless as she waited for him to unleash his anger all over her.

His jaw tightened, and the look in his eyes, for just a second, revealed a bleakness, a sadness she felt all the way to her stone-cold heart. He rolled away and sat on the edge of the bed. "We should dress. We have to leave soon."

Wondering what the hell had just happened, Chessa blinked away the moisture welling in her eyes. Damn him.

Knowing she'd disappointed him somehow, she watched as he rose and picked up clothing from the jumble of clothes on the floor.

She ached all over. Her ass was sore from the wild reaming he'd given her before. Her pussy was swollen and wet from unabated arousal.

Her chest tightened, and her anger spiked higher. Quietly, she left the bed and stalked him. When he turned, she sank on her knees in front of him and grasped his cock.

"What are you doing?" he asked, sounding tired.

"What do you think? You're the one who woke me up. If you don't take care of me, I'll have to jump the first man I meet."

"I'm not going to fuck you."

"What if I fuck you?"

His stillness told her he was listening. She'd never initiated sex with him. His hands settled on his hips as his expression hardened. "I don't want to be jerked off."

"What do you want?"

"To fuck your mouth."

Her nod was quick, sharp. "Okay."

"I won't get you off afterward. This isn't *quid pro quo*."

Nicolas had never left her wanting before. She counted on the fact he wouldn't start now. Planning to drive him out of his mind, she cupped his balls with one hand and trailed her tongue down his cock.

She gasped when his fingers threaded through her hair and tugged hard. Her mouth open, she let him guide her up his cock to the blunt, thick tip.

Quivering with rage, she understood now. No games. No reciprocal expectation of release.

He really was going to fuck her mouth and leave her wanting. With tears pricking her eyes, she opened wide and accepted the long glide of his cock as he pushed inside, sliding over her tongue and deep into her throat.

Without a demur, she relaxed the back of her throat and let him enter deeply, taking all of him, fighting the urge to gag and wondering what he'd do if she threw up on him.

Probably wouldn't faze him a bit. Hard, rigid anger radiated from his body as he stroked in and out.

The sharp, manly scent of his cock and balls nearly made her weep, so strong was the arousal building in her body. She settled her aching pussy on one heel and rubbed, trying to ease her arousal as he pumped into her mouth. When his strokes quickened and his breaths grew harsh, she cupped his balls again and squeezed gently, encouraging him to come.

His hands tightened around her skull and he sharpened his strokes just before salty, musky cum jetted onto the back of her tongue. "*Dieu!* Fuck!"

She swallowed, greedy for the taste, her throat clasping around the head of his cock as he came.

When he'd finished, he let go of her and backed away from her mouth. "Do you have a toy?"

"A toy?" she asked, feeling a little dim-witted with her overwhelming arousal. She licked her lips and gave him a helpless stare.

"A sex toy. I know you have them."

Beneath the biting edge of his anger, her confusion cleared. Of course, she did. She'd avoided sex with men for years, but she hadn't been able to resist altogether relieving that particular hunger.

Rising unsteadily from her feet, she circled him, heading to her nightstand and pulled out her bottom drawer. He reached around her, stirring her collection of dildos and vibrators until he found what he wanted.

A small silver bullet. Her favorite. Five speeds—from a gentle humming pulse to a raucous, roaring vibration that never failed to get her off.

"The remote?"

Her hand shook as she dug for it and handed it over.

"Go pee, but don't flush. There's no water pressure left."

Obediently, she headed to the bathroom and lifted the lid, settling down to relieve herself.

Nicolas entered, standing by the door.

"I need a little privacy," she gritted out.

"There's nothing you won't share with me."

Except tenderness.

She left it unsaid, but let her flow fill the basin while she glared daggers.

When she stood, he stepped close and lifted his hand between her legs, inserting the cool egg-shaped metal object into her vagina. "No underwear. And you can't take it out."

"It'll fall out. I won't remember to squeeze."

"Sure you will." He hit the remote button and a gentle throb tightened her inner muscles.

God, she was gonna kill him before the night was over.

Nicolas felt a smile tug at his lips, but tightened his mouth. Chessa looked ready to skin him.

With her mouth still swollen from being stretched around his cock, he felt a deep satisfaction that he'd managed to restrain himself from taking her to the floor and fucking her hard the way she'd practically begged him to.

But she had a lesson to learn. He wouldn't accept any rebellion from her. Nothing withheld. Not her body, not her emotions.

If she couldn't give either freely, he'd force her to accept everything she needed—from him. Her eyelids drifted down and a whimper tore from her.

He slid the dial of the remote to "off."

Her eyes slammed open. Rage burned in two hot, twin circles on her cheeks. She jerked past him and entered the bedroom, muttering as she drew clothes from her closet and tossed them on the messy bed.

Nicolas drew a washcloth from the cabinet and poured water from a bottle he'd taken from her refrigerator then tapped the dispenser to add a dab of rose-scented soap. "You need to bathe before we go out," he said, as he stepped behind her.

Her back stiffened. "I'll take a shower at the station."

"You aren't stepping outside that door smelling like sex."

"I thought you liked that, seeing as I smell like you."

"It's not just my scent all over you."

"Give me the goddamn cloth," she snarled and reached for the cloth in his hand.

He held it above his head and waited until she realized he wasn't done.

Her eyes closed and her whole body trembled, but she stomped her feet, widening her stance—giving him the access he demanded.

The first touch of the cold cloth to her hot, swollen cunt left her gasping.

Nicolas knelt in front of her, opening her lips with his fingers and washed her slowly, dragging the rough terry cloth over her tender flesh.

Her legs trembled, and her breaths gusted softly. When her hips began to follow his slow, sliding circles, he stopped and efficiently washed the insides of her thighs. "Turn around," he said, forcing his voice to remain light.

When she turned, he spread her cheeks and washed between them, spending more time than necessary to cleanse her delicate little asshole.

His cock jerked, filling between his legs, but he ignored his own arousal and tossed the cloth into the bathroom behind him. "Get dressed," he said, this time not able to hide the hoarseness of his tightening throat.

They had work to do tonight. A demon to capture.

That he planned to teach her a little lesson about obedience along the way was just . . . icing.

CHAPTER
7

C hessa was slipping her belt through the loops of her jeans, doing her best to ignore Nicolas's brooding presence, when the doorbell rang.

Before she could raise an objection to his high-handedness, Nicolas flung it open.

Alex stood on the threshold, his eyes lighting first on Nic, his gaze sweeping down Nicolas's bare chest. Then he glanced beyond, raising an eyebrow at Chessa.

She had to hand it to him, he didn't blink an eye at further evidence of her lurid life. Lord, he had to think she was a total slut. He'd never believe in a million years that before a few days ago, she'd been sexless for a decade.

Not that she cared what he thought.

She buckled her belt and sat on the edge of her

sofa to pull on her leather boots. "Wasn't expecting you here, Alex, and I know I didn't give you my address."

"Byron gave it to me, along with a satellite radio. That way we won't have to check in." He walked past Nicolas without another glance and flopped down on the chair beside her.

Byron? She didn't call her boss that even after all the years she put on the force. Not that she'd ever looked to be bosom buddies with the man. "What couldn't wait?" she asked, leaning back to pull the second boot over her heel.

"Another murder. This one's more interesting. Your 'family' man needs to have a look," he said, lifting his chin toward Nicolas.

"He's not mine."

A humming started deep inside her pussy and Chessa choked, delivering Nicolas a deadly glare.

Nicolas shrugged, a smile curling one corner of his sexy mouth. He walked nonchalantly toward the door, buttoning his shirt. "Coming Chessa?"

A garbled curse was all she could manage as she stood on wobbling legs, squeezing her inner muscles around the metal egg. Lord, wouldn't everyone be surprised if she just let the thing slide down her leg and drop on the floor.

Only the thought of Nicolas's punishment kept her putting one foot in front of the other as she followed him down the hallway.

"Is he always so quiet?" Alex asked, once they'd stepped onto the sidewalk.

"Only when I'm hunting," Nicolas called over his shoulder.

"Great hearing," Alex muttered.

Nicolas paused beside a low-slung convertible parked beside the curb. "Your car?"

"Yeah. How'd you know?"

Nicolas grinned and pulled open the back door, sliding onto the leather seat.

Chessa climbed in front, doing her best to ignore Nicolas and earning a jolt of pleasure edged another notch higher on the Richter scale. "I'm gonna kill you," she said softly, aiming a scowl behind her.

"Of course, you're not." He leaned forward to whisper in her ear. "You're dying for me to hit fifth gear."

"Only get as high as four in the city limit," Alex said, starting up the car.

Nicolas laughed softly while Chessa sank into her seat, gritting her teeth against the surging vibrations that elicited a steady dribble of desire. Her jeans would be soaked through before they'd reached their first stop. How would she explain that? She'd forgotten her Depends?

The little shop was just off of Bourbon Street in a long row of tiny, dingy establishments, sharing a single roof. Yellow tape already striped the door. Above it, a neon light proclaimed, "Tarot/Palms" in bright blue.

Chessa ducked beneath the tape, entered the shop and glanced around. On the shelves was the usual New Orleans kitsch—voodoo dolls, stuffed alligators, and black T-shirts with skeletal jazz bands.

At the rear of the shop was a doorway protected only by strings of glass beads and tiny bells that tinkled as the breeze from the street sifted through them.

Chessa swept them away and stepped into the dark little

room that smelled of incense, cigarette smoke, and a decaying corpse. A small table, covered in dark felt cloth and scattered tarot cards stood in the center. A chair sat undisturbed on one side. On the other, a chair rested on the floor lying on its side.

Beside it, left undisturbed by the uniforms outside, laid the body of Madame Fortun if the name was to be believed. In the center of her chest gaped a large bloody hole where her heart should have beat.

"She's a *bokor*."

Chessa spun toward the voice coming from a dark corner. Damn, she hadn't caught a whiff of his scent above the sour smell of drying blood.

Simon Jameson stepped closer, his expression grim.

"This is a crime scene. Should you be here?" Alex asked, from behind her.

Chessa snorted. "He's—"

"Family?"

"Definitely not!"

Simon's lips curved in a mirthless grin. "I'm a friend of the family."

"Does that mean I have to be polite when I kick his ass out the door?" Alex said, his voice low and lethal.

Chessa gritted her teeth. "He stays."

Simon gave Alex a narrowed, searching glance. "New partner, Chessa?"

Nicolas coughed behind her, a hint of laughter rumbling from his chest.

Alex's posture stiffened. "So, what's a *bokor*?"

Simon's gaze swept from Alex to Nicolas. "A practitioner of dark voodoo arts."

"This just gets better and better," Alex murmured.

"What are you doing here?" Chessa bit out.

"Looking for clues as to why our friend was here."

"Find anything?" Nicolas asked.

"Unfortunately, yes." Simon waved a hand to the sink in the corner. Beside it stretched a counter with bottles filled with desiccated bugs, dried plants, and powders.

A bottle lay on its side, spilling yellow-brown powder over the counter to the floor below.

Chessa stepped closer, but Simon stuck his arm out to keep her from drawing near. "Don't touch it."

"Why?"

"Walk away with any of it on your boots and you'll have zombie cockroaches crawling all over the floor. Touch that bitch's corpse with even a speck of this, and you'll have Madame Fortun gnawing on your shins."

Chessa wrinkled her nose. "Oh, come on! Zombies?"

Simon leveled his solemn gaze on the group. "I promise I'm not joking. Dark arts, remember?"

"You're not one for demon-hunting. What brought you here, Simon?" Nicolas asked.

"Not what. Who."

Chessa's gaze shifted from Simon to Nicolas and back again. "All right. Y'all gonna clue me in?"

"Inanna," Nicolas said, his jaw flexing tight.

"Give the man a cigar," Simon muttered.

Chessa's chest tightened. "She's here? In New Orleans?"

"At my place."

"With your kestrel?"

"Wreaking havoc with my love life. It is a full moon."

Chessa's lips twitched, imagining the regal Inanna being waited on by the mage's familiar. "Sorry about that."

"Sorry enough to take her home with you?"

"My place is too small to hold her ego."

"A little too crowded already, is it?" Simon said softly, his glance landing on Nicolas.

"We are not a twosome." Irritation sharpened her tone. She glared at Nicolas. "You give him that idea?"

"I kinda got that idea all on my own," Alex murmured. When she glowered at him, he raised his hands in mock surrender. "All right, I'll butt out."

Chessa huffed, letting her cheeks puff out. "Goddamn, I need a drink."

"That should be interesting," Nicolas whispered into her ear.

"Just keep your pointy little finger off that remote."

"Not a chance."

"I don't suppose I can talk you both into waiting out here?"

When both men gave her toothy grins, Chessa wondered whether Nicolas had let his dirty little secret out. Which was precisely what she planned to do if they'd let her at a bathroom for just a minute, but both stuck to her back like flypaper as they turned to enter the seedy little bar.

Choices of blood bars were narrowing, so many remained boarded up and more were closing with owners afraid to keep open due to rampant vandalism and a sordid blend of customers filing through the doors.

From the outside looking in, this place looked perfect. A generator hummed in the distance. Dark, music blared from a jukebox in the corner. The restroom stretched just beyond the dance floor down a dark hallway.

Perfect place to feed—after she got rid of the damn egg.

Nicolas was having a grand old time, selecting slow then fast on the drive there. Her jeans were soaked through, her legs quivering, her breaths rasping and moans slipping between her lips at the most inopportune moments. Dropping Simon at his door, she'd groaned a good-bye. He probably thought she'd miss him—as if!

She was feeling bitchy, hungry, and horny as hell.

Just as they entered, the phone bleated.

Alex answered quietly then handed it to Nicolas. "It's for you. They patched through a call."

Nicolas took it, his expression wiped clean of emotion.

Inanna.

Chessa pushed through the glass door into blessedly air-conditioned cool, tamping down a twinge of jealousy. What kind of hold did the ancient bitch have over him anyway?

"See you later," she called over her shoulder. It was now or never.

Alex fell into step behind her.

"I can find a meal on my own," she muttered over her shoulder.

"Not as much fun though." His voice rumbled with sensual promise.

"Nic will kill you," she whispered.

"Like I just said—"

"Suit yourself." She passed the long takeout counter and eyed the customers one by one.

"Hungry?" A waitress with bright red lipstick that gleamed bright against her cocoa-colored skin gave her a wink.

Chessa took in her muted excitement—the heightening thrum of her beating heart. "You know what my tastes are?"

"Rare, right?"

"Sure. Bleeding."

The woman's oversized white teeth bit into her full bottom lip. "I'll meet you in the back," she said, nodding toward the restrooms.

Chessa sighed. The waitress had made her as a vampire at first glance. She didn't recognize her, but maybe she'd seen Chessa in another blood bar. There had been so many.

Maybe she'd telegraphed her desperate hunger. She must be slipping.

Chessa headed to the restroom, intent on removing the bullet. She pushed through the swinging door, but turned when it whooshed behind her.

Alex leaned back against the wall. "Same deal as before?"

Her incisors were already descending when the door whipped open again and the waitress stepped inside, her expression alight with excitement. She tugged the T-shirt with the restaurant logo over her head. "Don't want to get it stained. Have to finish my shift, you know. Name's Maria."

"Sure," Chessa murmured, noting the vein pulsing at the side of the woman's dark throat.

"Is he hungry, too?" Maria said lifting her chin toward Alex. "He's not . . . into 'rare.'"

"That's all right if he wants to watch. Want it standing? I'm not too tall for you."

"Fine." Could anything be easier? If the woman whipped a straw from her pocket, she wouldn't have been surprised.

With her meal leaning close, Chessa licked Maria's neck, following the long artery, then tilted her head and sank her teeth just deep enough to puncture skin and the carotid. She sealed her lips around the wound to keep the blood from dripping down to the top of the woman's lacy bra.

Blood seeped around the wounds and slid down her throat, bubbling a little like fizzy champagne.

The woman moaned, and her breaths shortened. Her body pressed against Chessa's, her heavy breasts rubbing deliciously, exciting the tips of her own into aroused points.

Chessa rubbed against her, drinking deeply, letting her arms close around the woman's well-padded frame. The thought slipped through her blood-drugged mind that sharing an embrace with a host was pleasant, arousing—so unlike the dominating stance she usually took. She tightened her thighs, the egg seeming to swell in size inside her drenched pussy.

Strong arms encircled her from behind and a hand rucked up the hem of her shirt. When Alex's warm palm slid between them, cupping her breast, Chessa eased back her hips to grind against his heavy cock.

Heaven, after an evening of sheer, sensual hell.

With his free hand, he unbuckled her belt and pushed down her jeans. Then his hand was slipping between her legs, sliding between her slick folds. His thumb flicked her clit, and she trembled, drinking deeply while his fingers slipped inside her.

A muffled laugh gusted against her hair and he drew out the egg. "I wondered what the hell he was doing to you. Thought he had some kind of mind-fuck going on. Damn, you're wet!"

His fingers slid back inside a moment later, twisting into her, and she pulsed on them, encouraging him to delve deeper.

He obliged, stroking, swirling into her, drawing her moisture to paint her swollen labia.

"Want more?" he whispered.

"Mmmm-mmm," she murmured, around the woman's throat.

The woman's breath caught and she cried out, shivering hard as her orgasm crashed over her.

Chessa didn't stop drawing her blood into her mouth. Alex's fingers, all of them, tucked slowly into her cunt, curving and twisting—so thick she nearly blew then and there. She curved her back, lifting her ass to let him stroke deeper.

When his hand twisted and the thickness increased, she knew he'd crammed his thumb inside, too. So full her cunt burned, she pulsed on it, whimpering when cream seeped from her inner walls to ease him deeper.

Then she was riding his whole fist, her hot, dripping cunt sliding around him, pressing back to cram him deeper.

The door flew open, and Chessa's eyes widened. Her pussy clenched around Alex's fist. She retracted her teeth, lapping quickly to close the tiny punctures, reading the rage in the spots of burning color high on Nicolas's cheekbones.

"I better get back to my tables," Maria said, her eyes widening on Nicolas.

When she'd edged around him to flee out the door, Nicolas gave Chessa a look that held a simmering rage. "Interrupting anything?" he asked, acid etching his voice in harsh tones.

"I have her well in hand," Alex murmured, his breath still gusting against her neck.

"Alex," she warned, her teeth starting to chatter as Nicolas let the door close behind him. But she couldn't ease off Alex's fist, he was so high and tight inside her.

"Only filling in for you," Alex said, challenge in his words and the tightness of his voice.

Chessa closed her eyes, wondering if she'd be looking for a new partner after Nicolas had torn Alex limb for limb.

But Nicolas stepped closer, sandwiching her between himself and Alex. "This what you want? Both of us?" he asked, his voice raw.

Frightened and excited, she shook her head.

"Don't lie."

"It's too much," Chessa said, her voice trembling. "You had me so hot."

Nicolas knelt in front of her. "Ride his hand, baby." Then he brushed his thumb over her clitoris, lifting the hood, and leaned close to suck it with his lips.

Chessa came howling and quivering with Alex sliding in and out of her vagina, filling her to bursting, and Nicolas drawing hard on her clit. At the last, her legs gave way.

Both men murmured and reached out to hold her up.

Alex slowly pulled out and stepped to the side to wash his hand in the sink while Nicolas held her until the shivering stopped, and she could stand on her own two feet.

"Where's the bullet?" he asked.

Alex pulled it out of his jeans pocket and passed it to Nicolas. With a nod her way, he quietly left.

The silence that followed had Chessa feeling shaken and ashamed. "Nic—"

"Don't. I don't want to talk about this. Not yet." Then his fingers slipped between her legs, and he pushed the metal egg back inside her.

Groaning, Chessa bit her lip at the first little hum.

"There's something about him . . ."

She shook her head. "No. Nothing special at all."

"No, Chess. What I mean is I don't think he's quite . . . human."

"What are you thinking?" she asked, not mentioning the fact she'd had a similar thought.

"*Dieu!* I should have killed him. Or at the very least mopped the floor with him. Instead, this happened." His hand closed around hers and brought it to the front of his pants. His cock was full, heavy. Ready.

Her eyebrows drew together. "You wanted to screw him, too?"

Nicolas's lips thinned. "No, but I wanted him to have you. Wanted to watch."

"That's so strange?"

"Would you like to watch me fuck another woman?"

Chessa swallowed hard and shook her head. "No, I'd hate it."

Nicolas's arms closed around her, and he pulled her against his chest. "See what I mean?"

Chessa snuggled closer, enjoying his almond scent and the hardness of the muscle just beneath her cheek. "What does this all mean? Don't you think you're just wound tight because of all this trouble, and because you've been teasing me all night?"

"Maybe." But he didn't sound convinced.

"You gonna make me keep this thing in the rest of the night?"

"Are you going to complain?"

"You'd like that, wouldn't you?"

"All you have to do is say no."

"I can't." Rolling her forehead on his shoulder, she whispered, "Not to you."

His sigh sounded strained, maybe a little sad. "That's something anyway. Better get your pants up before someone else walks in."

Outside the restaurant, Alex lowered the phone.

"Any news?" she asked, her cheeks heating as his gaze slid down her body. She clenched her thighs together. Nicolas was right. There was something unusually alluring about Alex. "Any more bodies turn up?"

"It's quiet. The uniforms have more trouble than they can handle though."

"*Byron* asking us for help?"

"No. He knows we have our hands full." His eyebrows waggled wickedly.

Chessa gave him a frown. The man really liked walking on thin ice. "Shall we canvas the hotels again?" she said, wanting to change the subject.

"All quiet there, too."

"Weird."

"A lull before the storm?" Alex mused. He shrugged. "Shall I drop you both home?"

Chessa didn't bother reminding him, Nicolas's home wasn't hers. She figured he'd only make some smart ass comment anyway. Get himself killed for sure.

"Join us?" Nicolas asked, his voice a low growling rumble.

The bullet buzzed inside her, and Chessa's heart sped faster. What the hell was Nicolas up to now?

"I could use a cup of coffee."

"I'm all out," she said, her tone curt. Her message unmistakable. "And no electricity."

"No, you're not." Nicolas gave her a bland stare.

"I have a camp stove in my trunk," Alex said, lifting his shoulders at her glare.

"Do you have a map of the New Orleans area at home?" Nicolas asked.

Maybe he really was just thinking about work.

And maybe she was the Queen of Sheba.

"I do," she said, squeezing her thighs tight to keep the vibrator in place.

"Good. We'll start plotting the sightings. See if a pattern emerges over the next few days."

She wished she'd cleaned her apartment. Not that both men weren't aware she was a total slob. Maybe that's what she could do while the two of them got chummy over the map.

For sure, she wasn't planning on getting anywhere near either one. Her hormones were so out of whack she might have a meltdown.

CHAPTER

8

Alex noted things he'd missed the first time he'd crossed Chessa's threshold, surprising himself with his lack of attention.

He always noticed the details.

This time, the clutter struck him as slightly strange. Beneath the clothing that looked as though it had been dropped carelessly while she'd walked from one room to another and the shoes that must have flown as she kicked them off, the room was clean. The furniture polished. A floral scent permeated the air—soft and feminine, rather like the hint of perfume that clung to her skin the few times he'd stood close enough to notice.

Beneath messy stacks of books and opened mail, the sofa and armchairs were covered in soft corduroy in jewel tones—garnet, sapphire, and emerald. Plump silk pillows in Middle Eastern, embroidered patterns peeked from beneath the sofa and under a newspaper.

The walls of her apartment were a pale, soft gold and bare of photographs and paintings. Nothing to mark who she really was, or who had shared her past.

Just as she lived within her spiny demeanor, her home displayed the same urge to deflect warmth from without.

They'd opened the windows, pulling back pale sheer curtains to let in the muggy night air. They'd lit fat scented candles Chessa had seemed embarrassed to bring out of the cupboards. The flickering light painted her slightly angular features soft and feminine.

Nicolas watched her flutter around the room, seeming unable to sit still, his face growing hard, his gaze more feral as the night shadows deepened around them.

Alex had to remind them about their purpose for returning to her apartment. The map.

After he'd promised to repair the holes, Chessa let Nicolas tack the map to her living room wall. Then they'd stuck tacks next to Bayou St. John where the demon had exited the water and killed the three policemen and on the little street Madame Fortun had met her death.

Finally, sitting on the sofa opposite the map, they all three stared.

"It's scary we have to wait for more people to die before this will help," Chessa said, fidgeting between them.

Alex watched the byplay between Nicolas and Chessa, his amusement growing steadily.

By the frequent shifting of her legs, crossing, uncrossing, Nicolas had shoved the vibrator back inside her before they left the restaurant.

Chessa's cheeks were red, her gaze a little wild and desperate. She was delectable.

Everything he'd been promised.

Sexy, strong, moody . . . horny as hell.

And more. Chessa hid depths he wanted to plunder.

Nicolas was harder to read. His invitation had surprised Alex. Not sure if he was walking into an ambush, he'd played it loose, letting Nicolas lead the conversation.

Did he suspect Alex had secrets? Or was there another purpose to this night? Nicolas loved Chessa. That was apparent in every heated glance he gave her and how well he read her moods. His sly sideways glances that gauged her heightening arousal were impossible to miss.

Alex relaxed. Nicolas would never try to harm him, not while she watched anyway. Perhaps, he should give him a little nudge . . .

"How long have you two known each other?" he asked.

"Forty-two years." "Not long."

Nicolas's answer was telling. He'd counted. Chessa's said she didn't want it to be important.

"Not long in vampire years, I guess."

"Right." Chessa crossed her arms over her chest and scowled at them one at a time.

Such a spiny little porcupine.

Alex let his gaze slide over her, enjoying the blush reddening her cheeks and the way her eyes tried to shoot a warning his way.

He knew full well Nicolas noticed his slow appraisal. As casually as he could manage, he set his cup on the coffee table and stretched his arms above his head. "I guess I'd better be heading back home."

"Where would that be?" Nicolas asked.

"Not far," he replied, deliberately vague.

"There's no need." Nicolas's voice dipped into a rumbling growl.

The texture of that rumble appeared to be as alarming as a tiger's snarl to Chessa who shook her head when Alex's glance met hers.

So very funny. The two of them. Working at cross purposes.

"I don't want to intrude."

"You aren't," Nicolas's voice grated.

"Well, have you anything to spike this coffee? I am feeling a little edgy tonight."

"Whiskey?" Nicolas asked.

"I'm out," Chessa said in her trademark blunt tone.

"No, you're not," Nicolas said silkily.

"That'd be great." Alex suppressed a grin at Chessa's simmering anger.

Nicolas headed to a bookcase and reached behind a jumble of books and newspapers and pulled out a fifth of Jack Daniel's.

"How'd you know it was there?" Chessa groused. "I'd forgotten all about it."

"Good thing whiskey doesn't sour." Nicolas unscrewed the cap and held it over Alex's cup, pouring a couple fingers of liquor into the coffee.

Alex swirled his coffee cup and held it up. "Here's to a successful hunt."

Nicolas's lips curled upward. "We understand each other, I think," he murmured.

"Anything for a lady."

Nicolas held up the bottle. "To Chessa's pleasure." He drank deeply.

"A worthy toast." Alex turned his glance to Chessa and narrowed his gaze, flicking over her breasts, then lowering to her clenched thighs.

She popped off the sofa and quickly put the coffee table between herself and the two men. "Wait a second," Chessa said, her voice rising. "Nic, what are you up to? You've been so polite all night. You're never polite."

"Only with you, *ma petite*."

"You're only an asshole with me?"

"Of course. Would you take me any other way?"

His words struck her, and she flinched. Her hands tightened on her upper arms. "I don't mean to make you that way."

"I know. But you don't see that I'd do anything for you. Even share you."

"You never mentioned that before."

"I stood back when you desired Rene. I waited outside that hotel room, watching over you, while you made love with him and his love."

"And now?"

"You've a craving for this one," he said, lifting the bottle toward Alex. "I find I don't want to listen through a keyhole."

Chessa's eyes widened. "You want to watch?"

"I said I'd share."

"Both of you? At the same time?"

"Depends on his answer." Nicolas turned, his expression tight.

Alex felt a pang of regret for what he must do. Nicolas would suffer—and he truly didn't deserve it, but Chessa wasn't ready to commit. Each time she threw a challenge at Nic, he responded rather than throwing up his hands and walking away.

Alex needed them both. Needed them together and united. Leaving them to discover their love for each other wasn't an option. Time was of the essence.

With the *Grizashiat* closing ever closer to his goal and the unrest around them, both of human and inhuman origin, he didn't have the luxury of letting them find their way, naturally . . . to him.

"No biting," Alex said, directing his comment to Nicolas.

Nicolas lifted one dark brow. "Serving has its rewards."

"That's my preference. I'd just as soon earn an orgasm the old-fashioned way."

Nicolas nodded, his gaze narrowing.

Let him have his suspicions. Soon, he'd have to tell them the truth anyway. First, he had to win Nicolas's allegiance. Gain an advantage over Inanna.

Nicolas would come to love him. He detested Inanna. While he served her every need, resentment had to fester.

Alex would offer him another way to fulfill his oath. "Since I'm the guest, I'll follow your lead."

Chessa's hands fisted at her sides. "You two are making decisions without consulting me. What if I just say no?"

"You won't," Nicolas and Alex said at the same time.

Chessa stomped her foot. "Get your finger off that damn remote."

Nicolas's lips curved. "Your arousal is so strong I can smell it, Chessa."

"Doesn't mean I have to do anything about it."

"You don't have to do anything at all," Alex murmured.

She shot him a killing glance. "Shut up. You don't know what's happening here."

"Looks like I'm going to be fucking you."

Her breath caught. She'd liked the sound of that.

"I mean, so far I've fingered and fisted you to orgasm. Don't you think it's only fair I have a little pleasure, too?"

"I've got a bullet up my cunt. Bet it'd work just fine up your ass."

Alex grinned. "You'll have to put it there."

"Not exactly what I had in mind," Nicolas said softly. "But promising."

Anger drained from her face as she turned to Nicolas. "I don't understand you, Nic. Why are you doing this? I know you want me. Why do this?"

"I want you obedient. Compliant. Willing to follow my direction."

"You have that already," she said, her voice tight.

"Only when I fuck you. I want everything, Chessa. All of you."

"How does adding him to the mix help?"

"You've got walls around your heart. I've tried breaching them by force. Now, I'm changing my tactics. A bit."

She drew a deep, ragged breath. "I can't do this."

"You accepted Leo and Alex—"

"I didn't care about them." Her gaze landed switched to Alex. "Sorry."

"No offense taken. You don't know me. Yet." *But you will love me.*

"You take your pleasure, give your body over to other men. Easily," Nicolas said, his accent deepening with his rising passion.

"I'm not a whore."

"No, but you need to be held. To be made love to. You just won't allow yourself to feel too deeply."

"You think this will be any different?"

"You care about me," Nicolas said, his voice frightening in its quiet. "You know what this will do to me. You know how much I care when I invite this."

Her eyes welled with unshed tears. "Don't. Please."

"Not your decision," he said, regret tingeing his voice. "Take off your clothes."

Chessa's breath caught on another ragged breath.

His gaze swung to Alex. "You will follow my lead."

Alex nodded, understanding Nicolas had to have control. "You know the lady."

"Why are you going along with this, Alex?" Chessa asked, her voice tightening.

Alex gave her a crooked smile at the way she tried to change her tactic. "Chessa, I've been a walking hard-on since the moment I met you."

She rolled her eyes. "I don't fucking believe the both of you."

"Afraid?" Nicolas whispered.

Her chin shot up. "Of you?"

Nicolas didn't respond, just leveled a steady stare, one brow lifting in challenge.

She gripped the front of her T-shirt and pulled it over her head. "I don't fucking believe this."

Nicolas sat on the sofa next to Alex. "Tell me what you think of her body."

Chessa's lips formed a mutinous pout.

Alex settled deeper into the cushions, widening his legs around the arousal knotting at his groin. He swallowed hard and let his gaze slip from her burning cheeks to her small, round breasts. "A little small, but the nipples are lovely. Dark rose." They were already erect, and he hadn't telegraphed a single, sensual invitation since they'd left the restaurant restroom. *Interesting.*

Nicolas snorted. "They're perfect. You can take all of them into your mouth."

Chessa threw her wadded T-shirt against the wall, then stood with her fists curling at her sides.

Alex would have laid bets she wanted to cup her breasts to hide them.

"All your clothes, Chessa," Nicolas commanded, his tone brooking no arguments.

Hopping on one foot then the other, she huffed a string of curses as she pulled off her boots.

Alex didn't even try to withhold a grin, enjoying the way her small breasts jiggled as she fought her anger and the snugness of the boots. She didn't wait to be told to strip away the jeans, pushing them down her slim thighs and stepping out of them.

When she was naked, she stood opposite both men, her chin high. "Well, gonna comment on the rest?"

Although his mouth had gone dry, Alex cleared his throat and continued, his gaze sliding over her pale, creamy skin. "Beautiful. Muscular. Lithe." His glance fell to her pussy. "Wet."

"It's the damn vibrator."

"I haven't touched the remote, *ma jolie.*"

"Is that all?" Chessa asked, ignoring Nicolas.

Alex lifted his hand and twirled his finger, indicating she should turn.

Gritting her teeth, she spun, an ungraceful movement, made lovely by the view she presented.

"Chessa, love, you have a gorgeous ass. Tight, firm—"

"It's my ass," Nicolas bit out.

Alex nodded. "I won't go there."

"Not if you want to keep your dick."

"Maybe just a little kiss?"

Chessa choked and turned back around. "Satisfied?" she asked Nicolas.

"You're doing well. Now, I want you to come to the sofa and undress Alex."

Chessa bit back a moan. She was so damn horny cream seeped in a steady, embarrassing flow down her inner thighs. Now, he wanted her to touch Alex—while he watched? Was this a test?

If so, she was going to flunk. Already feeling weak with sexual hunger, her body burned. Her pussy was swollen from use, her inner tissues engorged and pulsating. Her breasts were tight, her nipples spiking hard. Even her skin felt too tight around her body and feverish.

Alex, the idiot, sat beside Nicolas without a clue how fine a line he was walking between any guy's wet dream and a soul sucking nightmare.

Not for a minute did she believe Nicolas would let this all unfold without losing the tight hold he'd kept over his emotions. His gaze burned too fiercely. His hands and jaw clenched too tightly.

Any minute now, he'd let loose.

She couldn't wait for it to happen.

"Undress him yourself," she said, lifting her chin.

"Now, now, Princess," he said, his tone so soft she knew one spark would ignite his fire. "You gave yourself to me. Called me 'Master.'"

Embarrassment flooded her face, the heat licking down her neck to her chest. "That was then. A moment."

Alex's eyebrows shot up. "I can manage my own clothes."

"Oh, no," Chessa snarled. "Nic wants to humiliate me. What he doesn't know is I've already seen you naked."

"Just my chest." Alex looked toward Nicolas and shrugged. "My shirt was covered in . . . ah . . . dust."

"Ash," Chessa purred. "Vampire ash."

"I'll get myself out of these clothes." Alex turned to the side and unbuttoned his shirt, shrugging it off his shoulders to strip down his arms. His hands went to the black cord that held his amulet, and he unfastened it, dropped it on the floor with his shirt. He kicked them both out of sight.

She swept his chest with a covetous stare, savoring the sight long enough that Nicolas's knuckles popped as he fisted his hands. Not waiting for the next command, she stepped around the table and gave it a little shove with her heel, sliding it backward, out of the way. Then she knelt in front of Alex and reached for the button at the top of his jeans.

Alex sucked in his breath as her fingers slid inside his waistband. She deftly flicked open his pants and pulled down the tongue of the zipper, taking her sweet time, making sure her fingers pressed the length of the thick ridge just beneath the placket.

His cock was huge, hard, and straining through the opening as it parted.

Chessa licked her lips and gauged Nicolas's reaction with a sly, sideways glance. "You can cry uncle any time now."

"Take it out," he said, his voice deadly even. "Play with it."

Chessa blew out a deep breath and slid her fingers beneath the elastic at the top of Alex's boxer shorts.

Again his stomach contracted and sweat broke out on his forehead. His breaths came faster.

Her fingertips brushed the head of his penis, and she paused to rub the soft skin, finding the slitted opening. She circled it.

Again, she licked her lips and leaned close, then pulled down his shorts just far enough to expose the purple tip of him. Her tongue swept out and lapped around his head. Then she opened her lips and sucked him into her mouth.

"Sweet Jesus!" he whispered, his hips lifting to press deeper.

She gripped the waist of his jeans, not letting up on the gentle suctioning as she eased them past his ass with his helpful little upward surges.

When she'd scraped them past his knees, he pressed his palm to her forehead, pushing her back. "Let me get them off."

Feeling wicked, she placed a boot between her legs and held tight as he slipped free his foot, then did the same with the other.

Both of them reached eager hands to slide away his pants and shorts until he too was naked.

Chessa pushed him back onto the sofa and straddled him.

The clearing of a throat, brought her back from the brink. She and Alex turned to Nicolas.

"You can undress yourself," Chessa said, challenge in the glare she gave him. "I'm kinda busy."

A tic pulsed beside his eye, but Nicolas held out his hand. "I want it back."

Alex understood what he asked before she did and fit his fingers into her vagina, curving to snag the vibrator and slowly pulling it out. He set it in the center of Nicolas's palm. "What next?" he asked, a small strained smile on his face.

Nicolas's eyes narrowed. "Chessa, fuck the grin off his face. Please."

Chessa grinned at Nic, thoroughly enjoying how bothered he was getting. Then she rose on her knees, staring down at Alex as she lifted his cock and fitted it to her opening. With his chest rising and falling fast, she braced her hands on his shoulders and slid down, taking him inside.

Alex groaned and his eyes closed tight.

Chessa understood the feeling and was right there with him. His cock was ridged with veins that rasped her inner channel all the way up. When she was fully seated, their groins snugly meshed, she leaned down to kiss him.

Alex's arms encircled her, his hands smoothing up and down her back.

She got the hint and started to move up and down, digging her knees into the soft cushion on either side of his hips as she rose and fell, and then rose again.

The ride was slow, savored by them both. Her tongue lapped along his, her lips suctioning, drinking him in. Her breaths mingled with his as she rode faster, beginning a motion that rocked forward and back while she lifted and fell, sliding him deep and grinding her clitoris into the crisp hairs surrounding the base of his cock.

Gradually, stroke by stroke, a fire lit deep in her womb, curling tightly, making her shudder and moan, causing his body to tighten like steel. She tore away her mouth and flung back her head, dragging deep gulps of air into her lungs.

Alex's hands gripped her sides and lifted her, bringing a breast to his mouth. He latched onto it, biting the swollen tip, causing her to cry out.

But she wanted him deeper, so she murmured a complaint and he let go, laughing softly against her skin. "Nic, so right," he panted. "Perfect. She's perfect."

Chessa smiled and continued to ride his thick cock. "Damn, right," she murmured, gripping his shoulders harder as she lunged against his lap now, her movements less measured, her breaths shortening.

When the rapture came, it snuck up on her slowly, unwinding in her womb, like a spring losing tension, curl by curl. Her body quivered, and she whimpered. She squeezed shut her eyes and simply rocked, letting her orgasm wash away in slow ebbs that left her feeling weak.

When she finally drew a deep breath, her forehead rested against his, and her body was snuggled close. His strong arms hugged her tight.

He hadn't come. Hadn't joined her on the summit. She lifted her head and gave him a questioning stare.

"That was just to shave your edges, sweetheart," he said, his lips blurred by her kisses, his face reddened, but still taut. "Seemed like you were a little nervous. Besides, he never said a thing about me coming."

Like a splash of cold water, she came fully to her senses and pushed against his chest to lift away.

Alex held her tight and kept her seated deep on his rock hard cock. He glanced to Nicolas. "What's next?"

Nicolas let out the breath he'd held while Chessa screwed Alex inches from him. All the while he'd sat beside them, his hands fisted on his knees, his teeth grinding while they'd cheerfully followed his instructions.

Chessa hadn't looked his way once—at least, not until the end. She'd ridden the other man slowly, seeming to savor a gradually rising passion. Together, their bodies had blended beautifully—Chessa's slim and taut, Alex's burly and powerful.

Her whimpers had held a soft mewling quality, like a kitten's when she'd come. The sound still reverberated in his mind.

Nothing like the wild moans she always gave him.

Stunned, a little sickened, he tamped down the urge to jerk her from the other man's cock and fuck her hard, the way she always demanded it. He wanted to remind her who held her reins—whose hands delivered the ultimate pleasure.

Alex surprised him, withholding his own pleasure, never using to his advantage the strength evident in his thick, toned muscles. His body had tightened, his muscles flexing into prominence, his breaths rasping loudly as she'd pumped on him. Still, he'd held back, resisting the creamy, rippling invitation of Chessa's tight, hot pussy to hammer deep toward her core.

That she'd enjoyed the man's thick cock, using it to ride toward her own fulfillment, had been evident in her soft cries.

He and Alex shared a similar size—something Nicolas planned to use to his advantage.

Nicolas wanted to hate Alex—*would* if Chessa ever came to love him more. For now, he'd tolerate his intrusion into their relationship—as long as the other man was needed. Nicolas would determine when to send him packing.

Between the two of them, Chessa didn't stand a chance of hiding behind her brittle façade. She'd stay on the edge of ecstasy, fulfilled beyond her dreams. Her emotions tested beyond her ability to sublimate them.

Surely, she'd shatter. Then he'd be there to gather together all the pieces of her life and help her form a new one. With him. Within the coven.

"Chessa," he said softly.

Her glazed eyes refocused, and she gave him a flaying glare.

Her defiance pleased him. He held out his hand, palm up.

Pretending extreme reluctance, she slowly placed her hand in his.

Nicolas stood and tugged her upward with Alex's help, guiding her off his cock. "Time for bed," he said, letting his anger and jealousy flare and bleed into his hardened tone.

Swaying slightly as she stood, she closed her eyes. "Can I bathe first?"

"Why waste the bottled water . . . and the lubrication?"

Chessa opened her eyes and nodded, her jaw firming for the coming battle of wills. She tugged away her hand and stepped past him.

Nicolas laid a hand on her backside and squeezed—a promise of things to come.

Her breath hissed between her teeth. "Does he have to see that, too?"

Was she ashamed of her particular fetish?

"I will decide what's needed."

"Damn you," she whispered, not looking back, but her body tightened.

Leaning close, he tucked her hair behind an ear and whispered, "Pull the covers from the bed. Bend over the mattress and wait for us."

"Jesus . . . *fuck*." Her slender frame quivered, her bottom tensing beneath his palm.

Oh, a spanking was definitely needed. But would he let Alex warm her soft ass?

"Go."

She flounced away, her feet slamming on the wooden floor.

When she'd passed the doorway, Nicolas nailed Alex with a warning stare.

Alex rose, smirking and rubbing an idle hand over his belly. "I know. Her ass is yours—and I follow your lead."

"In all things," Nicolas bit out. "No matter if she balks."

Alex returned his glare, his gaze narrowing. "Do you even know why you're doing this?"

Nicolas had enough of playing games. "You aren't what you appear. I felt your lure back at the restaurant."

Alex's lips curved in a rueful smile. His gaze raked Nicolas with sly assessment. "Did you now? Felt something like it before?"

"Yes," Nicolas gritted out. Only one other being had ever drawn him with a lick of a sensual noose. "No more tricks. Not with Chessa."

Alex's expression drained of humor. "I mean you no harm. And I like Chessa. I'll play by your rules."

"I know why I'm here. I'll figure out your purpose, and your nature, sooner or later."

"I'm counting on it." Alex lifted a brow and stared down at his cock. "I don't suppose you're going to let me get off, are you?"

Nicolas's lips stretched at the man's blatant frustration. "There are always rewards for gifts, at least among vampires."

Alex drew a grateful sigh. "We're cool, then?"

Nicolas shook his head. He'd seen everything, he'd thought.

But Alex was a puzzle. He just hoped his instincts weren't leading him deeper into treacherous water. He wanted to trust him—not just with earning Chessa's love.

He wanted to know that this "creature," whatever he was, would be strong enough to withstand Inanna's brand of hell. For he had no doubts Alex was trolling for the bitch.

Chessa, as always, was the key.

CHAPTER

9

Wondering why she'd followed his command like a damn ewe, Chessa waited in the bedroom, straining to make out the men's low voices.

No doubt Nicolas was planning his strategy, enlisting Alex in his demented game to drive her nuts.

Against the two of them, she'd melt like a soppy ball of wax, molded for their amusement and pleasure.

The pleasure part she had no qualms accepting. The amusement made her cringe. Before the night was over, Alex would know all her dirty little "go-buttons."

Why she didn't just back away from the bed and tell them both to go to hell, she couldn't have explained to anyone, least of all herself.

Yet, she was aware a part of her yearned to submit. Craved to be controlled. Only when forced, could she feel truly . . . free.

Steps sounded behind her and she groaned inwardly, fisting her hands in the soft cotton sheets.

"Spread your legs and lift your bottom, Princess."

"I hate it when you call me that," she said, hating even more the quaver in her voice. Still, she widened her bent legs and tilted up her ass, aware the two of them could see . . . well, everything.

A large palm smoothed over her ass, the glide deceptively soothing. Then it drew away and the sound of clothing sliding, dropping to the floor told her Nicolas stripped behind her.

"Her skin's cool to the touch, Alex. Use this to warm it."

Her eyes bugged. She only just resisted the urge to peek over her shoulder. When the first stinging slap landed, she tasted leather. His belt. *The bastard.*

Chessa couldn't help the fresh trickle of arousal that seeped from between her legs to wet her thighs and the sheets bunching beneath her hips. Nor could she help tipping higher to meet his strokes.

Alex wielded it with precision, delivering stinging snaps that while not exactly gentle, didn't cut too deeply. He striped her, working over every inch of her bottom until her ass had to be glowing.

"Flick her cunt."

"Oh God." She bit her bottom lip to halt the cry that tore at her throat when the leather singed her labia.

"Again."

The next slap sounded wet, and her pussy tightened.

"Close your eyes."

Chessa squeezed them tight, not knowing what to expect next, until a hot, blunt-tipped cock dipped inside her.

But whose? Not knowing only heightened her sensitivity. The heat of her stinging flesh, stretching around that nameless cock as it shoved forward, spearing deeply, grew unbearable. She moaned and pressed her forehead into the cool percale.

The cock pulled out, then slammed forward again, taking away her breath, then pulled out again—this time all the way.

Then a shuffling sounded behind her and another cock, this time dry, screwed into her.

God, they were taking turns! "Fuck. God. *Pleeease*," she moaned, unable to hold onto her prideful resistance. The thought of the two of them, standing behind her, cocks held in large, curved fists as they primed themselves staring at her wet pussy nearly had her weeping.

A deep stroke inside, a slow exit, another slow, burning stroke that crammed deep.

Her knees trembled, her thighs burned as she held the uncomfortable posture and welcomed the heat of thick thighs pressing against the backs of hers.

Another shuffle and long fingers stroked her folds, parted her, and fitted a wet cock to her vagina and rammed forward, delivering several faster thrusts.

Her pussy slurped when the cock withdrew and clasped noisily around air.

When another didn't immediately fill her, she moaned again.

Fingers thrust into her pussy, swirled, then painted a trail between her buttocks, sliding over her asshole. *Nic!*

A shudder wracked her body and her nipples grew engorged again, scraping the bedding. She rubbed them into the sheet, wriggled her rear and hoped like hell one of them intended to fuck her.

When a cock poised at her entrance, she sucked in a deep breath, then let it loose in a garbled scream when it drove hard toward her womb. This time, she'd get it for sure. This cock stroked deep, fast—faster, harder. A taut belly smacked her burning cheeks with satisfying furor. God, it had to be Nicolas!

Hands slid beneath her, cupping her breasts, then fingers clamped hard on her nipples, squeezing, twisting.

Just as she'd thought, he finally let loose, coming at her with pistoning, jerking hips that pounded his thick cock inside her.

When she began to unravel, he jerked hard, once, and cum spurted deep inside her in a pulsing stream. He collapsed over her, his face nuzzling the back of her neck. "Christ! I never thought you'd let me come."

Chessa's eyes slammed open as Alex pumped inside her, slower now, rocking against her ass as the last hot jets of his cum spilled into her.

JesusFuckingChrist! Nicolas hadn't even gotten started.

Her trembling increased along with lapping waves of shivers that ebbed and flowed as Alex's hot breath steamed the back of her neck.

The sound of fabric tearing drew her gaze to the side. Nicolas stared at her, his expression tight but triumphant as he ripped apart a pillowcase. Naked, his glistening erection rampant, she stared back, her eyes widening as she realized why he'd ripped apart her favorite pillowcase.

The strips were long and thick—two of them. One for each of her hands.

"When you're done fucking her, how about tying her to the bedposts?"

"Gimme a minute," Alex groused. "My legs are jelly."

Nicolas's smile didn't reach his eyes. "Thought he was me, *chérie*? I think my ego's crushed."

"Fuck you," she whispered, deciding then and there she was going to kill him—after he fucked her into tomorrow.

Alex sighed, kissed her shoulder, and leaned away, pulling out of her slowly as though reluctant to leave her moist heat.

When he backed away, Nicolas laid a strip of pale fabric in his palm. "Around the notches. I want her torso off the mattress."

Chessa sank to the floor beside the bed, her legs finally giving way.

"Sorry, sweetheart," Alex said, a wicked smile stretching his mouth. He grabbed her by the waist and lifted her, setting her in the center of the mattress, then straddled her, his waning erection tapping her chest. He lifted one hand and tied the strip around it, then stretched her arm above her head to tie it high above her.

Slipping to her side, he tightened the tether, raising her up.

"This isn't comfortable," she said, between teeth clenched tight to stop their chattering.

"Trust me," Nicolas said, his mirthless smile widening.

Alex tied her other hand, then stretched her arm bringing her shoulders off the mattress.

Sitting back on his haunches beside her, he glanced back, waiting for the next command.

"Crawl beneath her, support her back against your chest."

Chessa nearly screamed with anticipation, dangling while he maneuvered beneath her.

When he'd settled, her head rested on his shoulder, and his chest lifted her high enough the ties didn't pull her arms out of their sockets.

But she couldn't move her upper body either. With Alex's cock riding the crevice of her butt, she was entirely at Nicolas's mercy to do whatever he pleased.

The hard, grim set of his jaw heightened her trepidation. Her heartbeat fluttered. Her mouth went dry.

Nicolas walked to the end of the bed and climbed on, his legs thickening as they bent, his huge cock bouncing from his groin.

He reached to either side of him and pushed apart her legs, which were bracketed by Alex's, and forced his wider, driving his cock harder against her ass.

Apparently, that wasn't good enough, because Nicolas lifted her feet one at a time and hooked them over the outside of Alex's and pushed them up, bending her knees, tilting her pussy upward.

Now she had no leverage. And she felt obscenely open and exposed. Moisture trickled from between her swollen folds.

"Play with her breasts, Alex," he said softly.

Chessa had hoped her body was so well sated after so many orgasms that arousal would be impossible. If she could resist the curling desire growing inside her, she might survive what he had in mind.

But Alex palmed her breasts and squeezed them, then rolled the nipples between his fingers. Her stretched body and wide-open pussy heated once more.

"Please, Nic," she groaned. "I can't take any more."

"Will you deny me?"

She opened her mouth to do just that, but a look from his darkly glinting watchful gaze had her clamping her lips closed. If she hadn't seen a hint of bleak darkness at the back of it all, she'd have thought him a true sadist.

Her submission was important. But why? Because he wanted to lord his power over one of the Born? She dismissed that thought as quickly as it arose, recognizing she needed a reason to resent him. A barrier she could throw up to redirect her need for him.

Nicolas was the last man, living or dead, who needed to prove himself. Held above the others, given responsibilities reserved for those destined by birth to lead, he hadn't earned his place by climbing over anyone's shoulders.

Perhaps he thought her willingness to submit was a test of her affection.

Sweet Jesus! Was that it? She'd sworn never to let another soul touch hers. Yet, here she was. Opened. Accepting . . . anything he meant to give her.

Nicolas came over her, bracing himself above her and Alex. His gaze rose to Alex's and a thin-lipped smile spread over his face. Then his head swooped down. His lips touched hers. Hot, firm—his kiss slid and circled, wetting her mouth, building her hunger.

Her fangs slid from her gums, and she bit his lip.

His laughter vibrated against her chest. Wicked, dark, *pleased*.

Alex pinched her nipples harder, and she clamped onto Nicolas's lip, mouthing him to draw his blood across her tongue. His *Revenant* blood. Fired by the genetic chemistry that urged her to take control, she lifted her head, battling his mouth.

When his cock rubbed between her folds, she gasped, opening her jaws, and he pulled away, licking the blood that seeped from the shallow wounds she'd left.

"It's all right," he said, rocking his hips forward and back between her slick folds. "I want your bite. I accept your challenge."

"That was no challenge, *Revenant*," she hurled back, fighting the tug of his hard, ridged cock while trying to withhold any sign of her arousal. Although she guessed, he thought the kiss was proof enough. The moisture leaking from inside her to caress his cock was just the exclamation point.

"Perhaps, I should take a bite of my own, seeing as how it's such an inconsequential thing."

Alex's chest jerked beneath her, his laughter gusting into her hair.

"You wait until you need me at your back, asshole," she flung over her shoulder.

"I have yours," Alex purred, curving his hips to remind her whose dick she lay upon.

Nicolas dove in for another quick kiss, a hard mashing of lips, and then he moved down her squirming body. "Let me have this one, Alex," he said poised above the hand caressing her breast.

"You're just sore because you're the one tied up, and we get to have all the fun," Alex said to her, sliding a hand from her breast and slowly down her stomach.

"Touch my dick," Nicolas choked out, "and you'll be wearing a smile across your throat."

"Keep moving south, and we won't have a problem." Alex's fingers glided over her pussy lips where he started playfully massaging them, missing the hardened little kernel at the top of her cunt entirely.

Chessa drew a harsh breath as Nicolas's mouth closed around her distended nipple. "Alex, aren't you pissed you have to play like a mattress?" she gritted out, fighting the tug of Nicolas's hot lips.

"So long as something hot as you is stretched out on top, I don't mind a bit."

Nicolas nipped her nipple.

"God, you're both bastards."

"Running out of clever barbs so soon?" Alex drawled.

How could a girl be clever when she was sandwiched between two sexy men? "Ooooh!"

Laughter shook Alex's chest and spilled around the breast still tucked deep in Nicolas's mouth. A smile tugged at her lips at their playfulness, until Nicolas nipped her, harder this time. "Ouch! Watch it. That's not a chew toy."

"Nope," Alex said pulling at her opposite breast. "It's an all-day sucker."

Chessa flailed against her bonds, trying to shake them both loose.

Nicolas suckled hard, swirling the tip of his tongue around the engorged tip.

"Maybe you should move a little lower," Alex murmured, "before she figures out how much damage she can do with those feet."

If she'd really wanted to do either of them damage—she'd have already figured that one out. Now, the gauntlet had been thrown down, she was obliged to try to do her damnedest.

She untucked a foot from behind Alex's calf and stomped on Nicolas's ass. The second kick landed in his palm, and he pushed her foot high and wide. He quickly pressed the other up and outward.

Chessa blinked, realizing he'd been waiting for her to make some ridiculous move like that, because now her pussy tilted upward even more exposed and accessible.

Nicolas scooted down the bed and gave her gaping cunt a wide, wet licking. "Thanks, Alex."

"Anything to help the cause."

"The cause?" she said, her voice strangling from rage, while her sex trembled and tightened.

"Your complete surrender, sweetheart," Alex drawled.

"God, I'm so screwed."

"Not yet, but Nicolas's getting there."

The next laps proved her partner's claim. Nicolas nuzzled between her inner lips and suckled her tender flesh, drawing her moist lips between his to nibble, and then slanting his tongue over her center to lap at the fluids he seemed to crave the taste of.

All Chessa could do was wrap her hands around her ties and hold on tight. Unable to move in her restrained position, she couldn't nudge him toward the places she needed sucked the worst.

She revised her opinion of him when he glided past her clit again and again—he was a heartless sadist.

Her limbs and will stretched to their limits, she could only moan and thrash her head on Alex's chest, while he murmured filthy things in her ear.

"Let Nicolas have your sweet cream, Cheech. Give it up and he'll lick you like a snow cone."

"Sounds sticky," she gasped, when Nicolas slipped one of her feet onto the top of his shoulder and used his freed hand to screw two fingers into her cunt.

"Do you want him to lick your ass instead? Poke his tongue into your tight little hole?"

"Shut up, Alex," she said, her breath sobbing because that's exactly what she wanted at that moment.

Nicolas took Alex's hint. Keeping his fingers thrusting into her sopping pussy, he swirled his tongue lower, dipping the tip into the center of her anus.

"Shit! Jesus! Stop it, Nic," she said, pressing her foot on his shoulder to pump her hips up and down.

"Doesn't look like you want him to stop, love."

"Alex, butt out!" she bellowed.

His fingers plucked her nipples, letting them spring back, hard and tight. Distracted, Chessa missed the fact Nicolas had wet his thumb until it tunneled into her ass.

She squeezed shut her eyes, just letting herself feel. Both of them, hot, growing slick beneath her, over her—sweat dripping from Nicolas's brow to slide around her cunt and below.

"OhGodOhGod," she moaned, as a ripple worked its way inside her channel, clenching around her vagina. "I'm gonna come, Nic. Please!"

He drew hands away, abandoning her.

She howled, her body bowing with frustration.

"Shhhh, baby," Nicolas said, pressing a quick kiss to an inner thigh, and then he heaved himself over her, fitting his cock along her slit like a thick, nocked arrow. "How do you want it, love?"

Chessa shook her head. Her cunt! Her ass! Instead, she whimpered, "However you please."

"Perfect, Chessa. You're perfect." Alex's lips slid along her cheek, his hands cupped and caressed her breasts, soothing her now.

Chessa hiccuped, holding Nicolas's tender gaze.

He spread her inner lips with his fingers, wrapping his fist around his cock to stroke it base to tip, and placed himself at her entrance. Then hooking his arms beneath her knees, he lifted her bottom away from Alex and slammed forward.

Suspended on her ties and his cock, she hung there, completely without the will to escape.

For once, completely free.

His dark gaze locked with hers as he stroked forward, burying himself so deep she thought she should have felt a nudge at the back of her throat.

He drew back, dragging his big cock past her swollen and abused inner walls. Her pussy clung to his shaft, caressing its length, clutching at the last when all but the thick, round tip remained inside.

Then he plunged into her again, the muscles of his arms and chest flexing as he held her hips high, his abdomen rippling, tightening, and then he was pulling away again, leaving her empty.

Chessa's body was limp and boneless. She forgot to breathe when he entered her again, accepted his punctuated passion, gloried in his possession. She was his. Unconditionally.

When the next wave of heat wound itself tight around her womb, she ceased to be surprised he could wrest yet another sweeping orgasm. She floated on the crest, opening her mouth to cry weakly when it ebbed away.

Nicolas held her, sliding easily, gently inside her until she fell back into Alex's waiting arms.

"One more time," Nicolas rasped.

God, she couldn't. She really couldn't, but she nodded, not questioning when he pressed her thighs against her chest and ordered Alex to hold them tight.

When his cock pressed into her ass, she stirred, moaning. "Can't, Nic." Her voice sounded like someone else's lacking strength, seeming small.

"Once more," he demanded.

And she did, screaming when he stroked inside, filling her completely, remorselessly, again and again.

His shout echoed around her walls, dying down to tender whispers of praise that made her weep with their sweetness. Soft kisses pressed her lips and into her hair.

She woke when a cool cloth soothed her intimate flesh, but

quickly slipped back into sleep, cradled between the two men who'd gifted her with freedom from her memories.

Chessa woke at the first stroke of a thick cock sliding deep into her pussy. She moaned—a feeble, feigned protest.

Soft, deep-throated laughter shook the chest of the man she faced.

She pried open her eyes, her gaze colliding with Alex's lit by the moonlight that sifted through her open window. His lips were curved with wicked, sly amusement.

She lay on her side between the two of them, a thigh resting atop his hip, her sex open and filled with his rutting cock. Her nipples tightened immediately, scraping the sparse hair that covered his broad chest. "Been awake long?" she asked, striving for a bored tone, but her tongue felt thick and stuck to the roof of her mouth. Her voice creaked.

The two of them were up to no good. Many inches of wicked intentions if the other cock poking at her ass was any indication.

Oh God! A shiver caught her by surprise. She was already wet, moisture flooding her channel to ease his steady glide. How long had they gently plied her body? And how the hell had she managed to sleep through their preparations?

Nicolas's hand flowed over her shoulder, glided down her back, and dipped into the curve of her waist, halting as he palmed one cheek of her ass. "About time you joined us," he growled, squeezing her hard.

She gasped, her bottom still stinging from the lash of Nicolas's belt, and the bastard knew it from the soft chuckle that stirred the hair beside her ear.

"Did you think we were satisfied, *ma petite*?"

Her breath hitched, a whimper stealing between her lips.

His hand glided away then fingers parted her buttocks. Something cold and foreign pressed against her asshole. Cool, creamy gel slid inside her burning tissue.

"Oh God!" she groaned. "You've been in my drawer again."

"Such nasty things I found there, love." A finger pressed inside her, swirling in the gel, pushing easily into her depths, soothing her, exciting her unbearably as she realized what they meant to do.

"Mount him, Chessa," Nicolas said, his voice deepening with his command.

Another shiver racked her body, but she moved over Alex. His hands clasped her hips hard to keep his cock deeply embedded as she shifted, following his slow roll to his back. Her knees slid to either side of his hips as she braced her hands on his shoulders.

All the while, Nicolas's finger stayed deep inside her.

"Lean over him, love."

Chessa sank against Alex's chest, burying her burning face in the crook of his neck while Nicolas rose behind her, his knees bracketing hers.

Alex cupped the back of her head, his fingers combing through her hair in an oddly gentle gesture.

Her breaths deepened when another finger slipped inside her ass, and Alex's cock jerked inside her. "I don't believe this," she murmured, her heart skipping faster.

"Do you know why we're doing this, sweetheart?" Alex whispered.

"Because you're having fun?" she blurted.

His chuckle scraped his chest hair over her tender nipples, and she bit her lip.

"Fun is a very pale word," Alex chided, "and not the *only* reason."

"Because you're both trying to drive me crazy?"

"Guess again."

"Because I want this?" she said, her voice thin and quavering.

"Closer." His hands lifted her face so that she couldn't avoid meeting his gaze. "We're doing this because you need it."

"I need two men to fuck me senseless?"

His smile didn't match the softness of his gaze. "You need to be pushed beyond your limits. To yield to the pleasure. No holding back."

Like she'd been able to hold back a single choked groan before?

"You know what's going to happen, don't you?" Nicolas asked softly, pressing a kiss to the top of one shoulder.

"*God*. Yessss," she hissed.

"Is it more than you can take?"

His tenderness was already more than she wanted to accept. Now he wanted her to tell him she agreed? Wanted her complicity in their seduction? *Bastard!* She'd never be able to claim she'd been overwhelmed. *Taken.*

Her eyes filled. Her body tightening, beyond mere arousal. "Don't make me say it," she pleaded.

His fingers withdrew slowly. The heat radiating from his body left her, and she knew he was going to move away.

Something she couldn't bear. More painful than the emotions

swirling inside her, his disappointment for her lack of courage settled like a weight pressing against her heart. "Please, Nic," she whispered, meeting Alex's gaze. "Please, I want this. With you. With both of you."

Nicolas gripped her hair, angling her head to meet his lips. His kiss was fierce, harsh. "Don't hold back a whimper. Not a single moan."

Her breath sobbed. "I promise. Please." *Please love me!*

He released her and a hand pressed between her shoulder blades until once again, she lay against Alex's chest.

Shivering, her teeth starting to chatter with the tension building inside her, she kept still while he placed the plump head of his cock against her back entrance and pushed inside.

Chessa groaned, convinced she'd never take all of him, not with Alex's thick cock already buried inside her cunt—there wasn't room. But Nicolas pressed deep, inch by searing inch, until she was filled to bursting with both of them, pinned between them, held immobile by the painful, *sinful* pressure.

Then Nicolas smoothed his hands around her chest, cupping her breasts. "Take us both, Chessa. Move now," he said, his voice sounding strained.

"Easy for you to say," she gritted out, but she did move, up Alex's chest and back down, dragging off both their cocks, then cramming backward to take them deep again.

At first, neither man moved, letting her set the pace and the depth of each stroke.

Her nails dug into Alex's shoulders as she strained, and she realized she clamped her jaws tight to hold back her moans. She'd promised.

She gasped, opening her mouth and a thin wail tore from her throat. She moved faster.

"That's it, Chessa," Nicolas murmured, squeezing her breasts. Now, his hips lunged against her bottom, deepening his penetration when she thrust back.

She glided forward and back, faster now, her breaths harsh, her moans rising while he pumped harder, his cock stroking deeper as she rode Alex's cock.

"Jesus!" Alex gasped, lifting his head from the pillow to glide his lips along her jaw.

She turned her face downward to capture his mouth, breathing heavily through her nose as Nicolas forced her breaths from her lungs in sharp grunts that sounded animalistic and savage.

The thin, inner wall that separated the two men burned from friction, heat curling upward to tighten her womb, and then she broke the kiss, a cry breaking free as her orgasm burst over her, leaving her shuddering and boneless, tears slipping down her cheeks.

Nicolas stroked twice more, then pulled out, his cum jetting over her buttocks.

Alex gripped her hips and planted his feet in the mattress to pound upward, stiffening beneath her as his shout rang out.

Hands soothed over her hot skin, lips caressed her cheeks and neck, low murmured praise poured over her, and Chessa drifted toward sleep as the aching weight that had enclosed her heart, lifted and faded away.

CHAPTER
10

The mattress dipped opposite Chessa.

Bright, golden daylight peeked beneath the pale curtains, fluttering in a warm breeze that licked over the bodies still lying spooned close together.

Chessa had snuggled her sweet little bottom close to Nicolas's groin while she slept, instinctually seeking connection.

Nicolas yawned and lifted his head to peer over Chessa's shoulder to see Alex rising from the bed and heading toward the living room.

Curious, Nicolas unwound himself from Chessa and rose, snagging his jeans from the pile of clothing on the floor. As he walked inside, buttoning his pants closed, he found Alex slipping into his pants. "Going out?" he asked softly.

"Yeah," Alex said, glancing his way.

"It's the middle of the day."

Alex's lips curved and a single eyebrow rose. "So it is. All the more reason for me to get home and get some shut-eye. That bed's a little crowded."

"It's sunny outside."

"Your point being?"

Nicolas held his breath. He'd thought he had Alex figured out. If not a *Revenant*, he had to be some other night creature. He slumped into an armchair sitting in the shadows and watched as Alex reached for the shirt shoved beneath the couch.

When he lifted it, something thudded dully on the floor. A flash of red glinted in the sunlight.

Alex quickly swiped the object up, tucking it into his front pocket.

"That stone," Nicolas said, leaning forward.

Alex lifted his head. "What about it?"

"Can I see it?"

Alex's gaze sharpened on Nicolas. His shoulders drew back.

If it came to it, Nicolas wasn't going to fight him for a look, but his curiosity and suspicions burned. "I'd like to see the stone."

Alex shrugged and drew the cord out of his pocket, the stone along with it, and strode toward Nicolas to drop it into his palm.

Nicolas didn't have to examine it closely to know it was the same stone he'd held in his mouth when he'd confronted the demon in the water. While he hadn't looked closely at the etched inscription at the time, the stone was the same deep carnelian red, the same smooth oval shape and weight. His stomach clenched. "How'd you get this?"

"You tell me."

"Simon," he bit out.

Alex held his gaze, his expression shuttered. "He borrowed it from me."

"Why?"

"To protect you from the demon." Alex reached down and flipped the amulet to the other side.

Nicolas bent close and saw a depiction of three winged angels plucking at a nightmarish creature with dangling breasts whose long fangs were bared above the belly of a flailing infant boy. The relief sent a chill through Nicolas although he couldn't have explained why.

"The three angels are Semangelof, Senoy, and Sansenoy. The inscription on the other side is a prayer meant to repel the *lilum*."

"Fairy tales," Nicolas said, closing his hand tight around the amulet.

"Simon gave you the stone to place in your mouth to keep the demon from entering your body. He clings to his new host and enters through the mouth."

Nicolas sat still for a long moment, letting that bit of news sink in. Not that he believed any trinket could stop a demon. "I've been guarding him for over eight hundred years. Why the hell didn't he give me one of these before? Why aren't we all armed with these tokens?"

"This is one of a kind. Ancient. Carved and blessed by those three angels."

"Angels." Nicolas snorted. "Why is it yours?

For once, Alex's expression held no trace of humor." Because Simon kept it safe for me. Gifted me with it when I was a child."

"He kept it from me even though he believes it has power over The Devourer?"

"He swore an oath to hold it until he'd met me."

Nicolas understood oaths. Knew how powerful and costly they could be. A friendship he'd valued for centuries disintegrated like *Revenant* ash as he stared at the amulet.

"If it helps, Simon knew you wouldn't need it before yesterday."

"Is he a prophet now, too?" Nicolas asked, bitterness tightening his throat.

"I swear he's a friend," Alex said softly.

Nicolas bolted from the armchair, staring into Alex's steady blue gaze. "Who the fuck are you?"

"I'm Alex. Chessa's new partner," Alex said evenly. "Let's leave it at that, for now."

"Get out."

Alex nodded and strode toward the door, opened it, and turned. "You know, I'm on your side." He flashed a small, tight smile and closed the door quietly behind him.

Nicolas stared after him for a long time, wondering which fucking side he was talking about.

"Hi, I'm Bernie. I don't s'pose I can catch a ride with you? I'm headin' out to San Gabriel. Gotta grandma to find."

Standing beside the gas pump, the white-haired gentleman looked him up and down and must have concluded, erroneously, that Bernie didn't look like much of a threat.

Bernie's face had been an unexpected boon. His wide affable smile and glinting chocolate eyes had lulled several victims—up until the last moments of their lives.

This old man wouldn't be any different.

"You're a ways from the city," the old man said, eyeing Bernie's New Orleans T-shirt.

"They say they're shipping out bodies from New Orleans to a temporary morgue. Have to take a look for Grandma there."

The old man's expression softened. "Sure, I'll take you. I understand being worried about folks."

Bernie smiled and reached to shake his hand. "Pleased to meet you, sir."

"Dalton Allen. Hard times make fast friends."

Bernie suppressed a grin and slid into the car, burrowing his ass into the seat while enjoying the scent of leather and car. He knew the word, had seen the conveyances, and thought he remembered how to drive one from the memories he'd sucked from Officer Watson as he'd died.

He glanced at the old man as he climbed into the car beside him. His heart would be old, pruny—might make a nice snack, though.

Then again, he didn't want anyone knowing where he was heading, not just yet. They'd know soon enough. He'd want to savor the surprise.

Dalton started the car and pulled back onto the highway, pointing west.

Bernie let his gaze follow the sights through the bug-spattered windshield. The long black strip of tar-scented highway stretched like a ribbon, edged on either side by tall, green trees.

Bernie's human body, while it had a finite lifetime, could afford him the joy of sunshine warming his face.

"Well, you're in luck," Dalton said. "We don't have far to go. You been hitchin' your way out of the city?"

"Yes, since early this mornin'." Three rides, four meals. But he hadn't been able to use their cars after he'd killed them. He'd made too much of a mess when he hadn't convinced them to leave their cars.

He still had a stack of T-shirts from the witch's store in the plastic bag he clutched on his lap. At least he'd been able to wash up and make himself presentable to the next "ride."

They entered a small town, passing houses and shops and a surprising number of vehicles.

"This is it," Dalton said, pulling up across the street from a row of white tents, some fully erected, others surrounded by people in the process of raising them. "This is the morgue, but I don't think they'll let you just walk in there. Checkpoint's around that side," he said pointing. "They've been finding bodies all day long. Such a shame, all those folks drownin'."

Bernie nodded and murmured something.

Must have convinced the old man he gave a damn, because he kept rambling. "Even found a few old corpses washing up. Some have been in the ground for years. They just have to look at 'em all."

"You mean from cemeteries?" Bernie chortled inside.

"Caskets washing up, all floatin' down the river."

"Like Moses in a basket?"

Dalton gave him a quelling glare. "Hardly. It's ghoulish, grim. Wouldn't want the job of fishin' 'em out."

Bernie hadn't wanted that job either. See where it had gotten him?

"Guess they'll have to wait for the waters to recede before they find more."

Many, many more, Bernie hoped. He turned to the old man and gave him a smile. Dalton didn't know it, but it was his lucky day. He fingered the small cloth bag in his pocket and decided not to leave another clue on the morgue's doorstep. Soon enough, with the rising of the next moon, there'd be plenty of evidence of his fine plan.

Then let Nicolas and Inanna try to find him.

Chessa awoke with her nose smashed against Nicolas's neck. She leaned a little away and drew a deep breath, drinking in his rich, manly scent and the odor of stale sex. Every part of her body ached deliciously.

She needed a bath, but she didn't want to move, not yet. Not with the satin smooth skin beneath her fingertips and the beat of his heart thudding beneath her palm.

For the first time in a long time, she just wanted to savor being held by a man. His arms, even in sleep, clutched her close. As though she mattered. As though her absence would be noticed. As though he believed he possessed her.

And he did. Not through the force of his sensual seduction, powerful as that was. Rather, he'd trapped her through his dogged persistence so that she took note of how much he cared.

Seemed he'd always been there for her. He'd always been a fixture in her life. All the way back to *Ardeal*.

As a child she'd watched him training his team on the lush green grounds, or leaving on some dark mission with his face drawn sharp and hard, fierce determination etching his handsome features, making him seem larger than life.

Forever, Inanna had depended on him, kept him close and

seemingly tethered to her side. The ancient bitch understood his worth and manipulated his deep sense of honor.

Chessa had been attracted to him even before she'd been "reborn."

But she'd known from the time she was old enough to notice men, he wasn't to be hers—that she had to take a human mate. She'd been carefully educated, primed for her role among the coven, and knew that with her first bite of a living man would come true love.

If she'd fantasized about Nicolas, she'd been enough of a realist to know he would never be hers.

Inanna had chosen David Thibodaux as her mate. She'd picked him up in a bar and dragged him back to *Ardeal* when Chessa's season began.

David had thought he'd enjoy a quick tumble with the mysterious dark-haired woman who'd seduced him. Instead, Inanna had brought him nearly drunk with arousal to Chessa's bed.

He'd pierced her hymen and given her the first taste of blood. In that moment, they'd been bound.

Nine months later, she'd borne his child, and they moved into a cottage on the estate. David had taken to life as a *Revenant* with zest. Training with the security team. Running with the patrols. Cleansing New Orleans and the surrounding areas of rogue vampires who refused to recognize the authority of the coven.

With her little Ana to fill the hours when they were parted, Chessa had grown content with David, caught up in the excitement of her newly developing hungers. Sating her awakening sensuality with her lover and husband, while sharing blood and sex with the minions who served their needs.

Life was an orgy of self-absorbed pleasure. Only Ana kept her grounded, kept her hungers reined.

The night her life at *Ardeal* ended, she'd come fresh from a private dinner with Inanna, Pasqual, and a local man named Arnaud. Arnaud had been only too eager to bare his throat and cock. Filled, her body still tingling with pleasure, Chessa had walked along the graveled path to her cottage to find the front door gaping, blood smeared on the stoop.

Her heart thudded and her stomach clenched in horror as she stepped over the threshold to take in the sight of her husband and daughter, both lying dead among the shambles of their small, cozy home.

The first person who'd run to investigate the source of the screams had been Nicolas.

He's picked her up, carried her to the main house, shouting to his team to search the estate. He hadn't let her go until he'd stripped her, washed the blood from her, and settled into a chair with her until Inanna arrived to attend her.

He'd been so very tender in the days that followed, careful not to discuss the graphic details of what they'd found, but giving her enough to quell, at least for the moment, her insatiable desire for revenge.

When she'd gotten past the shock, she'd followed those leads, but never found the individuals responsible for the murders.

Her husband's handsome face she could barely remember now, but her little girl's, spattered with blood, her body savaged, pink ribbons still tied in her hair—that image remained imprinted on her memory.

Their loss had been the catalyst that determined she'd never care that deeply for anyone again. Her grief had nearly destroyed her. She'd fled *Ardeal*, drank her way through more bars than she could count, finally arriving one morning on a hotel balcony, waiting for the sunrise.

She'd stood naked, watching the sunlight climb down the wall beside her and halting on the trellised bougainvillea—waiting for the sun to scourge her flesh. Wanting to feel the agony before she died.

She'd closed her eyes and clenched her hands around the iron railing just as light peeled down the last few feet.

A thickly hewn arm encircled her waist and drew her back against a tall, hard body. His almondy musk, always recognizable to her, gave away his identity. "Dammit, Nic, what are you doing here?" So close. If he'd just waited a few minutes more . . .

He grunted softly behind her and pulled her from the balcony into the bedroom.

Pulling away from his embrace, she turned to face him, realizing her mistake. She'd only stood naked before him once before—the night her world had fallen apart.

Then he'd stripped them both with quiet efficiency, and stepped beneath the shower with her to wash away her husband's and sweet Ana's blood, which covered her from head to toe. His naked body had been a comfort—so tall and strong.

She'd quivered like a palsied human, her teeth chattering throughout, until he'd wrapped her in a towel and seated himself in an armchair to hold her, stroking her back and arms until Inanna roused to take charge.

This morning, she was all too aware he saw everything she was. Lost, alone, ready to die.

Not wanting to hear his disappointment, she'd tried to deflect him. "You're always underfoot lately," she complained, trying with bravado not to let him see how disturbed she was by her nakedness. "It's becoming annoying. People are talking."

One side of his mouth curled. "And since when do I care what people say?" His gaze swept down her nude body. "What were you planning, Chessa?" he asked softly.

Her chin came up. "None of your business. Why are you here? Have you been following me?"

"You need a keeper," he drawled.

"I don't need anyone," she'd retorted, her voice raw.

"I've come to take you home."

She shook her head. "It's not home. Not anymore."

His lips tightened. "Everyone's worried about you. No one's seen you in weeks."

"How did you find me?"

"You haven't been exactly . . . circumspect . . . since you left. I followed a trail of meals here."

With his gaze slipping downward, she curled her fists to resist the urge to place her hands over all the places he paused.

Even back then, his notice had disturbed her. Aroused her. That had been the problem.

She hadn't wanted to be drawn, to reawaken. That path led to painful yearnings she never wanted to feel again. "I'm staying here."

Nicolas hadn't left her alone that morning. He'd stayed for several weeks, redirecting her anguish. He'd found her a mentor on the police force, someone willing to teach her what she'd needed to know about investigative skills so she could find for herself her family's killers.

All along, she'd known finding the monsters who'd stolen away Ana would be an elusive goal, but it had been one that had kept her alive all these years.

Nicolas's chest wasn't moving as deeply as it had before.

"You're awake, aren't you?" she whispered.

"Have been for a good few minutes, but you were so deep in thought I didn't want to intrude." He turned his head to catch her gaze.

Feeling absurdly shy given all that had passed between them, her gaze fell away, drifting over his face.

Relaxed, his features were beautiful, perfectly symmetrical. His brows were dark wings that arched above deep brown eyes. His nose was straight, a little long, but well suited to his Gallic good looks. His lips were full, the upper bowed and stretching quickly into a soft smile as she continued to stare.

She lifted her gaze to his and found him waiting. "I never thanked you," she said softly.

His smile slid wider. "The pleasure was all mine."

"That's not what I was talking about."

Amusement slipped from his face, and his arm tightened around her. A large, warm hand moved down to her hip to draw her flush against him. "No thanks were necessary. I'm just glad I was there."

She didn't need to say what she was talking about, because, as always, Nicolas was already there.

So intuitive, he always seemed to know exactly what she was thinking and exactly what she needed.

Although she thought she already knew, she asked. "Why?"

He swallowed, this time his gaze flitting away. "I think you already know why. Until you can say the words, let's just leave it like this."

Relieved, and inexplicably disappointed, she nodded.

She was such a coward.

Chessa cupped his cheek and leaned forward to press a soft kiss to his lips. Then she rolled to her back, gently urging him over her. "I know missionary's not your thing, but . . ."

His face hovered over hers, studying her for a moment before he swooped down to kiss her lips. "If it means I can be close, I don't mind at all."

Chessa moved her legs from underneath him and opened them wide around his hips, bending her knees to tilt up and ease his entry.

He came slowly inside her, waiting for the moisture to ease his way. His hands smoothed down her arms, and his fingers threaded through hers. He brought them up to the pillow beneath her head as he began to move inside her. Pumping slowly, purposefully, he glided deep, straight, establishing a rhythm that didn't vary. He stroked as inexorably as a heartbeat.

The gradual rise was one she could note, step by step, within his expression—his slackening lips, reddened cheeks, the tightening of his jaw—and she knew he could see the clues of her heightening arousal written all over her face.

How much more intimate could this get? It wasn't just fucking anymore.

Nicolas was becoming part of her, twisting into her with a ruthlessly gentle determination.

Closer than she'd ever felt to him, her lips began to tremble, her eyes welled with tears. "I don't like feeling weak."

"This isn't weakness, *chérie*," he said, his voice a deepening rumble. "It's vulnerability. It's you giving yourself to me."

She shook her head, looking away, drawing deep inside for the courage to admit the truth. "I'm . . . afraid."

"I won't leave you."

"You can't promise me that."

His forehead met hers as he rasped, his voice thick with emotion, "Stick with me, and we can both watch each other's backs."

She shook her head, wanting to deny him, wanting to hold onto her stubborn promise, but not wanting to break the connection they were building.

A relationship with Nic, this deep, this potentially loving, would be all-consuming. She'd have to reconcile with her past and with Inanna.

She wasn't ready, not yet.

However, for once she wasn't completely resistant to the idea.

Nicolas resumed his steady pace, thrusting harder, then pausing to circle his hips, grinding the base of his groin against her clitoris. Finding the exact series of movements that left her gasping hard.

She lifted her legs to encircle his waist, riding the motion of his hips, pulling to cup him closer within the well of her thighs.

Sweat dampened their bodies, their bellies sliding easily together and apart. As deep and close as two people could get, but it wasn't enough.

Chessa leaned up to kiss him, promising with her body to try.

Nicolas murmured and lifted away his mouth to smooth his lips down her throat.

Chessa knew what was coming, steeled herself as best she could, knowing it would be too much. Too keenly felt.

He bit deeply, drawing her blood, exerting his irresistible vampiric lure that dragged her past a gentle orgasm straight into a fiery, orgiastic explosion that had her writhing beneath him, undulating to drag her hips down and up to meet his quickening thrusts. His cock lapped in silken, creamy delight.

Pleasure, so pure it pierced her chest, tightened around her core, rippling and pulsating along the length of his cock in ever tighter constrictions until, at last, she cried out and fell back against the bed, her arms landing limply on the mattress beside her.

Nicolas withdrew his fangs and licked her neck to close the tiny piercings. When he came back to kiss her mouth, he rubbed her lips and murmured again, "*Mon ange* . . . this is so fucking good."

Chessa lifted her lips, unable to respond.

He lunged inside her twice, then groaned deeply as his release swept over him, flooding her channel. Finally, he sank onto her, his heavy body squeezing the breath from her lungs.

"I think we're stuck together," Nicolas muttered.

"We just need a bath," she said, trying to draw a deeper breath over the top of his shoulder.

"No one would ever accuse you of being a romantic."

"Is the honeymoon already over?"

Nicolas dragged in a deep breath and raised on his elbows, a smile quirking one side of his lush mouth. "I rather like the sound of that."

CHAPTER

II

Just past dusk Nicolas and Chessa stepped off the curb in front of her apartment building to find Alex once again standing beside his car, waiting for them. She eyed his frayed jeans and stretchy black top. Interesting fashion choices, but both showed his honed body to perfection.

"You could have come up." A blush heated her cheeks at the intimate look he gave her, sweeping over her body, no doubt remembering all the places his lips, fingers, and cock had played.

No way was he ever going to pretend nothing had happened.

"So, any news of our friend?" Nicolas asked, a disquieting terseness to his tone.

"Yeah," Alex said easily, seeming indifferent to

Nicolas's deadly glare. "State troopers found three vehicles. All the victims fit the same M.O. We'll need to stick pins in a string along Highway 61."

"So, that's where we're heading?" Chessa asked.

"They've already taken the bodies to San Gabriel. Thought we might take a look."

"You'll have to go without me." Nicolas's expression was remote. All business.

Chessa remembered the phone call from the previous evening. "Checking in with Inanna?" she asked, keeping her tone even while jealousy boiled in her stomach.

"I need to talk to Simon," he said, still eyeing Alex.

"Need a lift?" Alex asked.

"I'll find my own way." When his gaze fell on Chessa, his expression softened. "I'll catch up with you later. I have the satellite phone number. I'll give you a ring."

Feeling awkward, Chessa looked at the ground, anywhere but into Nicolas's sharp-eyed gaze. Their relationship had undergone significant changes. She didn't quite know how to act.

Thankfully, Nicolas took the initiative, wrapping his hand around hers to pull her close. When his arms came around her waist, she lifted her face instinctively for a kiss.

"This," he whispered, "is how people falling in love say good-bye."

"We haven't had a chance yet to do an autopsy," the young man in medical scrubs said, as he led them into a tent in a long row of white tents that made up the temporary morgue.

"They'll be cleaned up first, then stored in one of the refrigerator cars."

Chessa shared a glance with Alex.

His nose wrinkled. His face was as green as the jacket he'd thrown on over his holster.

She grinned and wondered if he was going to throw up. The smell of disinfectant and the underlying odor of decaying corpses assailed them both—only it appeared she wasn't nearly as squeamish.

"How long have you been a cop, anyway?" she asked, under her breath. "Breathe through your mouth."

The bodies they'd come to inspect lay on a tarp floor in black bags. The young man knelt and unzipped the first one. A woman in her mid-forties, gray roots showing beneath auburn-colored hair, stared sightlessly upward. Her smocked denim dress with its embroidered flowers was marred by the large dark hole that sank in the center of her soft upper abdomen and the blood-spatter spotting the crisply ironed fabric.

"Looks like he used a post-hole digger to rip through her," the young man said, pushing his glasses up his nose. "What kind of person would do a thing like that?"

The next three bodies had similar injuries.

Working silently, they finished making notes, Alex holding his breath over each corpse.

"You have to sign out," their escort said. "I'll escort you to the checkpoint."

Lit as bright as any high school football field on Friday night, they made their way between the tents, passing people rolling gurneys with more bodies in FEMA black bags.

Alex was signing the checkout roster when screams ripped through the night, coming from the direction of the row of refrigerator cars.

Chessa sprinted back through the grounds, reaching for her weapon as medical personnel scrambled past, horror twisting their features. Chessa tried to halt one woman to ask what had happened, but she twisted away and kept on running.

At the corner of one trailer, she glanced over her shoulder to find Alex standing close by, his weapon drawn. He nodded to her, and she ducked around the corner, the stock of her Glock 40 gripped between both hands as she scanned the area.

Deep in the shadows she detected movement. The figure beyond the end of one truck ramp moved oddly, jerking, twitching, then stomping rapidly, almost too fast for the eye to follow.

Not human, that was for damn sure. She tightened her grip and took a stealthy step forward. When another twitching figure stepped suddenly in front of her, her mouth gaped.

The man was a walking corpse, his features bloated like a body too long in the water, the skin of his face peeling away to reveal underlying muscle and scraped bone. The odor that emanated from him had her stomach lurching.

Before she could do more than blink, his hand shot up so quickly she didn't have time to dodge.

"Shit!" she cried out, as he grabbed her throat and dragged her closer. His gaping maw of a mouth opened wide to reveal a row of jagged teeth.

Choking, she shoved the barrel of her weapon into his belly and fired off three rounds.

The shots passed through him, dinging against the trailer behind him, but he didn't loosen his grip.

Something large and solid barreled into her and the monster from the side, sending them both flying. Alex didn't stop, rolling quickly to his feet.

Chessa leapt to hers, but not as quickly as the ghoul who rose straight from his back to a standing position, his arms outstretched toward her. "What the fuck?" she cried out, this time ducking beneath his grasp, only to have his hand grab at the back of her jacket and jerk her off her feet.

She swung her foot forward and slammed it backward against his knee, but he seemed as immovable as a tree trunk.

Suddenly, a shot rang out from beside her and the monster's head exploded, splattering her with gray gelatin and coagulating blood. The hand gripping her tight, opened, dropping her to the ground. The corpse crumpled beside her.

Chessa kicked it, cursing, and scrambled away.

"Zombies, Cheech," Alex shouted, already searching the shadows for the next one. "Aim for their heads. Move it!"

Together, they raced down the row of tractor trailers while Chessa stretched her senses, scenting the air for the smell of rotting corpses, listening for the heartbeats of the living, and finding wildly beating hearts as workers huddled beneath wheel wells.

Scent proved an elusive clue as the breeze changed direction, but she found more of the creatures by their tell-tale jerking movements and eerily rapid advances.

With Alex's back sliding close to hers to watch for anything coming up behind them, she paused to pop off rounds when she spotted one, then moved forward again.

She fired until she ran out of bullets and dropped her clip, quickly reached for another from her pocket and rammed it up, filling the chamber with another round.

Knowing she had only one clip left, she crept forward, scanning left to right and back again, her Glock following the direction of her gaze.

More strange stomps sounded behind her. Alex squeezed off shots, another zombie then another stomped into view, their features twisted in frightening leers. She aimed, fired, missing as they rushed forward in their halting gait that looked like a film in fast forward. Her mouth dry, she drew a deep breath to steady her aim and dropped them.

They moved trailer to trailer, peeking inside, finding bodies writhing in body bags, finding more roaming the grounds. Only when the minutes dragged on without finding new targets did she draw a deep breath.

Chessa straightened and lowered her weapon, glancing behind her to find Alex sliding his gun into his holster.

"How many rounds do you have left?" she asked, dropping an empty clip and ramming her last one home.

"I have a box in my trunk."

"I have to reload."

Alex lifted his hand to glide his fingers over her cheek, drawing something sticky from her skin. "You know, we'll have to hit all the bodies left in the trailers. Can't take any chances."

Chessa nodded toward the people cautiously emerging from their hiding places. "What will we tell them?"

Alex smirked. "That a demon called The Devourer paid them a visit and sprinkled a voodoo priestess's powder over the bodies to make them rise from the dead?"

She rolled her eyes. "Uh . . . no. Think of something less absurd."

A grin broke across his face. "Good thing it was us here, huh?"

Realizing she'd missed a few clues while they'd battled zombies, she gave him a searching glance. "Yeah, who else would have known how to kill them?"

When she'd streaked toward the tractor trailers, he'd kept pace. He'd also managed better than she to sight their rapid movement and drop them before they'd crept too close.

Not something any human should have managed.

Cool air greeted Nicolas as he entered the long hallway leading toward Simon's apartment. A generator hummed somewhere in the distance.

Pasqual gave him a crooked smile and straightened from his post beside Simon's door. "Hey there, boss."

"She's inside?"

Pasqual lifted an eyebrow. "Would I be here?"

"Did she say why she came into the city herself?"

"I'm just a *Revenant*. She doesn't tell me what she's thinking." The words held no edge of resentment. So long as she welcomed him to her bed, Pasqual was happy to serve.

Nicolas understood that sentiment all too well. After all, once upon a time he'd been the eager supplicant. He drew a deep breath and lifted the brass doorknocker, knowing he was about to enter a minefield of treachery.

1308
Outside Poitiers, France

Nicolas put down the doorknocker and blew on his hands, rubbing his fingers together to warm them. The horses that had delivered them to her door were led away behind them. He and Armand shared a glance, and he frowned again at his brother's appearance.

Armand dressed plainly, his hair scraped back so hard his scalp shown white, as though he resented the fine trappings they'd been given. Why couldn't he just enjoy their new circumstances? Instead, he'd grown more withdrawn these past weeks as though something precious had been robbed from him.

Nicolas had come to the realization Armand loved God more than he loved him and would have welcomed a righteous death. While Nicolas had loved Armand above everything.

No longer. Nicolas was learning to love himself.

Still, a vague unease followed him, as though he was conditioned to expect the worst to happen after his long ordeal. Feeling like he'd been fattened and cosseted like a Christmas goose, he stood in his fine new clothing, freshly bathed and pink-cheeked. While truly grateful for his rescue, he felt a growing impatience to embrace his future.

The door swung open, and Nicolas stepped back from beneath the shaded entrance, shocked the lady herself answered the door.

Her glance slid from his newly shorn hair down the fine fit of his clothes then back up again. Slowly.

He felt a seductive curl of heat wash over him.

Her gaze inspected Armand much more quickly, and Nicolas knew a moment's satisfaction her interest appeared to be for only him.

"Follow me," she said, turning back into the dimly lit entry.

Nicolas gave Armand a dig in the ribs for his brother's nose was wrinkled, his lips thinned as though he disapproved of the fact she'd opened the door in a robe.

Nicolas found it *convenient* for he had no misconception he'd be sinking between her silky thighs before the afternoon was done. Whether or not they got down to the business of what she needed from them first was inconsequential. He'd thrown off his Templar's mantle, released from his lifelong duty to his brother by his anger over Armand's stubbornness that had nearly gotten them both killed.

Now he wanted to taste life. Wanted to taste this woman, with her slim round hips, burnished hair, and eyes that smoldered with Eastern knowledge promising she knew a thing or two about pleasuring a man.

She'd wanted a guardian—well, guardian would be his occupation—but he no longer believed in quests. He'd leave that sort of zealous devotion to his brother.

The lady Inanna showed them deep into the house to a parlor unlike any he'd ever seen. Rather than stately wooden furnishings, this room was draped in silky fabrics that covered the windows and encircled the center of the room, reminding him of the interior of an Arab's tent. Plush bolster cushions surrounded a low table; a thick hand-knotted Persian carpet stretched beneath it all, inviting him to sink his toes and body there.

Candlelight flickered within the intimate space, painting the woman's skin in golden tones that only enhanced the warmth already creeping beneath his cotte. The room was hot as any late desert afternoon. He spotted two braziers in the corners of the room and felt perspiration dot his forehead.

She waved a hand to the groupings of pillows. "Will you join me for a cup of *qahwa*?" she asked, dropping gracefully to her knees.

Eager to draw nearer, he took a seat close to her, his legs crossed in front of him, happy to be free of social restrictions.

Kneeling gracefully in the folds of her crimson and gold dressing gown, she poured two cups of the sweetened drink. Although he would have preferred ale, he accepted the dark, aromatic drink, served hot, and sipped it cautiously.

Armand sipped quietly beside him, his gaze resting on a curtain, his sleeve, finally the depth of his shallow cup. Nicolas knew he was uncomfortable sharing such an intimate setting with a woman dressed as though for bed.

Inanna's glance and secretive smile remained with Nicolas, sharing her amusement over his brother's discomfort. She plucked a deep red apple from the tray of fruit beside the tea urn—plump, out of season, but perfect, and extended it to Nicolas.

He accepted it, grinning at the symbolism of the act, and took a large bite, turned it, and handed it back to her.

Her white teeth bit the flesh he'd already laid bare, and she gave him a wicked smile as she chewed.

Beside him, his brother cleared his throat, clearly uncomfortable sitting on the floor beside them. "When will we be shown the crypt?"

Inanna lifted her hand, cupping her fingers in a beckoning wave to someone who hovered close to the door. "Will you take our friend out and show him belowstairs?"

"Will you not come with me brother?" Armand asked softly.

Nicolas didn't look his way. "No, I think I'll stay."

While Armand followed the servant out the door, Nicolas's cock thickened—so much so, he had to stretch his legs to the side and rest on an elbow, assuming a casual pose. That his arousal was clearly visible beneath the soft fabric encasing his groin didn't bother him a bit. They were alone now, and she didn't seem the modest sort.

In fact, her avid gaze clung to his groin for a long moment, before she gave him a wicked smile and lifted her hands to the front of her robe.

His breath held as she pulled apart the knotted ties and spread wide the lapels of her dressing gown, exposing her body for his viewing. Lovely as a goddess, she sat quietly while he stared, taking in the fullness of her breasts, the indention of her narrow waist and the soft, dark curls that pulled his gaze downward. "Do I please you, Nicolas?" she asked in her lilting voice.

His body tightened, his cock strained harder. He cleared an obstruction at the back of his throat. "Very much so, milady."

Her amusement shone in the sideways glance she gave him. "It's rather warm in here. I have no objection if you wish to make yourself more comfortable."

Since she'd been generous with her own disrobing, he decided to make his intentions indelibly clear. Ties, knots all flew open and he tore off his cotte and undertunic, tossing them to the side. Then he pulled off his soft leather boots and chausses, all the while looking for a signal he should stop.

But she watched, her glance burning over each bared expanse of his flesh.

At last naked, he stretched out, coming up on an elbow, turning so his cock pointed toward her, letting her look her fill, hoping she was pleased with how well his body had filled out with the food and care her servants had provided.

He grew sure of his attraction as her gaze followed the length of his body, lingering over his broad chest, lighting on his taut belly, and then resting on his thickening manhood.

"I think I'm hungry," she murmured.

His cock twitched, and he wondered if she meant to suckle him in the way a whore might pleasure a man. She rose on her knees, shrugged her shoulders and let the robe slide from her, then crawled toward him, grabbing his shoulders and pushing him to his back. Her strength surprised him. Her purpose did not.

Without a kiss or a single preliminary caress, she spread her thighs over his hips and sank on his sex, taking him deep into her body in a single glide, her inner flesh enclosing him like a wet, heated sheath.

He hadn't realized how intensely aroused he was until he erupted, embarrassingly, as soon as she was fully seated, his body shuddering beneath hers. "I apologize," he said, letting his head sink back against the floor, cursing himself for his weakness.

Her laughter held no disappointment. "You've been long without the comfort of a woman's body."

"An eternity, it seems," he averred, not wanting to admit he'd never been intimate with a woman.

"Don't berate yourself, my knight." Her eyes narrowed, capturing his glance, seeming to reach inside him and grasp an elusive curl of desire. His cock jerked, his waning erection arrested and filling once again.

Unbelievably, he was hard in seconds. His staff thickening like a post. Beneath her next deepening glance, he lifted his buttocks from the floor, spearing into her.

She rose on her knees, giving him room to labor against her. When he would have rolled her to her back, she gripped his shoulders hard and held him in place, her lips curling back in an almost feral snarl.

Each harsh upward stroke shook her breasts, pushed out her breaths in shallow gasps that gusted against his face. When release seemed imminent, a constriction seemed to grip the base of his cock, staving off the ecstasy threatening to burst. He pumped, tunneling his cock deep into her moist channel, rocking her forward and back until she flung back her head and cried out.

Only then did the constriction ease and his seed spilled as he trembled and stroked helplessly, endlessly upward.

When at last she fell to his chest, his hands lifted to slide around her back and hold her close.

They must have slept like that, her seated on his cock, his hand clutching her hair and her bottom. A rustling sounded behind the curtains and a cool breeze wafted over them.

When the curtains parted, his eyes opened to peer up into the steady gaze of a woman.

She entered, stepping around them, seeming unconcerned to find them intimately entwined. With unbound red hair that fell in shining waves to her hips, she appeared young. Her amber gaze when it rested on them lying locked and naked together didn't widen with shock. Curiosity lit her expression as Inanna stirred and lifted her head to smile at the woman.

"Is this the one?" the woman asked, her voice soft, yet throaty.

Inanna nodded sleepily and pushed back her hair.

Nicolas began to wonder whether they intended to take him together. He'd heard of such decadent acts, but only imagined them in his wicked night dreams.

However, Inanna rose from his thighs, letting his cock fall slick and flaccid against his belly. She touched her finger to his mouth, gliding her fingertip along his lower lip. "You will go with her. This is part of our bargain. You will mate with her. When she is done, then we will talk."

He nodded, wondering whether he'd have the energy to service this other woman, so relaxed and sated was his body. As strange and wicked as this day was becoming, he wondered if this would be part of his "duties" or just a benefit. He didn't care. He was free, and they were beautiful.

Already, he could feel arousal stirring in his exhausted belly. With the red-haired woman drinking in the sight of him, he rose slowly and bent to reach for his clothes.

The woman clucked, her lips twitching with amusement. "You won't be needing those."

Relieved he hadn't misconstrued the situation, he let the clothing drop beside his feet and straightened, enjoying the way her cheeks heated and her glance slid shyly away. "Is there no one else about in this house?" he asked, pleased when her gaze returned. "I don't wish to offend."

"You do not offend." The breathless quality of her voice appealed.

Passing close to Inanna's naked body, he threw her a smoldering promise and followed the younger woman out of the door.

He walked behind her, looking up and down the hallways they passed to see whether they were followed, feeling increasingly foolish with his cock dangling between his legs and a cool breeze licking his naked backside, wondering if this was a joke.

"I know you must be shocked by her behavior," the woman said, glancing over her shoulder. "I've lived so long with her I'm accustomed to her ways."

"Should I not be shocked with your behavior?" he murmured, watching the gentle roll of her hips as she preceded him, wondering at the curves her gown hid.

A blush stole over her cheeks, and she smiled. "It's true I'm not so experienced as she, but we are needful women."

Needful? A euphemism perhaps for lusty? By God, he hoped so. "Where is my brother?"

"He's being shown the crypt and apprised of his new duties."

"Are his duties as interesting?"

She shook her head. "He doesn't seem to have the temperament, or so I'm told. I haven't met him."

Nicolas nodded. Armand would have bolted for the door, sure the devil's minions were attempting to lure him into sin.

Let him assume the guardian duties.

Other, more pleasurable duties awaited Nicolas. He couldn't believe his luck. Not a celibate man by nature, but rather due to his brother's influence, he'd spent years praying for the strength to resist his body's rampant demands. He'd pleasured himself in private moments. Had fought his carnal nature in secret, hiding his true nature.

Walking naked behind the woman felt liberating. If it were a sin, he'd be gladly damned. He was a man in his prime. No longer a monk.

She led him to her chambers where more traditional furnishings filled the room, including a curtained bed with deep, plump pillows and a brazier that burned in the corner, warming the room to a perfect temperature for naked skin.

"My name is Anaïs," she said, and smiled, her intense gaze flowing over him and settling on his cock. Her breath paused. The pink of her cheeks deepened to rose.

Even with his limited knowledge, her fascination told him everything he needed to know.

Anaïs was a virgin.

CHAPTER

12

Present Day

Madeleine answered the door dressed in bronze silk pajamas that clung to her petite, feminine form. Her light brown hair fell in waves to her waist, glinting gold in the lamplight. She smelled lovely—perfumed, fresh—ready.

Nicolas smiled. Simon had to be grinding his teeth in frustration.

He gave a polite nod to Simon's "pet" who closed the door quietly behind him. "Madeleine, nice to see you."

Her smile seemed a little stiff. "Nice to see you too, Nicolas," she said, her words soft and precise. "Simon's hiding in his study."

"Hiding?"

She wrinkled her nose. "He's avoiding Inanna."

"Not very polite of her to linger. The full moon's nearly past."

"She knows she's intruding on our private time." She sighed. "But how does one ask a creature like that to leave?"

"Is she with him, now?"

"I told you he's hiding. She's dressing for dinner in the guest room," she said, her nose wrinkling with distaste.

Nicolas stalked past her in the direction of Simon's small, cramped study, and not bothering to knock, flung open the door.

"He said you were pissed," Simon said, as he sat back in his leather chair, fingering a polished green crystal in his palm.

Nicolas gave him a narrowed glance. "Who is he?"

Simon gave a quick shake of his head. "Chessa's new partner?" he called out a little louder than needed if he'd intended only for Nicolas to hear.

Nicolas's hands fisted in frustration. The mage wouldn't talk while the coven leader was near enough to eavesdrop.

"You're feeling . . . betrayed," Simon said softly. "I wish you wouldn't take this personally. This was necessary."

Knowing he was too angry to sort through the subtle messages Simon was trying to convey, Nicolas flopped into a chair opposite Simon and stared at him, willing his body to relax. "That *thing* you leant me, yesterday . . ."

"Was exactly what he described to you." Simon laid down the stone. "You resist believing, even though I've shown you unexplainable things, time and again."

"You want me to have faith—in you?"

"Have I ever lied to you?" Simon asked, his gaze steady.

Nicolas resisted a caustic retort. The mage had never lied, but he had kept secrets. This particular one stuck in his craw because he'd been forced to leave Chessa in Alex's company. "Should I trust him?"

"Implicitly."

"Since he wears it, should I assume he will be the one entrusted now with the demon's recapture?"

Simon's lips curved. "I've known many pasts, but I can't see into the future."

Nicolas felt a tic pulse at the side of one eye. Simon's deliberately vague and ridiculously mystical answer made him grind his teeth.

Sensing that was all Simon would offer for now, Nicolas took a deep breath. "I take it Inanna left the estate because of the escape?"

"She's taking a personal interest in this matter."

Another ambiguous answer that wasn't an answer. "Is she relieving me?"

Simon shrugged. "You'll have to ask her."

The last thing Nicolas wanted to do was face Inanna. Although they'd shared many things over the past centuries, he didn't trust her, didn't like her interest in his relationship with Chessa. He didn't trust her motives.

As if she'd read his mind, the door opened and Inanna swept inside, her exotic sandalwood and musk scent filling the room, her long Eastern caftan tinkling with the tiny golden bells that edged the hem above her bare feet.

Nicolas's skin tightened. Already she was throwing out lures. His stomach sinking, he surrendered to the inevitable. "Good evening, Mistress," he said, rising from his chair.

Inanna gave him a glowing smile and turned to Simon. "Are you going to linger here," she said in her singsong tone, "when time with your little bird is so fleeting?"

With a look of relief crossing his face, Simon gave Nicolas a nod and quickly exited the room.

"You've no doubt received a briefing from Pasqual," Nicolas said, his hands curling tightly when a wave of arousal assailed him—heavy, throbbing. He was drowning already.

"My love," she said, stepping close enough to trail her fingertips along his arm. "I didn't call you to discuss that creature. Although I'm concerned he's gained his freedom, I trust you to hunt him down. You did so before."

"Then why did you call me away from my investigation?"

Coming to stand directly in front of him, she held his gaze with her deep brown eyes. The golden halo that surrounded her pupils seemed to glow especially bright this night. "I was curious. Your voice when you spoke of Chessa betrayed a softness, an intimacy I haven't heard from you in a long, long time."

Nicolas stiffened when she leaned close and rubbed her silk-covered breasts against his chest. "Chessa's coming around."

"That's good. I have need of her." A small hand slipped between his legs and cupped his erection. "But I want this. Will your affection for the girl come between us, darling?"

"Of course not, Mistress," he murmured, closing his eyes as she squeezed.

"Her scent is all over you . . . mmmmm . . ." She rubbed her nose on his chest, breathing deeply. "I find I'm quite hungry." She tightened her hand around him. *"On your knees."*

As soon as she released his balls, he dropped, unable to do anything but her exact bidding, waiting while she drew her garment over her head, revealing her slim, nude body—dusky skin, black swirls at the apex of her thighs, brown nipples at the center of her soft, full breasts.

So lovely, his teeth ached.

So deadly, he shuddered at the thought of her ever finding out how he meant to betray her.

Her slender fingers cupped his head and pulled him toward her breasts. "Bite me, *Nico*."

His cock pressing hard against his zipper, he came up on one knee and latched onto her nipple, tonguing the tip before drawing it between his lips and sucking hard.

"I said, bite it."

Without any will of his own, his fangs descended from his gums, and he pierced her areola with one razor-sharp tooth while continuing to suckle.

Inanna's body writhed against him, her rich scent deepening. For several minutes, they remained like that, his mouth locked around her quivering breast, until her fingers dug into his scalp and pushed him away.

She grabbed for his shirt, but he leaned away and stripped it off, dropping it behind him. Then he opened his pants, releasing his hot, heavy cock, groaning with relief.

Her greedy gaze stared at him, her hands kneading her breasts as blood continued to trickle from the small puncture he'd made, trailing down her belly.

Without being told what she wanted next, he leaned forward and followed the trail of the blood, licking her nipple to close the wound, following the sweet curves downward, past her soft belly to the curling hair covering her mons.

When his tongue darted between her folds, she lifted her leg, planting her foot in his shoulder and shoved him onto his back.

Inanna squatted over him, her feet to either side of his hips, her legs drawn up. One dark-winged eyebrow rose to tell him to get on with it.

Supporting her bottom on one palm, he reached beneath her, slid his fingers into her cunt and swirled in the moisture gathering there.

He rubbed his wet fingers over the crown of his cock and fitted it to her opening. Her awkward positioning precluded any aid on her part, so he bent his knees, planted his feet in the carpet and lunged upward to impale her, squeezing into the tight opening of her channel, then pounding upward.

As he labored, his body grew more rigid, his emotions more desperate.

Inanna smiled. Her breasts jiggled as he thrust upward, her cheeks reddened, but her gaze never left his, seeming to inspect his expression for hints of his inner turmoil.

Did she suspect his divided loyalties? Was she testing him? Or would she use their relationship to hurt Chessa at some later, more advantageous date?

At the moment, he hadn't the intellect to ferret through the bitch's twisted motives. All he could manage to focus on was the molten heat surrounding his cock and the tension building in his balls.

When he thought he couldn't make it last a second longer, another wave of suggestion hit him dead in his cock, choking off his orgasm like a band constricting around the base of his shaft. He gritted his teeth, sweat dripping from his forehead into his hair, his breaths so jagged, he felt as though he'd run for miles.

"When I say so," she said softly, flicking his nipple with a long oval fingernail. "I'm not nearly done with you."

He groaned and stopped stroking into her.

Inanna rose, her feet on either side of him, her engorged sex open and pulsing, displayed for his viewing. She lifted her foot and placed the sole along the length of his cock and pressed down, the pressure uncomfortable, but not truly painful. "I want you to take me like you take Chessa. *Show me.*"

Nicolas closed his eyes while the pressure increased. He hadn't any real choices here. However, the tender violence he inflicted on Chessa was out of love, out of need to bring her past her walls.

With Inanna, he'd be pushed not to harm her.

"All right, but you have to do as I say," he said, his gaze nailing her.

"I'm yours, darling Nico," she purred. She lifted her foot and stood back.

He rose to his knees, taking deep breaths to fill his lungs with air and his spirit with strength. "I need you on your knees . . . Mistress."

Her chest rose, a lovely, rosy flush of color settling on her high cheekbones. She sank gracefully to her knees, her hands clasping her upper thighs.

"Face away and rest on your hands."

Her laughter bubbled, girlish, lighthearted.

If he didn't know any better, he'd swear she was a little nervous having given him the reins. When she'd faced away, her curvy bottom raised, he crawled to her side and forced her shoulders down, until her breasts scraped the carpet. He rested a hand on her rump. "No reprisals?"

"Did I not command you?" she asked, her voice rising with impatience.

All the encouragement he needed. He swept her bottom with his palm, fighting the overwhelming urge to let go of his control. He took a deep breath and lifted his hand, letting it fall hard on her soft flesh—so hard his palm stung.

She squealed and a short, shocked laugh erupted. "I want everything you give her, Nico."

He lifted his hand again, striking another part of her ass, then did it again and again, until his palm burned, and her skin glowed. He'd leave bruises he struck her so hard. Inside he cringed, but still felt a perverse satisfaction. The centuries of servicing her, bending to her will, brought out a hatred that wouldn't let him stop.

When her body trembled and her breaths sobbed, he shook himself and stopped. He crawled behind her and parted her buttocks, staring down at the neat little hole. He'd only ever desired to take Chessa that way. Only to conquer every last one of her inhibitions.

With Inanna, he thought only of conquering her body. He wedged his thumb into her, pressing past the muscles that tightened to repulse his invasion.

Her breath hissed between her teeth, and her head fell to the carpet.

Nicolas would have thought the sadistic bitch had never taken it in the ass. Spitting into his palm, he rubbed the moisture over the head of his cock and placed it at her back entrance.

Her bottom tensed and her fingernails dug into the carpet, but she didn't shy away when he pushed into her, meeting strong resistance.

He pressed his thumbs against the rim, opening her fractionally, and flexed his hips forward again.

She murmured, low and throaty, and her back sank, pushing her ass higher.

He dipped inside, tunneling in, groaning as her entrance clasped the head of his cock and engulfed him in sweet, hot heat.

When he was deep enough to begin stroking into her, he gripped her hips, positioning her bottom to take his thrusts as they grew steadily deeper and harsher.

Again and again, he crammed himself into her, pushing into lava-hot tissue that eased as he stroked, caressing his length.

Her body shuddered beneath him, her cries growing louder, more unrestricted.

When at last his groin smacked her bottom, he let loose, pounding hard, closing his ears to her high-pitched keening. She'd take him, all of him. For once, she'd be the one left wrung out as a dishrag.

He slammed forward, dragged his cock out and slammed back inside, pistoning faster. Just as her quickening cries indicated she approached the precipice, he reached around her hips and pinched her clitoris between his thumb and forefinger.

Inanna screamed, her cry sounding primordial, the deep, anguished caw of a wild bird.

Nicolas felt his own release explode from his balls, slamming through his cock to erupt in a stream of cum that eased the clasp of the tissue burning around his cock.

When they were both spent, he with his head flung back, his shaft riding her waning constrictions, she with her head resting on her clasped hands, Nicolas realized his relationship with Inanna, for better or worse, would never be the same.

A faint scratching at the door roused them both.

Inanna glanced over her shoulder as he pulled slowly out then lay on the carpet, her arms wrapped around herself.

Nicolas gave her a questioning glance but strode on shaking legs to the door and opened it a crack.

Pasqual stood on the other side, his gaze lifting beyond Nicolas's shoulder and widening.

Nicolas leaned into the opening to shut off the view, surprised to find some element of chivalry remaining in his conscience. Inanna needed time to recover.

"Yes," he said, his voice clipped. Anyone with a set of ears had to know they'd been screwing.

"Alex called Simon," Pasqual said, his cheeks reddening at Nicolas's pointed stare. "Zombies rose at the morgue in San Gabriel."

Nicolas stiffened. "Is Chessa all right?"

"Yes, they dispatched every one they found. They're on their way back now."

Nicolas nodded. "Is that all?"

Pasqual lifted his chin. "Does the mistress need anything?"

Did Pasqual really care? The resentment burning in his eyes said so.

"She's fine. Leave us."

Pasqual's back stiffened, and he turned on his heels, heading stiffly back toward the living room.

Nicolas closed the door and turned.

Inanna sat up, her chin rising. Her cool, sensual mask back in place.

Satisfaction filled him, knowing the effort it cost her.

"The zombies," she said. "He used the witch's powder?"

"Seems like it."

"Then he's west of the city?"

Nicolas shrugged, pulling his pants up and closing them. "He could have planted it any time today. Moonrise released them."

"He's clever," she said softly, slowly. "Cunning beyond your imagination."

"One question."

She eyed him warily, but nodded.

"I know he wants to punish me for keeping him imprisoned. You've had no contact all these years. Does he have a reason to come after you?"

Her glance slid away, but not before he'd detected a glistening hint of sorrow. "He'll want revenge on me most of all."

Chessa smoldered in the seat as Alex kept his rapt attention on the narrow, dark road.

Everything she'd learned about him, or hadn't, more precisely, came back to bite her in the ass.

No biting, for instance. She'd assumed he didn't enjoy being lunch to a bloodsucker. Now, she wondered what she would have discovered about him if she had.

Blood would always tell.

His speed during the chase through the morgue grounds wasn't something he could explain blithely away either, if he bothered to try.

Further, he'd known exactly how to take them out. She supposed he could have learned it watching horror films, but even if he'd believed those stories, they'd never have been able to outmaneuver the monsters. They'd been too damn fast. Hollywood's zombies moved so slow a child could outrun them.

His likability factor, the way he'd wormed his way into her bed and confidence so quickly—that should have been the ultimate clue.

Chessa didn't like anybody. Yet Alex with his sly amusement, as though he laughed constantly at a private joke, had intrigued her. He hadn't been fazed by what she was. Had helped her find her meals when she'd been beyond hungry. He'd slid his way under her clothes and into her body when she'd craved more than a little fast food.

The question now was what brand of night crawler was he?

A *Revenant*? Somehow, that seemed too easy an answer.

And mulling over her first meet and greet back in the office, she didn't know his full name, where he lived, where he'd come from.

Why hadn't she grilled him?

Sure, her mind was pretty consumed with her problems—Rene's defection, Nicolas's seduction. A city sinking beneath a seamy underworld of chaos, water, and creatures of the night come to prey on the defenseless.

Was he a *were*-creature? The possibility he hid an animalistic streak seemed just as unlikely seeing as he hadn't presented a single characteristic even in the throes of a powerful orgasm. And every vamp knew weres had little self-control.

Besides, why not bare his wolf's fangs and rip the heads off the zombies rather than risk his shots going wild in the heat of battle?

Too, weres and vampires had duked it out generations before she'd ever been born, finally dividing up the New World into regions, complete with intricate treaties that spelled out the consequences, savage ones, if any dared break them. Why would they mess with something that had worked and averted battles for so long?

A mage, then? Only he didn't seem to have the temperament, nor did he carry any of the trinkets mages were fond of—no crystals or magical powders. Nor did he appear to have an interminably dull fascination with fate and the roles of practitioners of the arts.

Could he be a demon, then? If a mage could wave his hand in front of his face to transform into a Generation X video store owner, why not a demon? With the use of darker magicks, why couldn't one present an irresistibly attractive package—a sexy, smirking cop with a body to die for?

Diabolical! That had to be it.

She straightened in her seat and shot him a glance, half

expecting him to change before her eyes. Demons came in many forms, amoeba-sized varmints that attached themselves to humans and burrowed into their cerebral cortex, causing all sorts of mental disease. Some possessed dark, twisted bodies to reflect the evil in their souls. Some possessed no form at all, except one they borrowed, like their friend The Devourer.

Could Alex, the real man, have been possessed like that? She could see the definite advantages a devious intellect would want to seize. Sexual gratification being high on most demons' lists, Alex's body offered endless opportunities.

Feeling a little relieved her mind was working again and pushing past the handsome package to look deeply into the man, she settled back, deciding to watch him closely and see what transpired over time.

He'd have to show his hand sooner or later.

"You're thinking too hard," he drawled. "I can hear the squeaking gears turning."

"Are you saying I'm not intellectual?"

"I'm saying I know you have questions. You've been too quiet since we left the morgue. You just haven't figured out the right ones to ask."

She narrowed her eyes. "Do you think I'm too stupid to figure it out myself?"

"Course not. Even if I did, do you think I'd say that?" he said, grinning. "I've seen you in action, sweetheart."

Chessa snorted. "All you've seen is me getting my butt kicked by a zombie."

"Chessa, I know you're smart. And I know you could have

determined how to take them out all on your own." He flashed her megawatt smile. "Mad at me for telling you how?"

She realized she was, actually. She hadn't liked the fact she'd gaped at the first one, uncomprehending even though she'd known about Madame Fortun's powder.

What she liked less was the reason for her inattention. A silver bullet up her cunt that had her half out of her mind with arousal.

That wasn't her. She was all about the job. Somewhere in the last few days she'd lost herself. "Are you going to answer my questions?"

"Maybe, but they're going to have to wait."

"Why's that?" she asked, her suspicions rousing again.

"We have a problem," he said, nodding ahead and slowing the car to a crawl.

She turned her gaze, her eyes widening as she spotted SUVs parked sideways in the road. A road block. "What do those knuckleheads think they're doing?"

"Waiting for us." Alex whipped the wheel, taking the car to the edge of the road and executing a neat U-turn in the center of the highway, but trucks barreled their way from the opposite direction.

"We're going to have to make a run for it, baby," he said, unbuckling his seat belt before he'd ground the car to a halt.

"You don't have to sound so cheerful about it."

"You'd rather I cry?"

"You and I are going to have a heart to heart when we get out of this mess." She unbuckled her belt as well and grabbed the door handle. "Who do you think they are?"

"Who else? *Revenants*."

Was he one of them after all? Had he led her into a trap? Would he pretend to put up a fight now and surrender when they were completely surrounded?

She didn't plan on waiting to find out, slamming open her door and rolling into the ditch beside the road, coming to her feet to sprint into the dark forest beyond.

Footsteps crunched hard and fast in the underbrush behind her, but she didn't stop to figure out who was on her tail. She shrugged out of her jacket, dropped her holster, and ripped her shirt off, never slowing her pace.

More rustling ahead forced her to change direction as two men stepped from behind trees and raced toward her.

She let the one on the left come close then shoved up her hand into his face at the last moment, breaking his nose. Then she spun on her heels and raised her leg to kick the chest of the man coming from her right, lifting him off his feet. She didn't pause to see whether he fell, just kept trucking through the woods.

She ran with the wind at her back, popped her wings from the long, slitted pouches between her shoulder blades, flapped down to catch the wind and lifted from the ground.

Behind her, footfalls silenced, which didn't mean she was out of the woods, so to speak, just yet. Scanning the ground below her she saw the first burst of gunfire before she heard the report of a weapon. She careened left in the air then right, then keeping close to the treetops soared until she was out of the bastards' line of sight.

Only then did she breathe a sigh of relief and give herself

over to the joy of a freedom she seldom indulged. Living in New Orleans, in close quarters with a thickly populated city, wasn't conducive to keeping a secret of this magnitude.

She followed the dark ribbon of highway heading East toward home, tamping down her worry for Alex. She'd abandoned him, but he hadn't exactly done a lot to win her trust.

He'd promised explanations, but now she might never know the truth. If he wasn't one of them, he was another sort of creature. Let him use his "gifts" and his cunning to figure out his own escape. Now, she had to worry about how she could sneak back into the city without someone claiming to see an angel falling from heaven.

A loud flap behind her drew her curious gaze. Her mouth gaped. Alex came like an avenging angel, his wingspread wider than hers, his face a mask of fury.

"Fucking unbelievable," she whispered as he bore down on her.

Alex was Born?

CHAPTER

13

"Not one fucking word," he'd said before leading her into the city, his powerful wings giving her enough of a draft to stay right on his tail, although by the time they crossed over the city limit, she was exhausted.

They passed the Quarter, eerily quiet due to the curfew and inky darkness, except for pockets of light where bars had rented generators to keep the refrigerators going, and apartment-dwellers kept candles burning in their windows.

They flew toward a neighborhood she knew only too well. She'd been there days ago. Had extracted a virgin vamp from her partner's home and discovered she'd lost him forever when he'd bedded the woman.

Not surprised at all, she touched down in Rene Broussard's courtyard.

A curtain fluttered in an upstairs window. Someone was home. But who?

Her heart beat fast, knowing the answer before Rene barreled out the door, Natalie fast on his heels.

She stared into her former partner's familiar face, and opened her mouth to greet him, but he shook his head and turned to lead the way into his home.

When she passed inside, Rene glanced back into the darkness, scanning the quiet rows of darkened houses, before closing them all inside and locking the door.

"Rene, how?" she asked, unable to curb her questions a moment longer.

His smile, a slow sexy stretch of lips she'd kissed intimately finally gave her the greeting she needed. His arms opened and she swooped toward him, wrapping hers around his shoulders for a tight hug.

After everything she'd been through the past few days, she finally felt as though something was wonderfully right.

A cough sounded behind her, and Rene's arms fell to his sides, releasing her. Chessa turned to Natalie who gave her a crooked smile.

Remembering Rene belonged to this woman now, Chessa faltered, feeling awkward, not knowing where she stood in this relationship. They'd grown close—just days ago for her, but who knew how many hundreds of years ago for them.

She crossed her arms over her bare breasts to cover them,

knowing how ridiculous that looked. She'd had sex with every one of the people surrounding her now, but their concentrated attention made her feel vulnerable. Something she resented and her chin rose.

It was all Nicolas's fault. He'd opened the door to her emotions. He'd instigated her need to make a move on Rene in the first place to prove Nicolas's attraction was only about the sex. Man, had that backfired.

Rene's gaze roamed her face and shoulders.

Chessa felt a heavy weight descend on her chest. He was likely trying to match his faded memory with the reality of her appearance.

"Miss me?" Rene asked, his sexy, growling voice sending a shiver up her spine.

Hell, yes! "I need some clothes," she demurred.

Natalie stood beside Alex, her smile pinched. Seemed she remembered too well Chessa's attraction for Rene. That last night they'd managed to share something pretty wonderful. Chessa hoped she remembered that, too.

Then her gaze landed on Alex, and the stuck gears in her head began to whir again. Standing with his arms folded over his bare chest, his wings tucked safely away, Alex's grin was broad, his white teeth gleaming in the silver moonlight sifting through the curtains covering the narrow windows that flanked the door.

She stared dumbly for a moment then opened her mouth, wondering if the inkling of suspicion creeping across her mind could be right. She'd been wrong about so many things. "Alex," she said, her voice trembling, "you know them?"

Alex leaned close, kissed her lips and whispered, "Hello, Auntie."

Nicolas found Simon and Madeleine in the kitchen. Their backs were to the door, their heads close as they whispered. Their intimacy was stamped in the idle hand Simon trailed down her back, and the way she nestled close. Her hair was mussed.

Their engrossment had enabled him to enter without being noticed. He knew he intruded. After all, it was the last night of the full moon.

He wondered how difficult it was for them both, knowing that in the morning, Madeleine would once again be consigned to her role as his familiar, perched on his arm, her intellect diminished.

He'd seen the bird and the way she sought the mage's affection. At least they had contact, even if they couldn't fully express their devotion to each other, except for a few short days each month.

An eternity of full moons stretched out before them.

Nicolas had no misconceptions that an eternity with Chessa was highly doubtful. As soon as she discovered the secrets he'd kept, her hedgehog spines would ruffle up and he'd be left in the cold again. Forever.

His subterfuge was no double-edged sword. There were three blades, and he always felt the weight of balancing his differing priorities because any one of them discovered would get him killed.

"Tell me, Nic, are you going to wait until I ravish her on the tabletop before you announce your presence?" Simon asked, casting a wry glance over his shoulder.

"I do have a purpose for being here," Nicolas growled.

"Questions about Chessa's partner?" Simon drawled while his hand encircled Madeleine's waist and drew her in front of him.

"I have the feeling if I asked, you'd still be reluctant to answer."

Simon nodded.

"So I won't waste your time. My question has to do with Inanna."

Simon's expression shuttered, wariness creeping in to tighten his mouth.

"She believes The Devourer will come for her." When Simon didn't respond, he continued. "Do you know why?" he asked, an edge of irritation making his words sharp.

Simon sighed and gave Madeleine a hug. "Why don't you go along to the bedroom? I promise I won't be a minute."

Madeleine gave Nicolas a small, tight smile and lifted her cheek for his kiss before she passed through the door.

"I know only that he hunted her in the time before I knew her," Simon said quietly, "and that she had somehow managed to trap him and imprison him in the sarcophagus before we met in Palestine. That was about the time she decided to make the leap to Europe and enlisted my aid in finding guardians."

"You don't know their connection?"

Simon lifted a sardonic brow. "Knowing Inanna, he probably has good reason to want revenge."

"If they have a past, do you think he'll toy with her?"

"Seems to be part of his personality. He doesn't kill every target of opportunity. Not when it suits his plans or he can draw out his enjoyment."

Nicolas drew a deep breath. Simon didn't know any more than he did.

"Have you heard from Alex and Chessa yet?" Simon said, his tone even, but his words needling.

Nicolas refused to rise to the bait, replying dryly, "I tried their satellite phone number. There's no answer."

"Ah well, they can both take care of themselves."

Nicolas knew this was true, but he worried about the fact they spent so much time together. Chessa would be unable to resist if Alex cast his attraction her way.

Why was he her partner? Nicolas didn't believe in coincidence. Although he trusted Alex's interest in Chessa would keep her from harm, he didn't want him toying with her affections, not when Nicolas had finally made headway. For he intended to enjoy this fleeting relationship as long as he could.

"I'm hungry," Inanna's melodic voice came from behind him.

Nicolas stood still, fighting the instinctive urge to stiffen in rejection.

"I want to try some of Chessa's haunts. *Take me.*"

What was her obsession with Chessa? Nicolas sighed. He really didn't have a choice. Besides he hadn't heard from Chessa and Alex. Perhaps he'd meet them when Chessa sought replenishment.

The trip was organized quickly. Inanna's limousine was followed by the security team's SUVs back into The Quarter without incident.

Dressed again in her gold caftan, Inanna drew all gazes as she gracefully entered the establishment.

A step behind her, Nicolas touched her arm, causing her to turn. "The private room's back there," he said, nodding toward a corridor, hoping she'd move along quickly.

Nicolas would watch her back and ensure she had a private moment with her meal. But he was bored, edgy. Dawn would be upon them soon, and he'd head back to Chessa's apartment and hope to catch her there.

As Inanna entered the private room at the end of the dark corridor, she paused at the entrance, staring around her, her eyes wide and curious.

The music seemed muted for once, the feeding restrained. Still, an orgy was an orgy. Couples, threesomes, sharing blood and sex, some doing it standing in the middle of the dance floor.

"You don't get out much," he said, close to her ear. "Why is that?"

She shook her head. "I don't know. I think I have been in a rut." She lifted her nose and inhaled the rich, intermingled scents of liquor, sex, and blood. "*Revenants*, everywhere."

Nicolas knew well her aversion to free *Revenants*. Her preference would be to kill them all rather than risk an uprising, but calmer heads had prevailed so far within the council. Preemptive killing of their "children" wasn't their way.

Enough of the New Orleans crowd knew of her preference that bringing her here was probably a mistake. As the head of the *sabat*, and the oldest living Born on the continent, she was legendary. The news she had entered their lair, their territory, would spread like wildfire.

And it did. One person at a time. Heads nodded in her direction. Whispers rose like a hissing tide above the din of the music.

In the midst of the growing storm, Inanna stood surveying them all as though she were their queen. The haughty lift of her chin, the superior tilt of her nose, the narrow-eyed challenge in her glance—added to the vision of her sultry perfection—held them all enthralled. If only for the moment.

Nicolas wished he'd brought more backup besides Pasqual and the crew surrounding the place outside. If the crowd turned ugly, he'd have a battle on his hands he might not win.

Although a Born, Chessa was accepted here in their midst. Tolerated, and even respected, because of her fighting skills and dogged neutrality.

Inanna might incite a riot.

She stepped deeper into the room and turned, and the shoulder of her caftan slid down, exposing her left breast.

As all gazes fell to the lush, round globe, eyes widened when they realized she was nude beneath the caftan. The mood of those watching changed subtly from bristling menace to excited arousal when they realized what she'd come for this evening.

She looked like a goddess, an Eastern deity. Sloe eyes, black hair falling straight and shining past her shoulders. Skin a dusky, light cocoa. Lips painted red, so lush and full that any man would crave their caress on his intimate flesh.

Tension, sensual and primal, rose in the room as every male *Revenant's* body tightened, primed, wondering who'd be chosen. While they might consider whether this was an opportunity to capture or kill the ancient vampire, the thought of fucking her had to be preeminent.

He and Pasqual shared a worried glance. The other man's lips thinned, his shoulders bunched. He gave away too much. If he wasn't careful and became too possessive, Inanna would cast him aside. Nicolas thought he should warn him, but then again, it might suit his purposes later to let Pasqual slide down that slippery slope.

Inanna continued surveying the crowd and locked gazes with one particularly tall, handsome, dark-skinned man. She approached him slowly, her breaths deepening.

His eyelids dropped, his glance clinging to her exposed breast, then sliding down the rest of her body.

Suddenly, he dropped to his knees, and Nicolas realized she'd cast out a suggestion. The man buried his face between her legs, licking her through the caftan and offering up his hand.

As her fangs sank into his wrist, her gaze scanned the crowd.

Nicolas understood now, this wasn't Inanna wanting what Chessa had, but a show of power, a reminder to *Revenant* and Born alike of how she was different from them.

Different and *more*. Every male present wondered what it would be like to taste her cunt or feel her bite. Nicolas watched their smoldering gazes and wondered how many she'd go through tonight and how the hell he'd get her out of here when she'd had her fill.

Because she hadn't cast a targeted lure, his own body reacted. His cock hardened, his balls ached for release. His gaze clung to her perfect breast.

Damn her. Damn Chessa for putting him in this position.

While he fought the arousal slowly tightening in his groin, he wondered what Inanna's underlying purpose was and worried that she'd decided to extend her influence, and perhaps play a more dominant role in the territory. She'd remained at *Ardeal*, a potent but shadowy presence for so long, dipping her fingers in the politics of the *sabat*, stirring trouble occasionally, but seeming content not to swim with the sharks.

Had it only been The Devourer's escape that provided her impetus to cast out her influence afar? Had this new strategy started with The Devourer . . . or with Chessa?

"Do you have a shirt I can borrow?" Chessa asked, wondering when the four of them would make a move from the entryway. They stood like posts, watching each other's reactions. Her own emotions were so stretched, she feared she'd snap and let them see just how uncertain she felt. How vulnerable she truly was.

Natalie's gaze swept her chest, and she nodded. "Follow me, Chessa," she said softly. She gave a pointed stare to the men who appeared rooted to the floor. "You two, make coffee."

As though accustomed to taking orders from Natalie, they shuffled off to the kitchen, while Natalie led the way upstairs.

In Rene's bedroom, she pointed toward the bathroom. "There's a basin of water if you want to wash up."

Chessa gave her a grateful smile and entered the room, inhaling the scents of Rene's musk and Natalie's citrusy perfume. Together, they were delicious.

She dipped her hand into the basin, washing away the stench of carbon residue that clung to her hands and the fine droplets of blood that spotted her face.

With a grimace, she realized she must have made a gory sight standing in the entrance while she'd been worried about her breasts hanging out.

When she was drying her upper body with a towel, Natalie walked up behind her and began to brush her hair.

Chessa closed her eyes and sighed.

"I missed you," Natalie said, the careful strokes matching her serene tone. "It felt as though we were just becoming friends. Then I had this whole life apart from you."

Chessa opened her eyes and swallowed past the lump at the back of her throat. "Where did Simon send you? He wouldn't say."

Natalie smiled into the mirror. "He sent us to find himself."

Chessa drew a deep breath. He'd known all along what had happened, what was to come. "What year?"

"1310."

Chessa nodded slowly, knowing at least part of his history. "That was after Black Sunday, after the roundup of the Templars. He took refuge in Scotland in a monastery sympathetic to them."

Natalie's blue gaze grew thoughtful. "That's the place."

Chessa's lips tightened. "Living among all those bitter monks must have been hard."

"Not really. They became family." The softening of her expression told the rest of the story. She'd been happy.

Chessa wondered how many of the knights had also been mages. Alex had been raised in their midst, trusted by them. A powerful weapon for a Born.

When the women entered the kitchen, candles were lit on the table as they sat down with coffee. Rene had boarded the windows so no light would expose their presence here. She wondered how they'd managed to heat the coffee without running a generator, but spotted a Coleman stove on the counter.

For all intents and purposes, the house from the outside still appeared abandoned since the night it had been ransacked by *Revenants* seeking to destroy Natalie and her unborn child.

Unspoken for the moment was the fact the *Revenants* hadn't given up their quest. That she was no longer pregnant with a Born child might not dissuade them from violence.

Chessa wrapped her fingers around the warm cup, feeling a little numbed by all she'd learned. She'd hoped the couple would survive, and that she'd see them again one day. However, the space of days from her viewpoint seemed a yawning chasm.

She glanced again at Rene, who was once again staring at her.

His jaw tightened. Then his gaze slid to Natalie. The softening of his granite jaw told her the whole story.

Rene had fallen in love with Natalie.

An ache grew at the back of her throat. She didn't hurt because Rene had found love, but rather because she knew she'd lost her friend, her partner for good. For him, too much time had passed for a bond to remain between them. Natalie and Rene had a shared past, had raised a child together. The glances they shared were charged and loving.

Her present partner stood silently to the side, his expression set, but his gaze watchful.

Damn him. He'd played with her—had known all along that this moment of reckoning was coming.

Chessa straightened her shoulders and tore her glance away from the couple. Natalie and Rene had put much of the house back to rights. With only gouged furniture and the dents in the walls as the remaining evidence of the attack a couple of nights ago, she had no doubt they'd have those taken care of quickly too once the dangers they faced had passed. If they passed.

Alex cleared his throat.

Reluctantly, she came back to him. Then her gaze went from Alex's piercing blue eyes to Natalie's softer blue. It finally clicked.

Why hadn't she guessed at their relationship? So many things fell into place as she cataloged the features he'd inherited from both his parents. Rene's rugged build. His square jaw. His hair was a blend of Rene's deep brown and Natalie's pale locks. The familiarity she'd felt had a reason now.

"Fuck!" She scowled. "You knew about . . . them . . . and me, yet you . . ." She blew out a breath, ready to scream. "That's just wrong."

Alex laughed, a sexy deep rumble that filled his chest. God, he sounded just like his dad. "A little too incestuous for you, sweetheart?"

Natalie smiled, but her gaze fell to her cup. Rene sat back in his chair, his glance roaming over Chessa once again.

For the first time, his interest didn't stir her. He seemed a different man from the cocky, growling man she'd known. Of course, he'd changed.

So had she. In ways she didn't fully recognize yet. She met Alex's amused glance. His smile slid into a sensual smirk, and she glared harder. "So Born males are possible."

Alex nodded, his gaze narrowing. "They are if someone isn't waiting to destroy them as they're born."

Shock made her hand tremble, and she set down her cup. "You think there have been more of you?"

"I can't say. But I do know why Born females might not want us around."

"Tell me."

He shook his head. "A secret's not a secret if it's shared."

"Now you sound like Simon," she grumbled.

His shrug seemed a little too casual. "I can't say whether all males might be born with the same gifts, but would you want someone around who was more physically powerful? With unimaginable powers? Wouldn't someone like that upset the balance of power?"

Chessa's eyes widened. "You think this goes beyond Inanna. To the *sabat*. That there's been some kind of conspiracy."

"My existence proves it. I wasn't born within a coven as all Born children are. They didn't have a chance to dispose of me before I'd reached my full powers."

"Why are you here, Alex?" She glanced at Rene and Natalie. "Why did you return knowing what you do—knowing they'll want to destroy you?"

Natalie reached across the table to close her hand around Chessa's clenched fist. "There's more. The Devourer's escape is just the start. Simon has lived many pasts, and he's seen what's coming."

"And he told you what it is?"

Natalie shrugged. "He hasn't. He's only hinted. Something about not changing the warp and weave of time. But he has prepared us. Trained us. As warriors and as leaders. We've been gathering . . . troops."

Something in the careful way she'd said that and the steadiness of her gaze had Chessa stiffening. "You want me to join you?"

"You already have," Natalie said, her gaze boring into hers.

Chessa shot a narrowed glance at Rene then Alex.

For once, Alex's expression held no hint of humor, just a soft, penetrating intent.

Her back stiffened. "I don't know what you're thinking, but I'm not your girl. Mages scry all sorts of ominous portents all the time. I live in the here and now. Preparing for some kind of Armageddon isn't in my job description."

Beneath their concentrated stares, she bristled, feeling as though if she didn't make a move quick they'd suck her into their fantasy. "I have to get back to work. I'll understand if you think you need to be somewhere else," she added, glaring at Alex.

His lips curved, but the smile didn't reach his eyes. "Chessa, love. While I'd like to bring you into the fold, we weren't talking about you."

"Who then?" she shot back, irritated and filling with an unease that burbled in her stomach. "Why involve me at all?"

Alex leaned back in his chair, his expression darkening. "I need the child you carry."

CHAPTER

14

Inanna pulled up the shoulder of her caftan, at last covering her breast.

Nicolas felt only mild relief. Tension gripped him in an iron vise. His teeth ached he'd gritted them so hard against the need to find release from the sensual spell she'd wrapped around him—around every man and woman in that room.

She'd remained regal, in control, as first one man stepped forward and slowly slid her caftan up her thighs to give the man tonguing her access to her folds, and another caressed her breasts from behind. All sound had died inside the room except from the moist sounds between her legs and the pained sighs of the men who'd offered their wrists, one after another, to feed her.

It had been an awesome display of power. When she was through, the men had fallen back as one, letting her gown slide back into place. She'd turned without a word, sweeping away before they'd collected themselves to realize what had just happened.

At any time, they could have been overcome, but she'd held them back with just her will and her sensual allure. She'd radiated womanhood, donned a mantle of authority only the strongest of men could match.

With a nod to her driver, she slipped into the back of the limo and stared straight ahead.

Nicolas slid in the seat across from her, and stared at the entrance of the bar as the limo pulled away. "That was quite a scene back there. I left half the crew inside to make sure the humans in the room aren't savaged by the lust you stirred up."

"It was necessary," she said, flicking on the interior light.

"Are you going to tell me why?" he grumbled, expecting a refusal. Inanna never explained herself.

"I will," she whispered, "but first, let me see to your problem so you can listen to what I say."

His breath hitched, and he spread his legs to ease the tightness that grew impossibly more urgent.

"Open your pants for me," she said, scooting to the edge of her seat.

Nicolas's hands shook as he flicked open the button and eased down his zipper.

Inanna reached inside, pulling down the band at the top of his underwear to free his cock. *Dieu!* Would she take him in her mouth? She'd serviced him only once before.

Her hand reached inside to cup his length, smoothing down to grasp his balls and she squeezed. "Are you still mine, Nicolas?" she asked, her stare boring into him.

Did she guess his loyalty had been compromised? Although he wanted to close his eyes, he willed himself to hold her gaze. "I'm yours. Always."

Her head bent over his lap and she opened her mouth, taking him into heat and moisture that soothed and aroused his swollen cock.

He gripped the back of her head, not to urge her down, for he'd never force her where she didn't want to go, but to tell her, *Yes! More, please!*

And amazingly, she took him deep into her mouth, her tongue gliding along his shaft as she sank, her throat opening to swallow around him, constricting then opening as she mimicked the motion of drinking to caress the head of his cock.

Nicolas gasped, his breath catching on a moan as she came up his cock, then slid back down, her motions graceful, measured, while inside, his belly tightened with urgent tension.

Her small, soft hand began to tug and release his balls, over and over, until the fullness reached a painful peak of need.

"Inanna, back off," he gritted out. "I'm going to come."

But she kneaded his balls harder, sank her mouth deeper around his cock and he exploded, his hips driving upward to spear the back of her clasping throat, cum jetting into her while his body trembled wildly.

When the lapping waves of release ebbed away, he sat with his head resting on the back of his seat, staring into the face of the woman who'd been his mentor, his mistress, *his keeper* for so long. Power had shifted, however subtly, between them. He didn't for a minute think it had a damn thing to do with the sex they'd shared in Simon's office.

Inanna was calculating, never rash. She'd come to a decision before that day, reinforced it with this act.

"You are mine," she said, still holding his penis in her hand. "As I am yours."

His chest lifted, regret and tempered anger filling him. Why now? He'd been with her for centuries, only in the last years had he finally shed the shackles of her obsessive need for control. He fucked her when she commanded, but his heart and emotions were no longer hers.

She waited for him to reply, her lips tightening. "Yes, I am yours," he lied.

Her gaze slid away, and she released him to sit back in her seat. "We need to talk, Nico. I have no one else I trust."

"About what? The demon?"

"No, he's a danger to us, but not the reason I am here." Her arms crossed her chest, her hands gripping her upper arms as though she felt a chill.

"Tell me."

Her expression grew taut. "The *sabat* has called a meeting."

"They called the meeting? They aren't answering your summons?"

Her lips tightened. "They summoned me here."

He let a deep breath out. "Are they challenging you?"

A swift shake of her head sifted the dark locks of her hair. "They claim there are reports of a daywalker—here in New Orleans."

Nicolas held himself still, careful not to betray the quickening that arrested his heartbeat. A daywalker? Was that what the bastard was? "I thought daywalkers were a myth."

"They think I've been lax, inattentive," she said, ignoring his comment. "First, the demon. Now, this creature. Both here in New Orleans. What if it's not a coincidence?" Her eyebrows drew together in a fierce frown. "I want him found."

"And when we capture him?"

"Destroy him."

Wondering how far she'd let him question her, he asked, "Should we? Do you know what he is?"

Her lips twisted. "I suppose we should determine whether he's Born or *Revenant*, first—and whether he's using a mage's skills to deflect the sunlight. You're right."

"A mage can do that?"

"They can do most anything, depending on how powerful, how old they are."

Simon, again. "Aren't they supposed to remain neutral?"

"It's what enables them to live among us and the other kin—without borders—but this could change everything."

"We maintain a balance of power," he said thoughtfully. "A status quo." He understood the status quo—it was what kept *Revenants* subservient to the whims of the *sabat*. "This daywalker could threaten that balance?"

Her gaze hardened. "He's an abomination. Depending on his true nature, he could endanger us all."

Nicolas pressed again. "How does he threaten us?"

Her gaze slid away. Her shoulders straightened. "That, you don't need to know."

"So, in addition to my duties as guardian, I must divide my attention between The Devourer and the daywalker. What about the *sabat* members? Must I provide protection for them?"

"They will bring their own security."

"To New Orleans? How can we hope to host them here?"

"They will descend on *Ardeal*."

Nicolas filed that away. "I'm going to be busy," he murmured. "Does this mean you will be heading home, soon?" he asked, hoping for a hint of how much time he had to get things into place.

"Tonight. Before dawn."

He nodded, his mind already racing ahead.

"Nicolas?" she asked, her tone changing, softening, as did her gaze.

"Yes, mistress?"

"Will you take me again?"

She hadn't allowed herself release with the men in the bar. Her expression was still taut with unabated arousal, her nipples still hard and dragging at the silk of her gown. She asked, didn't demand, when only a tentative wave of her allure could so easily pull him beyond his will. Things had truly changed.

"Of course. Take off your gown."

A soft sigh escaped her, and she slowly drew the gown over her head, depositing it on the seat beside her. The golden light of the overhead lamp painted deep shadows beneath her full breasts and between her closed legs.

"Bend over the seat, mistress."

A strangled laugh erupted from her, but she knelt on the

floor and turned, giving him a look that held the tension of uncertainty. Her shoulders were stiff, her back straight.

He gripped her hair hard and pulled her backward for a kiss.

Her shock caught her breath. Kisses weren't a common occurrence between them. Kisses were a shared act—too intimate for one who wanted to hold all the power.

Nicolas punished her mouth with his, driving his fangs against his lips and into hers, scraping to draw blood, which she sucked down eagerly.

When he drew back, his breaths were harsh, hers more so, labored, her body quivering. He liked that. Liked the new vulnerability she surrendered to him.

Gripping her hair harder, he forced her to face forward and pressed her over the seat.

She hissed as her nipples hit the cool leather. Her bottom lifted into his groin.

Nicolas knelt on the floor behind her and pushed down his pants, then brought his hands up her inner thighs and shoved them wide, gentling his grip to smooth up her soft skin and cup her moist cunt.

With the picture of Alex's fist disappearing into Chessa's sweet, hot pussy, he thrust three fingers into Inanna, twisting to stretch her, pushing deep to capture the wetness coating her vagina. She was a woman. Beneath the power she wore like a cloak, she melted beneath a man.

Her bottom rose to take him deep, pulsing up and down, her hands stretched wide over the leather, her fingernails digging in to scrape the leather as she groaned.

He pulled out, folded his thumb into his palm, curled his fingers, and inserted his hand inside her, pushing hard to overcome the resistance that gripped him tighter than a glove. He leaned close and nipped one cheek, warning her. Promising punishment if she didn't relax and let him have his way.

Her head thrashed side to side, and her groan deepened. "Please, Nic. Don't!"

However, she relaxed the stricture of her inner muscles, and he slipped his fist through her opening, cramming higher. He kissed the imprint of his teeth on her cheek, and twisted his hand, coating it in her arousal and pulling away slightly, only to ram forward harder, deeper.

A whimper—soft, feminine, *helpless*—broke from her, and his chest expanded with his grim satisfaction. He twisted again, driving inward then pulling out, listening to the moist sounds as her channel convulsed around his fist.

With his free hand, he reached beneath to pluck and massage her stretched labia, circling downward toward the erect knot freed by stretching flesh. When he glanced over it, she drew a harsh breath, her back arching.

He circled again then squeezed it, knowing he'd pushed her past pleasure into pain.

She screeched, the sound loosed like the breaking cry of an eagle. Her vagina tightened, fluid rushing past his hand to dribble down his forearm.

But he didn't relent. He leaned over her back, ramming his hand as high as she could take, and gripped her shoulders with his fangs, sinking into her flesh, mouthing her as blood seeped around his bite faster than he could swallow.

Her whole body shuddered, and she writhed as her orgasm squeezed around him, numbing his hand.

His cock, full and aching, bumped against her thigh, reminding him of his own urgent, painful need and he withdrew his fist while still gripping her neck and slid easily inside her stretched cunt.

He stroked deep, gliding in the excess of moisture, warming his cock within her hot inner walls.

"Nicolas," she groaned, reaching behind her to grip the back of his head as he fucked into her, hammering her, not letting up until the second tightening wave of orgasm swept over her and she keened. Her arms dropped, her body hung limply in the grip of his jaws and upon the spike of his cock.

Still, he didn't stop, fucking her with a fury built over years of submission breaking free, punishing her body with the harsh stroke of his cock and his deepening bite.

Only when his own orgasm sucked the breath from his lungs, did he release her neck, letting her body slump against the cushions. His fingers bit into her ass as he pumped hard, riding the crest in jouncing thrusts that rattled his teeth so hard he clenched them tight.

At last, the anger drained, and he closed his eyes, dragging deep breaths into his starved lungs, letting the waves of shivering, ebbing ecstasy dissipate slowly.

Leaving him quivering in the blast of cool conditioned air, and finally, staring down at the woman he'd savaged.

Alex stared at the doorway after Chessa fled the kitchen.

"Seems you've been busy," Rene bit out between clenched teeth.

Alex shrugged. "The moment was there. An opportunity I couldn't pass up."

"You were to woo her," Natalie said, feminine recrimination in her tight expression.

"I didn't rape her."

"She doesn't give herself easily," Rene bit out.

"Could have fooled me," Alex drawled.

"She's off-balance," his mother said softly. "She's still acting under the influence of my allure."

"Not yours, mother," Alex said, letting a grin slide along his lips.

"You cast yours for her?" she said, stiffening.

"I cast it to draw in Nicolas. I needed his compliance. She was just there."

Rene choked. "You cast for Nic? God, I almost wish I'd been there. The arrogant bastard had to be fighting hard."

"Surprisingly, no. He was right there. I think he was actually thinking of Chessa's best interests."

Natalie's frown deepened. "Her best interests included going to bed with you?"

"You had to be there to understand," Alex said with a sly smile. "Oh wait, you know exactly what I'm talking about. You seduced her—to draw farther into your ménage."

"Knock it off, Alex," Rene said, his voice low and lethal.

"You've been behaving like an ass," Natalie said. "She doesn't deserve any of this."

"She doesn't have any choice—any more than I do," he bit out. "She was destined for this."

"Chessa doesn't understand why," his mother said, her

brows drawing together now in concern. "She hasn't mourned her first child. Not fully."

"She'll come around," Alex said blithely even while his stomach started to knot with unease. They'd known her long before he ever met Chessa Tomas. "Maybe she'll even be grateful. I've given her a second chance at motherhood."

"One more word and I swear I'll knock you into tomorrow," his father said, his hands fisting on the tabletop.

Natalie settled her hand over her husband's and squeezed. Rene's gaze swung toward her, softening instantly.

Alex backed off, settling deeper into his chair, uncomfortable with his parents' show of affection. All these centuries and their love for each other had never waned. "Nicolas is the one I'm worried about," he said, changing the subject to something his father could really get worked up about.

"You think he's going to figure out what you are?" Natalie asked, looking away at last from Rene's taut face.

"He's gonna want to take a bite."

"Will you force it?"

"Let's see how it plays."

Natalie's gaze went to the empty doorway, and her tight expression reflected feminine concern. "You should go after her."

Alex followed her glance and let loose a deep sigh. "What can I say?"

"You're the damn genius," she snapped, revealing her deep annoyance. She rarely cursed. "You figure it out."

Alex found Chessa half a block away, walking with her head bent, her hands stuffed deep inside her pockets.

"Get the fuck away from me," she said, not bothering to look back.

He drew closer, noting that her shoulders shrugged as though trying to throw him off. He reached for her arm and swung her around to face him. "We need to talk."

Keeping her head down, she tore away and kept walking.

Alex reached out and wrapped his arms around her, halting her and drawing her back against him, holding her while she silently struggled inside his embrace.

Only after she stood still, trembling in his arms, did he loosen his hold. He leaned down to press a kiss to her temple. "We really do have to talk, Cheech."

"Don't call me that," she growled. "You're not my friend."

Alex slipped his hand beneath her borrowed shirt and edged his fingers under her waistband to palm her soft belly, reminding her just how close they really were.

"It's not possible," she whispered, her voice breaking. "I can't be pregnant."

"You don't know much about Born males."

"I know they aren't supposed to exist." Her tone said she wished it were true.

"You don't know about our—"

"Our?" she asked, her tone sharpening.

Alex cursed his loose tongue. "*My* capabilities." He sent out a subtle flare of arousal that had her sighing and tilting her head to the side.

"Bastard," she whispered.

He kissed the spot behind her ear. "I can impregnate human women—"

"Have you?" she groaned.

He ignored her question. "And Born females."

"But I haven't had a cycle in four decades. We only have one."

"It isn't needed." He rubbed her belly, heating her skin, soothing her.

"I don't believe you," she said, her voice trailing into a sigh. "I don't feel any different."

"You will. And soon. This child will quicken in your belly. You'll give birth in weeks."

A shudder racked her slender frame. "How is this possible?" she asked, grabbing his arm to stop his motions.

"A little magic. I can't have you vulnerable for long."

"Me? Or the baby?" she asked, resentment telegraphing in her even tone.

"Both of you."

"Will it grow quickly, too?"

He nodded against her hair as she fell silent for a long moment.

"Is this Simon's doing?" she asked, her voice tight and thick.

"He understood the need." He slipped his hand from her waistband and glided upward to capture her breast.

Her nipple spiked hard against his palm, and she gave him a delicious little moan. "Why do you want this child?"

"You accept you're pregnant?" he asked, squeezing her.

"Only the possibility . . . for conjecture's sake." She cleared her throat and tried to hold her body away from his. "Why me?"

"You're special, Chessa. Even the *sabat* recognizes it."

"I'm not," she said flatly. "I'm just like any other Born female."

"*Liar*," he whispered in her ear. "You feel different. Apart."

"Only because of what happened with my family."

"Isn't that enough? Have you ever wondered why they died?"

"Because the rogue *Revenants* want to usurp power from the Born," she said, her voice strengthening with anger that started to make her shake. "To take control of the council."

"That's true in itself, but why start with your child?"

"Because they had the opportunity," she gritted out. "They wised up. Got bold."

Keeping his tone soft, he kissed her ear and whispered. "They didn't make the decision. They were only the instrument."

Chessa turned to stone; her breath caught. "Someone else wanted them dead? Inanna?"

"I don't think so. She wants you close. I believe she wanted to control the destiny of your child."

"Why?" she asked, emotion thickening her voice again. "Why am I any different from the others?"

"Because your father wasn't human."

"Of course, he was." Only a hint of doubt made her words sound halting, hesitant.

"Did you know him? How did your mother meet him?"

"My mother died just after I was born. My father along with her."

"How, Chessa?"

"They were attacked."

"By whom?"

"They were traveling, through the buffer zone, near Baton Rouge. They must have crossed the border without ever realizing it. Weres killed them."

Alex tightened his arms around her. "But they weren't outside the territory."

"How can you know that?"

"*I remember.*"

"You were there? That was part of your past?"

"Of course not. If you'll think, you know the answer. I remember because Natalie's grandmother was there."

Chessa's breath halted and her back tightened against him. "You inherited her memories? Is that even possible?"

"It's called genetic memory, and yes, I know everything my ancestors experienced, up to the point of each conception. The point of all this, Cheech, is your father's nature was revealed. The *sabat* arrested him. They set a death sentence."

"Lies!" she said, struggling in earnest again. "What about my mother?"

"His death started her labor. She committed suicide as soon as you were born."

Suicide? Not unheard of when a Born lost her first true love. Hadn't she attempted the same thing? She didn't want to believe it, but it made sense. "What was my father?"

"A mage—natural-born, eternal. Not a practitioner. You carry his blood. So did your child. Once the council disposed of him, they wanted to murder you, but Inanna saved you."

"Because she wanted to use me?"

"She watched, keeping you close to see whether you showed any signs of talent. But the characteristics must have recessed."

"So she spared me." She stayed silent for a long moment while he waited for her to make the next logical leap, which she did unerringly. "If I'm pregnant again, will she—"

"She'll have no choice but to kill you both. You can't ever be in her presence. She'll sense you're quickening."

"That's why Simon put his hex on me. So I can get back out in the open . . . in weeks?"

"Yes."

She slumped against his chest, her face lifting toward the moon that shone hard and bright in the night sky. He heard her heart begin to thud harder in her chest as the reality of her situation began to sink in. "What about the child?" she asked in a thin voice. "How will we hide it? Keep it safe?"

Alex relaxed. She understood the dangers now. "You'll give it into my care. I'll raise it."

"Do you intend to slip into the past?"

"Probably," he kissed her temple again. "But I'll miss you."

She wrenched away and faced him, her lips twisting in a snarl. "Do you really think I'd give away any child of mine? That I wouldn't have to be there to protect it myself?"

"You must take your place on the council. Prepare our way for when we return."

"I'm not anyone's pawn, and certainly never yours!"

"You're not a pawn," he said, reaching for her again. "You're my dark Madonna."

She snorted. "And you're what? God?"

"No, but I am the prince who'll fight the good battle."

"What's this really all about?" she asked, fisting her hands at her sides. "Is it Armageddon?"

Alex held her troubled glare. "It's worse. It's Hell on Earth."

CHAPTER
15

Once he'd shaken off his rage, Nicolas closed the wound on Inanna's neck, wincing at the deep red, ragged oval he'd left on the top of Inanna's shoulder.

Then he pulled her into his arms and held her close to his chest, watching her chest rise and fall in shallow, labored gasps. For the first time, he realized how delicate and slight her frame really was. Without the burning fire of her personality, she seemed young. Vulnerable. Womanly.

Goose bumps rose on her flesh; her skin and lips were tinged blue. He'd done this. Rage had blinded him.

Sickened with his actions, he brought his wrist to his mouth and sliced it viciously with his fangs then held it over her gaping mouth.

He didn't relax until blood pooled in her mouth, and she swallowed reflexively. Slowly, the underlying tones of her skin warmed, her cheeks reddened. Her eyes blinked open, and her gaze met his.

"I'm sorry, Inanna," he said. He meant it. "I went too far."

Her hand lifted to cup his cheek, and she smiled. "See how much I trust you?"

"Are you saying you knew what I'd do? And you let me unleash my anger on you?"

"Do you feel remorse?" she said softly.

He closed his eyes and swallowed. "Yes."

"Then we put this behind us. I belong to you, in the same way you belong to me. We have both taken and used and hurt each other."

Nicolas drew in a jagged breath. "Is pain the measure of your love?"

"Is that what we feel?"

Not in the same way he loved and desired Chessa, but he recognized there was a bond. He sighed deeply and slumped against the seat behind him. "You shouldn't have let me do this."

"Then how am I to ever know you truly care?"

He snorted. "Do you hear yourself?"

She smiled the winsome smile of a girl. "You forget. I've lived long. This life you enjoy is a blinking light."

"Are you saying I'm a baby?"

"I'm saying you don't understand everything. You can't." Her eyes gleamed in the darkness. "I need you, Nico. I trust no one. Only you. You can have your Chessa. But I must know you love me, too."

His stomach churned. Doubt crowded in to raise the bile of betrayal to burn the back of his throat. "I do love you. You are my mistress."

She slipped her arm around his back and settled her cheek on his shoulder. "I'm chilled. And tired."

Nicolas pressed a kiss to her forehead, feeling a new tenderness well inside him. "Rest. I'll hold you."

As her eyes closed, Nicolas wondered how things had gotten so complicated.

All he'd ever wanted was to live. That had been the core of their bargain all those years ago. When he'd been human and seduced by her exotic, lithe body and the gift of a pretty wife.

1308
Outside Poitiers, France

Anaïs had been a sprite. A funny, golden elf who stripped him of his clothes and tugged him to her bed the first afternoon they'd met. She'd shed her overgown and bliaut, revealing her pale, rosy skin.

His eyes had widened on her slender curves and slight, mounded breasts, his body hardening again although he'd spent a decadent afternoon with the experienced Lady Inanna.

Gluttony, he discovered, was a glorious sin. He feasted on Anaïs's small peach-tipped breasts. Tasted her fragrant woman's flesh, sliding his tongue inside her to collect the cream she released as he slowly built her arousal.

When he'd nudged apart her thighs and placed his cock at

her entrance, she'd gripped him by the ears and kissed him hard, mashing her lips inexpertly against his.

His own kiss had been as unpracticed, but he learned her taste, slipping his tongue into her mouth, playing with hers, dueling until they both laughed with the joy of being together.

He'd felt alive, young, filled with hope and burgeoning passion. With a flex of his hips, he'd entered her, pushing past her maidenhead, sheathing himself in her moist depths, stroking them both toward fulfillment.

When her release milked his cock of his essence, he rested his head on the pillow beside her, unable to move. Sated, at last. Dragging in breaths flavored by their combined scents.

Her lips had kissed him indolently, gliding along his cheek, licking the lobe of his ear until he shivered, and then sliding down his neck.

Her first bite reinvigorated his passion, and he thrust helplessly against her, taking her murmured praise as she drank him. Lost in the powerful feelings that swirled inside him, he spent himself again, falling asleep in her embrace.

He'd awoken suddenly, his body bending double against the pain that racked him.

Anaïs's sweet voice murmured. Her hands soothed his back and flanks. Then he'd felt the bed dip behind him and more hands glided over him. Inanna's voice whispered in his ear, giving encouragements he didn't understand for she spoke in a lilting, guttural tongue—one he almost recognized, one that put him to mind of searing white-hot heat and golden sand.

His belly knotted, and he cried out. A warm mound pressed into his mouth. "Bite. Drink," Inanna crooned.

He'd felt an itching in the roof of his mouth and the strange downward tug of his teeth as they slid from his gums. He bit the breast filling his mouth and knew it was Inanna's ripe, generous breast. He'd suckled her like a child on his mother's tit, only he'd swallowed blood that roiled inside his belly. The urge to gag was soothed by the warmth of her skin pressing close and the many hands stroking him.

Slowly, his stomach relaxed and a new heat filled him, hardening his ballocks to stones that ached with the pressure to release, filling his cock so that it nudged the thigh opening beside him.

He'd burrowed until his crown glided into wetness that surrounded him, gloving him lovingly in moist, rhythmic caresses.

Kisses landed on his mouth, his ears, his shoulders. Hands glided over his back and buttocks, fingers slid between the twin halves and burrowed, entering him as he thrust into Inanna's depths.

Surrounded by the women, he'd drawn in their distinct scents, one laced with exotic sandalwood, the other fresh and floral. Almost like a dream, images merged illuminated in candle glow—pale skin, dusky, flowing together and apart. Voices, soft and soothing, growing more urgent and pained. Breath brushed his face, and all the length of his body.

Through it all he stroked to the beating of his heart that grew louder and faster in his ears, until a soft caress cupped his balls and he shouted, jerking upward, hammering into the sweet flesh that squeezed the length of his shaft, wringing his seed from his cock in a stream of searing heat.

When he had the strength to move again, he enclosed the woman perched across his flanks in his arms, bringing her closer for a kiss—wondering when the women had switched places. "What has happened to me?" he whispered against her lips.

"You are ours," Anaïs whispered back, her lips stretching into a tentative smile. "Forever."

"Ours?"

Her gaze slid away. "You don't remember?"

"I remember . . ." He shook his head then looked quickly around. "We're alone?" Had he been dreaming?

"Now, we are. To rest."

"But before?"

"*Grand-mère* thought it necessary to bind us both to you."

"I thought . . . maybe I had dreamed." He reached up to slide a kiss along her naked shoulder. "*Grand-mère?*"

She smiled and shook her head. "Do you remember my bite?" she asked, her finger touching the side of his throat, circling over an aching patch.

"It doesn't hurt." His lips stretched into a grin. "I didn't mind."

Her smile slipped. "There's no going back."

He touched his lips to hers, not really listening. But ready to fuck this winsome creature again. "I'm where I want to be."

He hadn't known, didn't realize that he had died. That he'd spent days in bed recovering. Days spent in the arms of the two women who'd turned him.

One he'd wed. The other he served.

Still served, for he was bound by blood to her.

But he was bound by his own will to betray her.

Present Day

Alone in her apartment, Chessa locked the door behind her and grabbed several bottles of water from the kitchen counter before heading to the bathroom.

With candlelight casting shadows over her naked skin, she stopped up the sink and filled the basin with water. Then slowly, she worked a rich, scented lather into a washcloth and washed every part of her body, working methodically from her face to her shoulders and underarms, then working faster as she moved down, at last lifting her feet one at a time to the counter to complete her task.

She didn't want to finish. Didn't want time to think. She wanted to be clean, and then crawl between fresh sheets and pull them over her head, never to waken until this whole nightmare had ended.

Perhaps, if she slept long enough, she'd wake up to a world where everything worked again. Where the sound of the dump truck growling up the street tugged her into awareness in the early morning. She'd roll over again and sleep until the mailman buzzed the outer door to fill their boxes.

She'd waken to find that everything that had happened over the past week had been nothing more than a really bad dream. A pizza with jalapeño type of dream, the kind that gave her indigestion and burned the back of her throat, but the ache passed as she hurried through her evening.

She tossed the washcloth on top of the overfilled hamper and walked back into the bedroom to find Nicolas stretched across the bed, dressed in black and looking devilishly seductive, two pillows stuffed beneath his shoulders.

"Not now," she said, her chest tightening at the sight of him.

"Then when?" he growled.

"You stick to your turf—"

He shook his head. "So we won't talk. That's fine by me. I want to sleep."

"Sure you do. She exhaust you?" Chessa sniped, feeling gloriously bitchy. "Or does the smell of Inanna just happen to be your latest cologne?"

Nicolas didn't blink. "She dropped me off. She's heading back to *Ardeal*."

"Good riddance. Tired of slumming already?"

Nicolas closed his eyes for a brief moment. His chest rose with a deep inward breath. "I didn't come here to talk about her."

"You follow her around like a lap dog," Chessa snarled. "You use me to get rid of the kinks she leaves in your neck."

"How about we make a deal?" he said, sounding tired. "You don't mention Inanna, and I won't ask what happened between you and Alex tonight."

She winced. Nicolas could never know. Another reason she needed him out of her life. When it came down to it, if Inanna wanted the dirty work taken care of, Nicolas would be the one given the job.

The thought made her want to vomit.

Damn, she really was pregnant.

She crossed her arms over her naked chest. "You want a place to sleep—take the couch."

He gave another heavy sigh. "We have to capture our demon. We both need rest. Shut up and get under the covers. I promise I won't touch you."

He swung his legs over the side of the bed and walked toward her, his gaze giving her a single heated once-over before he passed her and shut the bathroom door behind himself.

"Fine," she called over her shoulder. "You just stick to your side of the bed." For added measure, she hunted for a set of pajamas and jerked them on. Then she knelt on the bed to pull open the window to let in a breeze, but found the latch was already turned.

So that's how he'd gotten inside. She peered over the narrow ledge that ran to the balcony. The man had wanted in here bad.

Thoughtful, she lay down and pulled up a sheet then turned on her side to face away from the bathroom door. Tonight might be torture, but she couldn't pass up the opportunity to share the same bed with Nicolas one last time. Tomorrow, she had to make plans.

Number one, catch a monster. Next, pack a bag and head to somewhere no one knew her. Somewhere she could blend in. Somewhere a night owl wouldn't stick out like a sore thumb.

Maybe Vegas, although it was were-country. As long as she kept her snacks below the radar, she should be all right. And no way would any of the coven break treaty to follow her.

The door opened. Nicolas padded toward the bed, lifted the sheet, and slid in beside her.

Such an intimate thing, sliding between the same sheets. If she didn't have to go, maybe it wouldn't have been such an awful thing going back home. Knowing Inanna had saved her all those years ago, for whatever reason, eased her resentment against the woman who tried to manage all their lives.

A deep sigh sounded behind her and arms enclosed her, bringing her flush with a long, muscled body. Nicolas's erection felt thick as it pressed into her backside. "Sleep," he growled.

"Serves you right," she said grumpily. "You should have taken the couch."

After several minutes holding herself still, ready to fight off an amorous advance she just wasn't ready to handle, she relaxed.

"This is nice," he said, his breath stirring her hair.

He can never know. "I'm sleepy."

"You smell good."

I'll never see him again. "It's gardenias."

"I like flowers."

"I'm pregnant."

His breath stopped, and his arms tightened. "What did you say?"

She closed her eyes, starting to shake. "I'm pregnant."

He sucked in a deep, hard breath. "Can't be."

"Believe me, I've already had that conversation."

"How?" he asked, his voice a harsh scrape.

"It's the 'who' that made it possible."

"Alex," he hissed.

She didn't have to answer. The rigidity that gripped his body told her he'd made the correct leap of deduction. For long moments, they lay next to each other, both tense, both measuring their breaths and listening to the sounds of each other's heartbeats.

When the trembling started anew, Chessa couldn't help the soft sniff that shook her chest, or the tears that slid to the pillow beneath her cheek.

A sigh ruffled her hair. "Don't cry, *mon ange*," he whispered, coming up on his elbow to slide her hair behind her ear.

Chessa squeezed shut her eyes and sobbed, turning her face into the pillow. "Go away," she choked out. She felt fragile as glass, ready to break at the slightest touch.

"Not a chance, love." He forced her to her back, tugged off her pajama bottoms, and slid over her body. His large hands cupped her cheeks, his thumbs sliding over her tears.

She sniffed again, knowing she was getting sloppy and embarrassed about it. "Nic, I can't do this again. Can't have a baby."

His throat worked, his jaw tensed. Then he bent and kissed her cheeks, her chin. "Shhh . . ."

His tenderness was too much. She felt her face crumble. Tears blurred his features. "I can't lose this one, too."

An arm slid beneath her shoulders to raise her head. Another kiss landed on her forehead. "You won't. Nothing will happen." He nudged apart her thighs, his cock unerringly sliding between her folds.

She opened eagerly, relishing the gentle thrust as he entered her, joining them. "He wants to take my child from me."

"We'll stop him." His lips sipped at hers as he started to stroke inside.

Her arms reached around his back, her fingers digging into hard, firm flesh and muscle. As he eased away her tears with his body, she felt her chest lighten. She kissed him back and lifted her legs to grip his hips, urging him deeper, surrendering to his mastery, trusting he would make everything right.

Slowly, they surged together and apart, their breaths intermingling, their bodies sealing their unspoken bond. When his thrusts grew harder, shorter, she tensed and squeezed her inner muscles around his gliding cock.

Nicolas groaned into her mouth, then drew his head back sharply, his face screwed tight in an anguished grimace.

Chessa dug her fingernails into his flanks. "Fuck me, Nic! Fuck me, harder!"

"*Dieu!* Fuck!"

His cock powered into her, ramming toward her core, tapping her womb with his deep, sharp thrusts until she felt her orgasm unravel, releasing moist, rhythmic pulses that shivered along her vagina.

Chessa cried out, digging the back of her head into the pillow as she strained higher, cresting the peak while jagged lights exploded behind her closed lids.

Nicolas's tightening groan accompanied a spurt of cum that washed against her womb. He languished in the wet heat, rocking between her thighs until the storm had passed, and they both collapsed to the bed.

"We'll flee to Mexico," he said between ragged breaths.

She sank her fingers into his thick hair. "I thought Vegas."

A sharp shake of his head. "Were-country. It's not safe. Fleas."

A short, gasped laugh caught her by surprise. "So, I'll wear a collar. No one will look for me there."

"I like the collar idea. But two of us can't exactly blend in."

"Really? You'd do that? Come with me?"

His features softened. "You're mine, Chessa."

Old, ugly doubts intruded between them. "But what about Inanna?"

His eyes closed. "I'll have to leave her."

"You're bound to her in some way, aren't you? Did she turn you, Nic?"

He nodded, his forehead falling to her shoulder.

Chessa rubbed her hands slowly up and down his back and pressed her cheek against this hair. "How can you leave her?"

"I must," he whispered. "I won't let you leave alone."

"Do you love her?" she asked then wished she hadn't.

"Yes."

Damn, damn, damn. "Can you resist her?"

"I can, if there's distance between us."

"She'll haunt you."

He lifted his head and gazed down at her in the darkness. "Since she and Anaïs, my wife, turned me together, the bond is diluted somewhat. I won't pine for her, if that's what you think."

He believed what he said. If only it could be true. "I wondered about you and her. You seem so aloof from her at times. Almost angry. Yet, she commands you."

"I don't approve of everything she does."

Alex's warning still fresh in her mind, she hesitated to reveal everything. "She will want this child dead. The *sabat* will demand it. They'll want me dead as well."

His eyebrows drew together. "Every Born child is a reason for rejoicing. Why do you think they'll turn on you? Inanna cares for you."

Chessa bit her lip, afraid, but hoping she could place her trust in him. He'd always been there for her. "I know they won't be happy about this child," she began, wrestling one last time before blurting the truth. "I know, because we've conceived something more than just another Born child. Alex and I. *He's* Born. That's the first curse. The second is that I'm . . . special."

One corner of his mouth lifted in a wry smile. "I already knew that." A gentle swirl of his hips emphasized his point.

"No." She shook her head. "I'm a hybrid. Mage and Born vampire."

His eyebrows rose. "Alex knew this?" he asked, his tone so even, she knew he was disturbed.

She nodded slowly.

His shoulders tensed, his chest rippling with the flash of anger that hardened his frame. "Another nail in his bloody coffin. I'm going to kill him."

"You can't."

His lips firmed into a narrow, hard line. "Because he's the father of your child?"

"Because he's needed."

"Explain," he said in that low, deadly drawl that never failed to arouse her.

"I can't. I don't know very much."

"Then don't tell me," he said, with a bitter twist of his lips. "He's the dark prince, come to fight a horde of demons on earth."

She shrugged, feeling a little foolish to hear it said aloud. "Maybe."

"I've heard that story before."

"From whom?"

"Inanna. A long time ago. It's a load of shit. Order. Treaties. That's what keeps back the hordes."

"This sounded more . . . dire . . . what he hinted at."

"Well, all the more reason for us to get a long, long way from here. He's going to start something."

"I agree. We need to get the hell away from here, whatever's going to happen." She dropped her gaze to his wide shoulders and ran her palms across the top, trying to avoid his knowing gaze. "Are you angry with me?" she said in a small voice.

"Angry? Because you're pregnant?" At her nod, he sighed. "How can I be? I invited him into your body, didn't I? Although I'm starting to suspect, he probably dropped the hint somewhere in the back of my mind."

"He might have. I don't know what all he's capable of doing."

"So, we have two adversaries we must flee. Alex and the *sabat*."

His anger. His acceptance. Both warmed her. She felt a thawing of the panicked ice that had enclosed her heart and mind. "Can we start tomorrow?"

"Tired, love?"

"Exhausted."

"You're definitely pregnant." He gave her a short kiss and started to pull away.

Her legs tightened around his hips. "Not too tired," she said, walking her fingers down his chest.

His lips curved in a wicked, smoldering smile. "How do you want it?"

As it turned out, trust wasn't all that hard to give up. Not to someone who'd demanded it every step of the way and had never failed to show his care—however high-handed he was.

"Surprise me."

CHAPTER
16

Nicolas stuck more tacks in the map on the wall and stood back. With the latest reports, there was no doubt about where their demon was headed. Disregarding the first bodies beside the bayou, he tapped the pin for Madame Fortun's. The victims along the highway. The mortuary. All heading inexorably in one direction.

"He's going straight to *Ardeal*. Doesn't he care he's dropping bread crumbs all along the way?"

Nicolas smiled at the grumpiness in Chessa's voice. After searching her closet for the one pair of dark slacks she owned with a stretchy waist, she'd fallen silent while he'd pulled together a meal of sorts from whatever dry goods he could find in her pantry. Roughage to fill her growling belly until they could find a live meal.

Alex hadn't shown up after dusk. Probably knew he was *persona non grata* with him now. Still, Nicolas would have felt better keeping him in his sight. "Maybe you should stay at home, tonight," he said quietly.

Her laser-hot glare had him holding back a smile. "You think I'm fragile or something? I'm just pregnant. No different than I was yesterday. Besides, this is my investigation—you're just the consultant."

"You'd be safer," he said, biting back a flare of anger for her obstinacy. That it was mixed with an equal amount of pride for her courage didn't escape him.

"I'll be just fine. I'm a big girl. Getting bigger by the minute," she said, tugging at her waistline.

She didn't even show a bump, but he bit back another caution. Nothing would make her dig in her heels faster than being told she shouldn't do something.

"You would go to *Ardeal*, then?" he drawled.

Her gaze snapped to his. "I'll follow The Devourer there. But I'll have to be careful not to be in Inanna's company."

"I'll shield you. Distract her, perhaps?"

"How?" Her eyebrows lowered. "Oh, never mind. Tell me, do you play your rough games with her?"

His lips tightened.

Chessa snorted. "Of course, you do. You like it that way. Does she?"

He turned, unwilling to share the part of him that could never be totally hers. "We understand each other."

"Will you tell her good-bye?"

Irritated, he growled, "Leave off, Chessa."

"Guess we better get going. It's a long drive. We're wasting the night away here."

They left her apartment, stepping to the pavement. He lifted a hand to summon the SUV he'd arranged the night before. When he'd dismissed the driver and they were both seated inside, he said, "What more can you tell me about Alex?"

Her gaze slid away to the dark streets. Every corner and alley hid shadows and secrets. Just like Chessa.

His hand gripped the steering wheel. "How is he one of the Born? And who is his mother?"

"Natalie."

Shock struck him like a blow to his midsection. Simon was at the bottom of this. He'd known all along. So much for friendship. The man who had lived many pasts had learned treachery during one of his evolutions.

"Then she and Rene are back?"

"I saw them last night. Inanna can never know they left in the first place."

"She'll know something's happened when she sees Natalie is no longer carrying. Do they plan to hide from her?"

"I don't know what they plan. A lot happened yesterday. Too much." She clasped her hands together in her lap. "I'm hungry."

An unsubtle change of subject, but he had a lot on his mind as well. For now, he'd let the subject drop. "I'll stop once we're out of the city."

Chessa shifted restlessly in her seat for several minutes. She wasn't much for small talk, but he could hear the gears creaking. "You know everything about me," she began. "I know almost nothing about you. Why's that, Nic?"

"What do you want to know?" he asked, pretending nonchalance he didn't feel. He knew exactly what she was curious about.

"Tell me about your wife, Anaïs. How did she die?"

"The Devourer," he said, biting out the words, hoping she'd get the hint and drop her line of questioning. He seldom let himself think of it.

"Of course. Explains a lot about your devotion to your duty."

He swung hard to avoid a fallen tree whose limbs reached into his lane then back onto his own side of the road.

"I'm glad you're driving," she whispered. "I'd never find my way."

The landscape had changed that much. A few signs remained to point the direction. "That's right, you've been in The Quarter since the storm hit," he said, relieved at the new tangent their conversation took while disturbed they seemed to be dancing around each other. Despite the accord they'd reached when lying locked together in bed, a deep chasm still yawned wide between them. He glanced in his rearview mirror. One misstep . . .

"I knew it was bad, but . . ." She fell silent for a long while. Long enough to leave the city behind. As he neared the outskirts of a small community, she stirred in her seat.

"I know," he murmured. "We'll find something here."

He pulled into a diner, the windows still covered in battered plywood. As she pulled open the door to enter the restaurant, he hung back. "I'll be along in a minute."

"Sure," she said, not looking over her shoulder. "I already see something tasty."

Nicolas walked back to the edge of the parking lot and up to the truck that had been trailing them out of the city.

As he came abreast of the driver, the truck's window rolled down. The man behind the wheel gave him a hard, glinting stare.

"Malcolm," Nicolas said, standing so that he could keep an eye on the restaurant door in case Chessa returned too soon.

"Are you still in?"

"Yes, but we will have to move tonight."

"I'll radio the others. Why the rush?"

"The Devourer's closing in on *Ardeal*. We can use this."

"Why not just let him have the bitch?"

Nicolas reached into the cab and gripped his throat, squeezing him until Malcolm's face turned purple. "Nothing happens to Inanna, you understand? Or you'd better be prepared to battle me as well." He let go, and stood back while Malcolm dragged in deep breaths.

"I understand," he rasped. "I just don't think you're taking this far enough. She'll never agree. No matter what we do."

"She's not stupid. Once she knows we're serious, and that we have the numbers to back us, she'll bend. Find a way to use us to her benefit while addressing our demands."

"What about her?" Malcolm said, lifting his chin toward the restaurant. "Is she with us?"

Nicolas shook his head. "I'm working on it," he lied. "Just make sure your men hold back until I give the word. If The Devourer shows himself, be ready to take him down."

Malcolm nodded. "We'll score some big points if we capture him. We'll keep our eyes peeled."

"Make sure Chessa doesn't spot you. I have to go."

Nicolas took a slow turn around the parking lot, spotted more of the men he'd recruited, and decided he'd taken enough time. When he entered the restaurant, Chessa wasn't anywhere in sight. "*Merde!*"

By the time he made it back into the parking lot, the tail lights of the SUV were glowing red as she hit the brakes at the exit of the parking lot then peeled out, churning up gravel. She'd made him.

"Looks like you need a ride, Nic," Malcolm drawled as he pulled up beside him.

Nicolas cursed again and slid into the passenger seat. He'd known he walked a fine line, but had arrogantly thought he could balance the needs of the coven with his own ambitions and desires. Now, he faced the possibility of loosing Chessa forever.

But how much had she overheard? Would she betray him?

Knowing he could be facing a death sentence if his plot were revealed, he gripped the dashboard, silently urging the truck faster as Chessa's lights grew dim in the distance.

"What the fuck?" Chessa shouted, slamming her palm against the dashboard. Nicolas was in league with rogue *Revenants*? Possibly, the same crew that had threatened Natalie's life and trashed Rene's apartment? Maybe the same ones responsible for her family's deaths?

As unbelievable as it seemed, she couldn't have been mistaken about the man she saw him casually talking to at the rear of the parking lot. She'd spied on Nicolas through the restaurant window, wondering what he was up to and whether he needed backup. She'd run through the restaurant, through the kitchen and out the back door, skirting the edge of the lot to get close enough to see whether he needed help.

What she heard had her stomach churning. "What the fuck?" She hit the dash again, mad at herself for believing in him when he'd only been using her. But for what purpose?

If he wanted to take *Ardeal*, why get cozy with her? He all but said they'd make a move on Inanna, and as much as she resented and sometimes hated the matriarch of the coven, she'd never conspire against her.

Nicolas was bound to Inanna by first blood! This level of betrayal was unheard of, impossible to contemplate. Didn't he know his complicity in any plot against a Born, but especially Inanna, would mean instant death?

A chill gripped the base of her spine and shivered upward. She had to stop him. Save him from himself. But how?

For certain, her relationship, or whatever it had been, was over. Any affection dried up as vampire ash.

"What the fuck were you thinking, Nic?" she whispered, and realized she was crying when she couldn't see the road for the shimmering moisture filling her eyes. She dashed away her tears with the back of her hand and stomped on the accelerator. "I trusted you. I was ready to love you. You fucking bastard!"

No one was going to kill him before she got to him. He was hers. She'd kick his ass all over *Ardeal* and leave him frying in the sunshine. She'd strip his skin inch by inch from his body, while he writhed and moaned.

Only the thought of Nicolas writhing and moaning re-minded her how much she was going to miss the writhing and moaning he caused in her. "You sonofabitch!"

She almost missed her turn, turning hard to the left, lift-ing the SUV's tires from the pavement for one heart-stopping moment, before it crashed down, righting itself.

Her rear tires fishtailed as she fought for control. It was all his damn fault. He'd made her care. Made her think she mat-tered to him. Forty freaking years, he'd been there for her. Had he been nurturing their relationship all the while?

It seemed inconceivable.

Yet, she'd seen him with her own eyes. Heard him with her own ears. Had she gotten it right? Could she have jumped to conclusions?

Her foot eased off the gas, slowing while her mind reengaged.

Then she caught the flash of headlights in her rearview mirror. A truck's headlights. The bastard from the parking lot? With Nic?

Her heart slowed, her mind slipped into a numb state where muscle memory handled the SUV, keeping her on the road and pointing in the direction of home.

When the gates appeared in front of her, she slammed on her brakes and slowed, rolling down her window to shout a warn-ing to the gatekeeper. Only no one was there.

And the gates were wide open.

Had Nicolas's friends already struck? She pulled beyond the gate, cognizant the truck wasn't far behind her and turned off her headlights, rolling past the gate to park in the shadows of trees alongside the road.

Then she stepped out, stripped her upper body of impediments and popped her wings. Taking a running head start, she lifted swiftly, flying over the tall concrete and brick wall surrounding the compound. She flew straight for the house, uneasy at finding the sprawling, white Victorian mansion cloaked in darkness like a pale ghost.

She circled overhead then landed on a gabled rooftop, crouching when the truck's headlights passed through the gates, more vehicles pulling in behind it to line up side-by-side, dark-clad figures spilling from them to take up positions throughout the grounds.

What the hell was happening inside? Did they know they were under attack? She stepped lightly over the peak of the roof, peering over the backside of the mansion toward the security force's barracks. Even with her sensitive night vision, she detected no movement.

Then she saw a figure and then another crashing through bushes, telltale jerking movements indicating zombies were on the premises. She cursed, wishing she hadn't been so quick to drop her weapon when she'd stripped.

She ran for the edge of the roof and soared toward the barracks, determined to raid the arsenal for a firearm, and wondering how she'd manage to take on zombies and an army of rogues all by herself, when the sound of wind catching the edge of wings powering toward her halted her in midair.

Alex flew into view, Natalie at his side. He drew up, hovering in front of her and beckoned her with a wave toward the barracks.

What the hell were they doing here?

No time to ask. At the entrance of the barracks she touched down alongside them, and they filed silently inside, rushing down the long corridor toward the arms room. The door was shut. She hit the key pad, glad they hadn't bothered to change the number in the last ten years, waited impatiently for the faint snick of the lock releasing, and slammed her hand down on the lever to open it.

Once inside the room, she and Alex went straight for the rack of weapons, standing chained in a long rack. "Natalie, get the rounds from the lockboxes behind you," she whispered, as she slid her hand beneath the desk for the hidden key Nicolas left for emergencies in a magnetic case. She unlocked the chain and slid three rifles from the end of the rack.

Silently, they loaded their weapons, slipping more rounds into their pockets.

"Head shots, only," she reminded them.

Then they were racing for the exit. They met Rene as he barreled through the door. "Did you see? Fucking zombies," he whispered, reaching for the weapon Natalie slapped across his palm.

Then Nicolas entered, his rogues at his back.

Chessa lifted her weapon and aimed it straight at his heart.

"You know that won't stop me," Nicolas said, his face hard, his expression remote.

"It'll sure hurt like hell," she said, keeping her tone flat. "That's good enough for me."

"I'm not feeling the love," Alex said quietly behind her.

"We don't have time for this," Nicolas said. "He's on the grounds."

Who "he" was didn't need to be said.

"Why shouldn't I blow a hole right through you? Give me one good reason," she said, her voice even. Deadly.

"Hell hath no fury," Alex drawled. "But I'd second him on the fact this isn't the time for a lover's spat."

"This is no spat," Chessa said, her finger slipping around the trigger.

Nicolas set his hands on his hips, and his brows lowered in an irritated frown.

The one Nicolas had called Malcolm uttered a curse and stepped from behind Nic, raising his hands. He was as tall as Nic, his brown hair pulled back in a ponytail to reveal a firm, rugged jaw. Probably ex-military by the look of his broad shoulders and thick arms. "You need us, Chessa Tomas." To Nicolas, he muttered, "Looks like she still needs some work, buddy."

"You arrange this?" Chessa snarled at Nicolas. "This part of your plan?"

Nicolas's dark brows snapped together. "Of course not. This isn't anyone's plan but that fucking demon's."

"And you expect me to believe you, why?"

"Because I'd never cause you harm," he said, his voice rising. "You know that."

Chessa firmed her lips to keep them from trembling. "You already have," she said, her voice hoarse.

A muscle flexed along his jaw. "Princess, this isn't the time. We'll talk later."

"Later, you'll be dead."

"So be it. In the meantime, let us get to the arsenal."

Alex wrapped his hand around the barrel of her weapon and pushed it toward the ceiling. "He's right. Let them pass."

"Because you know how this ends?" she gritted out.

"Of course, I don't. Simon only tells me so much. But I do know Nicolas's not going to hurt those he's loyal to," he said, his gaze narrowing on Nic, until Nicolas nodded.

She bit out a curse and shoved past the men gathered at the door. "Just keep out of my line of sight, or I swear I'll fill your asses with lead."

Low rumbling laughter followed her outside, but she didn't have time to ponder what the hell they thought was so damn funny. The first zombie sped into view and she dropped to her knee, aimed a laser sight between its eyes, and pulled back the trigger.

She jumped up as it slid to the ground, ready to take another on and pushing to the back of her mind the fact the compound was deserted except for the rogues and the walking corpses. No one was rushing to their aid. At least she hadn't found any Born bodies or piles of smoking ash.

Behind her, shuffling footsteps came at a fast pace. She spun on her heels, slamming the stock of her rifle into her shoulder, but she didn't get a chance to squeeze off a shot. The head of the gaping zombie exploded like a water balloon, splattering her with brain and blood.

"Yuck! Could you let him get any closer," she snarled at Alex who was already facing away to find the next target. All around them, Nicolas's men slipped into the shadows, the sound of sporadic gunfire filling the night as they dropped zombies like rag dolls in their tracks.

And like a bag of popcorn too long in the microwave, the pops slowed, until all that remained was the stench of carbon and putrified bodies. Slowly, the team gathered outside the barracks.

They'd fought like a military team. Trained, controlled. Working with silent precision. Rather like *Ardeal's* own security force.

As well, they should. Nicolas had trained them both.

Chessa glanced around quickly and realized that Alex, Natalie, and Rene had faded away quickly, which was just as well. Alex's nature wasn't ready to be revealed just yet. Although why she felt any loyalty to the bastard, she didn't know.

She straightened her shoulders as Nicolas stepped in front of her. His expression was remote, his jaw firmed. Her heart sank. Now that the danger had passed, the enormity of what he planned slammed into her hard.

He'd betrayed her. He'd betrayed them all. But why?

He glanced over his shoulders at the team assembling around them. "Search the grounds. We have to figure out what the hell's happening here."

With their weapons still held in meaty fists, the men turned. Malcolm gestured with one hand, silently giving the orders to disseminate the team.

Dressed in dark clothing, they started to fade into the shadows.

Only to halt in their tracks, when men and women melted from beneath trailing fronds of Spanish moss and stepped from behind thick oak trunks.

They too wore black SWAT gear, but carried crossbows, the

stocks nestled against their shoulders as they took aim on the rogues.

Chessa realized with a start she hadn't even noticed the weapons had been missing from the opposite side of the arms room, she'd been so intent on getting to the rifles. But then, she'd been worried about zombies, not dusting vampires.

Everyone froze. For a long tense second, they stared at each other, and then Nicolas gave a sharp nod and the rogues dropped their weapons to the ground and raised their hands.

Chessa blew out a breath, her heart thudding loudly in her chest. He'd surrendered? Just like that? His expression was shuttered, empty. His gaze raised above the line of the security team as they fanned around them, ringing them.

From above, came the sound of wings cracking like bed-sheets in a stiff wind. Chessa turned to see Inanna and Erika touch down in a pool of moonlight in front of *Ardeal's* security force.

Chessa trembled, her anger at Nicolas's betrayal draining away as a cold knot of fear settled in her stomach.

If hot fury had reflected in Inanna's expression, she would have understood, even been relieved, but the cold tension that tightened the matriarch's expression as she held her lover's gaze, set Chessa's heartbeat pounding faster. *Oh God, she's going to kill him.*

She had to distract Inanna long enough to think of a way to save him. "So, how did you know they were coming?" she blurted into the silence.

Inanna's glance swung toward her, her expression losing a

little of the grim tension. Pasqual walked up behind Inanna with a smirk on his face, and Inanna gave him an approving glance. "Someone sounded the alarm, saying rogues were entering *Ardeal*."

"Good thing Nic and his men were about, " Chessa brazened out. "They followed the zombies here."

"How convenient," Inanna murmured, "that the trap we laid for the zombies caught these men. We left the gates opened and let them come inside." She turned to Nicolas, stepping close to him. "Your force was impressive."

His jaw flexed, but he didn't meet her gaze, keeping it pinned to the distance. "I enjoy my work," he rasped.

Inanna curved a palm around his cheek. A muscle flinched. She gripped his hair and pulled his face toward hers, capturing his glance at last. "I really wish you had trusted me more," she said softly. Over her shoulder, she raised her voice, "Take him to the room."

As members of the team swarmed around Nic, Inanna turned to Chessa, her lashes sweeping downward. A frown wrinkled her smooth forehead.

She stepped closer, her naked chest rising sharply on an indrawn breath.

Chessa lifted her chin, feeling a blanket of suffocating dread settle around her shoulders.

Inanna's hand lifted to touch Chessa's breast, and she squeezed it.

Chessa couldn't help wincing, her nipples were beyond sensitive.

The matriarch's lips curved in a mirthless smile, and her

hand slipped down Chessa's belly. "Interesting," she purred. "You've been a busy girl. Take this one to the room as well."

Chessa supposed she could try to escape, take to the sky, but with so many armed men around her, she wasn't willing to risk the life of the child she carried inside her. With a dull nod to Inanna, she let herself be led toward the house where she'd grown up as lights flickered inside then glowed, beckoning her up the winding iron staircase to the same room Natalie and Rene had been imprisoned the first days of Natalie's season.

The same room she'd observed through television monitors while the man she thought she loved was taken bite by bite by another woman.

And now she was to stay there, but for how long? If Alex was correct, the *sabat* would demand her death. The child she bore would be too much of a threat to the balance of their powers.

The door opened, and her guard gestured for her to step inside. Once in the room, there would be no escape. Iron bars covered the tiny window. Armed guards would remain outside the door for the length of her imprisonment.

Nicolas waited inside. She wished Inanna had given her another room, but likely she didn't want to split the guards further among so many prisoners.

Taking a deep breath to gird herself for the coming confrontation, she entered, flinching at the snick of the lock as it closed behind her.

Her gaze found Nicolas bound to the bed, manacles around his hands and feet, stretched out like a supplicant. *Nude.*

Gone, too, was the quiet surrender he'd worn like a mask

when he'd confronted Inanna. Fury battled in his expression as he shook the chains that draped beyond the edge of the mattress.

For a moment she felt exultant as righteous anger washed over her. This humiliation was no more than he deserved.

And yet somehow, even chained, his power wasn't diminished. His long, lean frame glistened with sweat, strength radiating from the sculpted muscle of his abdomen and arms as he struggled against the manacles. She remembered every time he'd mastered her, every time she'd come screaming, sobbing in his arms.

Just looking at him, filled her with aching longing for what should have been. She would lose again, and this time Nicolas wouldn't be there to draw her back from the sunlight.

"Damn you, Nicolas," she whispered. "Why did you make me love you?"

CHAPTER 17

Nicolas avoided meeting her gaze when she strode into the room. He didn't want to see hatred in her eyes. However, the aching regret in her voice clamped around his chest like a vise.

He stopped fighting the chains and lay back, lifting his gaze to find her eyes glassy with unshed tears, recrimination crimping the corners of her mouth. Fighting for stoicism, he waited to see what more she might say. He needed a clue how she felt about him now. Whether she was willing to fight for him . . . for them. He'd let her talk first, because honestly, he didn't know what he could say that would make her understand how he'd come to be here.

He wasn't sure he understood himself. Maybe he'd had a death wish after outliving nearly everyone he'd ever loved. The longer he'd lived, the strictures of his existence had tightened, smothering him.

Would she understand he'd never truly accepted becoming anyone's minion—not Inanna's, certainly not hers. It had been a poison brewing for a very long time until he'd set into motion plans he couldn't unravel. But he'd hesitated at the last moment when he realized there was something worthwhile enough for him to consider surrendering his pride, his freedom.

And she stood in front of him now with tears in her eyes, looking fragile, brittle—looking ready to rage or cry.

He hoped she'd use rage to battle the hurt he'd done her, because he wasn't in any position to soothe her. If she folded now, he wouldn't be there to draw her back into the shadows.

Her glance seemed to linger over his body, perhaps remembering the loving they'd shared. Unbidden, his cock stirred where it lay curved along his thigh.

"I need a shower," she choked out and headed to the bathroom.

Without a clue what was going through her mind, he closed his eyes, cursing himself. He'd failed her, just as he had Anaïs.

Outside Poitiers, France

Nicolas trod down the dark steps to the room beneath the house where the prisoner lived. He was late, having decided to clear his mind with a ride before dawn on the new horse Inanna had gifted him after he'd finally left his marriage bed.

A black gelding with a fiery temperament. His body ached deliciously. So much time in bed had left him a little soft.

He smiled at the thought of mentioning that to Anaïs. She'd blush adoringly and offer a delicious remedy. How had he lived before having women in his life? How could Armand bear the loneliness and the ache of unquenched desires?

His martyrdom had made him a surly, dour companion of late.

Guilt niggled at Nicolas's conscience that he really ought to have invited him to join him for the ride. They'd seen little of each other, Armand preferring his prayers and the dank cellar beneath the house to the delights enjoyed by the inhabitants above.

In fact, Nicolas hoped to find him here now, to see whether he could tempt him with a game or a walk—anything to get him past the disappointment that darkened his face each time he caught a glimpse of Nicolas with his lovers.

This day, the dungeon seemed particularly gloomy, the air damp and chilled. Inanna called it a dungeon, but there were only three rooms. One for storage for the kitchen, one for the guards to while away the hours of their duty, and the demon's room.

While Nicolas conceded something lived inside the sarcophagus, for he'd heard its scrape for himself, he didn't think too deeply concerning its nature.

Let Armand recite his prayers each time he entered the last room to inspect the seal. Nicolas trusted the heavy stone cover and the thick bands they'd tied around it.

As he entered the guard's room, he hesitated. It was empty.

Thinking the men must be in the last chamber, he lifted a torch from its sconce and walked inside.

His heart froze for second as light flickered over the bodies strewn over the floor. His brother's wasn't among them.

The sarcophagus lid lay across the chest of one of the guards. From the spray of blood that dotted his face the force with which it had been thrown had crushed him. The other man lay slumped against the wall, a huge hole in his upper belly.

A quick glance into the coffin, and his fears were confirmed. The creature they'd imprisoned, tied inside the sarcophagus, fed to keep his body fleshy and whole, had died, swallowing his own vomit. The body lay inside, sightless eyes staring upward. The men littering the floor served as proof of the tale Inanna had told. The demon Devourer had escaped death.

He tossed down the torch, drew his sword and rushed out of the room, down the darkened corridor to the steps, shouting as he sped upward.

Above, the house was already in an uproar. Liveried guards swept into the hall.

"Scour the grounds," he shouted. "He has escaped! Question everyone. Trust no one who's been out of your company. He could be wearing your companion's face."

The sergeant-at-arms quickly turned and shouted more orders, breaking the men into teams to spread out around the estate. Nicolas didn't stay to see to the preparations. His concern now was with his wife whom he'd left sleeping in bed and his brother whom he hadn't seen among the men who'd rushed into the hall.

With his heart at the back of his throat, he ran up the steps to the apartment he shared with Anaïs, his steps slowing as he heard muffled, feminine laughter from beyond the door—and a man's voice, low and straining.

Dread tightening his belly, he pushed open the door. Anaïs gasped beneath Armand and dove beneath the covers, calling out his brother's name.

Something in Nicolas's expression must have registered, for her eyes widened with shock and her gaze sliced toward the man who rolled naked from the opposite side of the mattress.

His brother stood, a small, sly smile curving his lips. "I was only getting a little taste of this freedom you've been enjoying, brother," he murmured.

Nicolas stared, a dawning horror sending a rush of heated rage through his veins. Armand's hair was loosed from its perpetual queue. His expression had lost its pinched, dour displeasure that made his appearance so discernible from his own that no one ever mistook them.

"Haven't you always urged me to enjoy my life?"

"Not with my wife," Nicolas said, his voice taut with fury.

"She's delicious, you know," Armand said, stepping away from the bed. "Why shouldn't we share? We've always been like one, brother."

Nicolas's jaw clamped tight at Anaïs's choking sobs.

Armand's gaze glittered feverishly, excitement reddening his cheeks. "I've seen you together. I've seen all three of you together."

Nicolas continued to stare at his brother's face. He heard the words Armand spoke, but though the voice was the same, he knew it wasn't Armand who uttered them.

His brother, with his unbreakable vow of celibacy, stood with his cock glistening with his wife's fluids. In that moment, Nicolas finally believed the myth of The Devourer, understood the true horror of his nature.

His brother was possessed by a demon.

"Armand?" he asked, his voice shaking. It was his brother's face, but his soul no longer resided in that body.

Anaïs looked at Nicolas and shook her head. "Nico, I thought he was you!" she sobbed. "He bears your face. Smiled your smile. Touched me like you do."

"I don't blame you, Anaïs," he whispered, at last realizing how precarious their situation was. Armand stood between him and his wife. "I don't blame you at all, love. Armand?" He stepped toward him.

Armand smiled, his lips widening, his expression losing its gleeful excitement, becoming cold, sharp-edged. Feral. For a moment his eyes seemed to glow red, then faded.

Anaïs's eyes widened. "It's him!" she cried out. "It's him, isn't it?"

"Come around the bed, wife," Nicolas said, edging closer to Armand. "Get behind me." He held out his hand to her for she seemed rooted on the mattress.

Naked, she slid her back along the wall then slipped from the end of the mattress and scurried behind him and out the opened door.

"She's so lovely. So fragrant," Armand drawled. His hand slid down his belly to caress his slick cock. "Such a generous piece of flesh. She thoroughly enjoyed it, moaned so sweetly when I thrust it into her—"

"Silence!" Nicolas shouted, gripping his sword tight.

Armand gave his cock another slow stroke then let it go. "What will you do? Slay me? You will only free me to find another body." His eyes narrowed. "Shall I take yours? Will your cock please her any better?"

Nicolas hoped Anaïs called for more guards to arrive and help restrain his brother, because he didn't know if he could resist killing the beast who'd stolen Armand's life.

Both he and his brother had transformed, his brother to carry out his duty, he to enjoy this life he'd bargained for. At last his brother had earned his peace.

"Your wife, Anaïs . . . she's very sweet," the creature wearing Armand's face said, sipping on his fingertips. "But will she bear your child . . . or mine?"

Nicolas threw down his sword and lunged for him, ready to tear him limb from limb.

Armand rolled, grasping Nicolas's face, kissing his lips as Nicolas squeezed his hands around his brother's throat.

Only when arms encircled his waist and fingers pulled back on his, did he release his grip and let the guards pull him away.

As they held him from Armand, restraining his arms behind his back, he stared into his brother's face—his twin. He'd failed him. Let him be taken.

While he'd ridden a black gelding—a gift from the woman who had taken his own soul.

Armand smiled, his teeth gleaming brightly, his grin stretching into a wide, savage grin. "Will it be my child or yours?" he repeated then laughed, even as fists pummeled his belly and face.

Nicolas looked away, shrugging off the men who backed up, their glances averted. He strode through the door of the apartment, but didn't find Anaïs hovering outside, waiting for him.

Some inborn instinct led him down the hallway to Inanna's room. At first it appeared empty, and then an odor he recognized all too well assailed his nostrils.

Burned flesh.

Sunlight streamed inside from between curtains that had been thrown apart to reveal the balcony overlooking the garden below. Dawn had broken.

Dread knotting his belly, he forced one foot in front of the other until he stood just beyond the streaming light and looked onto the balcony with its pretty, scrolled iron balustrade. A body laid draped over the rail, long red hair the only part of the scorched remnant of a person to indicate her identity.

Nicolas's breath caught on a sob, and he reached into the light, ignoring the blisters that bubbled on the back of his hand, to snag the long hair and pull Anaïs's body inside. Despite the horror he embraced, he knelt and cuddled her form against his chest, tears leaking down his cheeks.

"Who did this?" he cried out, his voice echoing in the room.

"She did it to herself." Inanna's quiet voice came from the doorway.

"Why?" he asked, his throat thickening.

"She didn't wish to bear the demon's child," she said, tonelessly. "She couldn't risk it. She sacrificed herself for us all."

"I don't believe you."

Inanna's tense expression crumpled and she sped toward

him, falling to her knees beside him to cup his cheeks. "Nico, what do you mean? Do you think I would harm her? She's my *damu*, my granddaughter," she said, tears streaming from her eyes. "And you are my dearest servant. Do you truly think I would cause you pain apurpose?"

Nicolas shook his head, his jaw tightening to hold back a sob, yet unwilling to believe his Anaïs, his impish sprite, was gone. That she'd destroyed herself.

She'd been alone while he wrestled with a demon. He'd spent his anger on Armand's killer while his wife stepped into sunlight. His tears spilled faster.

"Focus your anger on the one responsible for this tragedy, Nico," Inanna said, her voice growing harsh and urgent. "It is him, The Devourer, who has robbed you of your wife and your child! Stay with me. Guard him. Make him suffer for an eternity for what he has taken."

Nicolas closed his eyes and pulled his face from her hands. He pressed a kiss to his wife's hair and settled her body on the ground.

He let Inanna lead him from the room, down the hall-way past the silent retainers who quickly filed into the room behind them. Inanna took him into another chamber, stripped his clothes from body, and bathed him while he stood silently, woodenly aloof. When she'd finished, she led him to the bed and pulled a blanket over his naked body.

Nicolas closed his eyes, wanting to sleep forever.

The bed dipped beside him and Inanna came over him.

He murmured and reached out to push her away, but she stretched over him, warming his chilled flesh.

He must have slept for a while, because he woke to find her deep beneath the covers, her warm breath and lips kissing his belly. His cock was already rigid, swollen, his balls filled with urgent, painful need.

Inanna's hands enclosed his shaft, and she worked the skin clothing his cock, up and down, up and down, relentlessly, robbing him of his mind and his grief.

Awash in sensation, he closed out the memories, concentrating instead on the needs of his flesh and sex. He widened his legs, raising his knees to flatten his feet on the mattress and push deep into her throat. With her approving murmurs vibrating along his length, he let the pressure in his balls explode, spilling his seed into her throat as her swallows caressed the tip of him with her greedy gulps.

Long after he'd spent himself, he stopped pumping into her mouth and waited for her to come off his cock. When she slid up his body, he enfolded her in his arms, letting her fill a small portion of the deep, endless void of his immortal life that stretched before him.

"Did you speak with her before she died?" he rasped.

"Sleep, darling," she whispered, but her heart thudded heavily against his chest.

So she had. Nicolas wondered silently whether she'd tried to dissuade Anaïs from her course or had told her what she must do. He didn't want to know the answer. They never spoke of it again.

That day, he'd finally become The Guardian to The Devourer.

His resolve had hardened to ensure the monster who'd

taken his family from him would remain in his dark, cramped prison forever.

There Nicolas had stayed—with Inanna. Until he'd met a girl with suspicion shadowing her dark eyes, a chin that tilted toward the sky, and a heart as fierce and loyal as any knight's.

Chessa stood beneath the shower for a long time, letting the stinging pulses of water wash away zombie gore and her tears. She stayed there long enough her toes and fingers pruned.

Only then did she turn off the water and reach for a towel. Only then did she let her thoughts drift back to the *Revenant* tied to the bed in the other room.

Her anger fading, she could finally think, finally try to make sense of everything that had happened.

She knew Nicolas. Deep inside, past all the secrets and the memories of a life they never shared, she knew him. He was, at his core, an honorable man. If he'd enlisted rogue *Revenants* to attack the compound, he must have a powerful motive.

He'd risked his immortality for it. Risked his life with her—and deep inside, she knew she mattered to him. Knew he might even love her.

That didn't change the fact he'd landed them both in deep shit. She wished she could hold onto her anger. Sarcasm and fury were her favorite weapons, and she needed them now to protect what little pride she had left.

Instead, she wanted to go to him. To slip into bed beside him and love him for whatever time they had left. Damn the tiny cameras hidden around the room.

In the end, lust and want—and the need to hold him one last time—won out. She straightened her shoulders and strolled naked into the bedroom.

Nicolas's gaze swung toward her and his eyes widened. "Thinking of adding a little torture to my misery, Princess?"

She almost smiled. The man had guts. Just one of the many qualities she admired about him. "I'm just thinking I'm horny as hell and hungry. Never did get that meal you promised."

"I know how you like it, *ma petite*, but sadly, my hands aren't free to give you what you need."

Her gaze fell to his cock, which was perking up, lengthening along his thigh as it filled. Chessa strode to the bed, stepped onto the mattress and placed her hands on her hips. "Maybe," she said, dipping her toes between his legs to nudge his balls, "I like playing a little rough, too."

His gaze narrowed, his nostrils flaring as he caught her ripening scent. "Have you forgotten the cameras?"

"Do you care?" she asked, sliding her foot over his cock.

One dark brow rose. "Not really." His lips curved slightly.

"For a man trussed up like a turkey, you look awfully relaxed," she said, then dipped her gaze to examine his cock, "Well at least most of you."

His hips undulated, sliding beneath her foot to stroke her sole. His expression sharpened. "Unless you intend to kick my balls up my throat, don't you think you should . . . take a seat?"

"I'm still thinking," she drawled. But who was she kidding? Her arousal wafted in the air like a damn plug-in air freshener. She knelt over his hips, pressing his cock to his belly. Then she leaned down with an elbow planted on his chest and rested her chin in her palm. "So, I'm still wondering what you would have done had the coven been in residence when you arrived."

"Interrupted dinner," he drawled, his easy tone at war with his darkening expression.

She teased a flat nipple into a tiny bead with her fingernail, giving her an excuse not to hold his knowing gaze. "Would you have hurt her?" she whispered.

"Never," he said softly.

"I don't understand your relationship with her. How you can want me. How you can resist doing her will."

His chest rose, his gaze grew shuttered. He wouldn't discuss the woman who'd turned him. "*Ma chérie*, you act as though we have all the time in the world. Know something I don't?"

"You're right. I'm wasting time." She lunged for his mouth, sliding her lips over his, moaning when his tongue thrust deep into her mouth. She tucked a hand between their straining bodies and lifted slightly, just enough to grip his cock and push it where she needed it. Right into her cunt.

She broke the kiss and stared at him as she took him inside her body, already trembling, already rippling around him with delicious little shivering shocks that had her bouncing on his cock to keep them coming.

Pressing her hands against his chest she curved her back upward and rolled her hips to circle on his cock while she drove down harder.

His teeth ground together and his eyelids closed and opened. "If I were free, I'd make you come screaming in seconds, love."

"Tell me. Tell me, how you'd touch me," she moaned.

"I'd pinch your nipples and slide a hand down to cup your ass. Give you a swat to get you moving faster."

A snort of laughter surprised her and she bit her lip, but ground down harder.

"I'd slide my fingers into the cleft between your buttocks and tickle your sweet little asshole."

"*Oh God*, shut up," she said, afraid she wouldn't be able to hold it together for another moment longer.

"I'd press inside, circle, *Dieu!* Just like that," he groaned as she circled her hips again and bounced. "Then I'd buck beneath you, driving my cock so deep I'd spoil you for any other man. Fill you up with my cock and my seed—"

"*Jesus, I mean it. Shut up*," she said, leaning down to take his mouth again because she was coming and he wasn't and she'd wanted to wait, to take him along, but her body was shuddering, convulsions shimmering along her vagina, milking his cock for his release.

When she slowed her movements, he laughed. A soft, husky sound that stirred the hair at her temple.

She pressed a kiss to his chest and buried her nose against his skin, breathing him in. Loving the almond and musk scent of him, wanting that to be the thing she thought of at the last moment. That and how perfect it felt to be connected with him, body and soul.

"I love you," she whispered.

"And I you."

"About damn time," a low voice said from above them.

Chessa jerked up to find Pasqual standing over them, a crooked grin on his face.

"Bastard!" Nicolas gritted out, shaking his chains.

"Wait a second," Pasqual said, sweeping his hand in front of him. Before he'd finished, Pasqual's coarse dark looks melted into Simon's familiar, rugged face. "Better."

"Not much," Nicolas said, his voice evening.

Chessa grimaced and knelt up to let Nicolas's cock slide from inside her, then she rolled to the side of the bed to stand. Although standing in the nude was only slightly less embarrassing than being found sitting on a man's cock. "Why am I not surprised to see you here, Simon? You already know what's going to happen. Want to clue us in?"

"Since I'm here, I've already changed the future. I can't guarantee the outcome." He shrugged. "I'm sorry."

"Then what are you doing here?"

"I'm here to offer a warning."

"Too late," Chessa bit out. "We're already up to our necks in trouble."

"When she calls you before her," Simon said, his face hardening, "try for subdued apology. Don't force her to deal harshly with you."

Chessa snorted. "Force her? She's the one holding all the cards here—a straight goddamn flush."

"Let him speak, Chessa," Nicolas said, before turning his gaze to Simon. "Should you be saying this with the team monitoring us from the next room?"

Simon waggled his dark eyebrows. "I played a little with

the feed. They will see Chessa here writhing on your cock for another few minutes. Since it's Erika and Sergio watching, my guess is we'll have a few minutes more while they decide to try out a few of Chessa's moves."

Chessa scowled at the smirking smiles the two men shared. "I still don't know what being quiet will buy us."

"Give her a chance to be the winner here, Chessa," Simon said, his voice holding a warning.

"She doesn't care about saving face," Nicolas said.

"No, and it's not about her pride or your betrayal. She'll be worried about how the *sabat* will read her actions." His grin faded. "You're not safe. Not yet. But there is hope. Now, Chessa, climb back on Nicolas while I let myself out."

Chessa sighed and crawled back onto the mattress, assuming the position she'd held a few minutes earlier.

Not until the door closed quietly, did she relax.

"You're blushing."

"Am not," she bit out, feeling the heat deepen on her cheeks.

"You can't take it back."

"Take what back?" Although she already knew. "So maybe this isn't the last night of our lives."

"Thinking you were a little rash?"

Finally, she met his gaze. "It needed to be said."

"I meant it too," he said, his gaze softening.

She melted against his chest and leaned down to kiss his mouth. When she'd thoroughly plundered his lips, she lifted her head and arched one eyebrow. "Such a shame you didn't come when you had the chance."

"I was being a gentleman," he growled.

"Think I'm a lady?" She snuggled her pussy onto his cock, rocking to let it slide between her slick folds—a slow, sexy tease.

"I think you're ready for a second round, *ma chérie*."

"Damn straight," she said, her breath catching as she eased back down his cock. "But I'm thinking you've never felt what I feel when I'm completely at your mercy."

His eyes gleamed with wicked humor as his chest rose, his hands clasping the chains attached to his manacles. "Do your worst."

CHAPTER

18

When the summons came, Nicolas felt relief. His fate, whatever it might be, would be set in the next hour. He only hoped he could convince Inanna to spare Chessa.

Clothed, his body deliciously relaxed after Chessa's impassioned loving, he rubbed his raw wrists as he was led to the salon where Inanna awaited them, flanked by Pasqual and Sergio, her favorites among her minions now that he'd fallen from grace.

Inanna's hard gaze skimmed over him to rest on Chessa. "It's too much of a coincidence that the arrival of a daywalker and your current state aren't somehow connected. I don't suppose you'll explain?"

Chessa's jaw clamped.

Nicolas sighed. Chessa would never reveal Alex's identity. Inanna might know what he was, but she wouldn't know exactly who he was until Alex was ready to emerge. He hoped Chessa's resistance wouldn't seal her fate.

Inanna's lips curled in a small strained smile that didn't reach her eyes. "I didn't think you would. I have the feeling, stubborn Chessa, that the more I demand, the more determined to remain silent you will become."

Chessa lifted her chin. "So what are you going to do with us?"

Inanna took a deep breath and glanced away. When she reached for the goblet of wine on the side table, her hand shook.

For the first time, Inanna revealed before an audience a chink in her armor. She'd always held herself aloof, using sly amusement or an intimidating hauteur to maintain a distance.

Now, he understood why she felt the need. Having lived so long, she had to have experienced loss, time and again. Once she'd been a doting grandmother to a motherless child. Chessa likely assumed she'd only done it to cement their bond. Another weapon in Inanna's immense arsenal.

Inanna sipped her wine, and then set it aside, finally raising her head to level a cold stare on Chessa. "The *sabat* will demand your death This is too big a secret to keep for long."

Chessa lifted her gaze beyond Inanna, her deep indrawn breath and the rigid set of her shoulders indicating she was already resigning herself to die.

Then Inanna turned to Nicolas. "You, with your band of rogues, was this just a show of power or did you intend to take me?"

Nicolas met her glare with a steady gaze. "I would never have done you harm."

The corners of her lips lifted in a slight smile. "I believe you, but you have betrayed me." She drew a deep breath and strummed her fingers on the arm of her chair. "You've made things very . . . complicated. What am I to do with you?"

"Banishment for Chessa?" Nicolas suggested.

Her eyes narrowed. "Nothing for yourself?" she asked evenly, each word distinct and cutting.

"I'd take her place. Accept her fate."

"You love her so much?"

Nicolas's throat closed around a thickness that threatened to choke him. He gave a sharp nod in response.

Chessa closed her eyes, swallowing.

"Your men have all been questioned. They have the same story. A show of force. No harm." She relaxed against the back of her chair, her shoulders softening, her expression pinched. "They fought well. I did notice that fact, before I gave the signal to surround them. I should kill you both. Now. But the truth is I have need of your men . . . and of you."

Her eyes closed for a moment, before she lifted her chin and pinned him with a glare. "I don't know of any other way to assure your loyalty than to hold her. Keep her here. So, hold and keep her, I will."

Nicolas's chest rose, his mind spinning. A reprieve for them both? Would Chessa balk at the restriction? And she'd said nothing of what would happen to the child.

"The demon is still loose, and I've been warned there are darker portents. I have need of your force, but they follow you.

You wanted a seat on the council. You shall have it. Perhaps you can sway them concerning Chessa's fate, and that of her child's when it is born. For now, for her protection, she must remain here."

Nicolas nodded, and he flashed Chessa a warning glance. For a long charged moment, her gaze flashed with angry, bitter defeat.

He couldn't help but be happy with the outcome. She'd just have to get over it. He reached out his hand to her, trying to tell her silently they were in this together, whatever the future held.

Chessa's jaw flexed as she ground together her teeth, but she placed her hand inside his. They clasped their fingers tightly, as they turned to face the woman who'd given them a second chance.

"Go now. I don't want to look at either of you."

Nicolas wasted no time and tugged Chessa along, knowing by her wooden steps she wanted to say more. He squeezed her hand. *Later.* They had time now to think of a way out of their bonds.

As the door closed behind the couple, Inanna relaxed the grip she'd had on the arm of her chair when she'd rendered her decision. She couldn't quite believe she'd done that. Given them a reprieve, when an hour ago she'd wanted to rip Nicolas's throat open, tear him apart and feed him to the dogs she'd kenneled when the zombies started pouring through the gate. When Pasqual had whispered of Nicolas's plot in her ears, she'd screamed, vowing to kill him with her own hands.

She'd loved him. In her own fashion.

Trusted him, as much as she could any man, any *Revenant*. Hadn't he understood the privilege she'd given him from the very start? His handsome body had called to her when she first gazed on him in the dark, filthy prison. She'd seen the pride that canted his chin, the sardonic humor in the lift of his dark brows. She'd guessed correctly just how beautifully he'd fatten up once he'd been freed.

His devotion after she'd saved him had made him the perfect pet. He'd never failed to see to her pleasure, fucked her with the strength and burning focus that made her come outside herself, forget she was the Born, the one who should rule.

When sweet Anaïs had died, he'd let her turn his grief to determination. The harder edges of his personality that had emerged in his grim pursuit of duty had gratified her, excited her. She'd used his anger and his hunger for control to her benefit.

She'd never known such a lover. She'd never give him up.

But what could she do with Chessa? If she died, so would Nicolas. His mind was set to sacrifice himself for her. Well, she would use that. The softer feelings she'd begun to experience, she'd shove ruthlessly behind her.

She wanted sex with him. Hard, painful release. She'd have it—even if she had to share his favors. And maybe, she'd enjoy seeing the pain she caused the couple as she came between them.

Liquid heat flooded her cunt, and she looked up at Pasqual. "You have served me well."

His expression was warm, adoring. He'd given her loyalty

above his commander. She had need of that kind of loyalty. Especially now. "Come. I wish to rest."

"Rest, mistress?" he drawled, his face tightening with ardor as he realized she had honored him with her choice of paramour this night.

She gave him a small, sly smile, relieved to have a reason to put Nico and his new love to the back of her mind. "Well, perhaps we'll rest after a while."

Pasqual's body was pleasingly strong and virile. She wondered how he might behave if she gave him certain freedoms when they were alone in her chamber. "I'm hungry."

"That's what this was all about?" Chessa shouted, her hands fisted on her hips. "A seat on the bloody goddamned *sabat*? You wanted to be on the council?"

Nicolas crossed his arms across his chest and leaned back against the bedroom door. Chessa in a snit provided a fabulous show. Her cheeks were reddened, her eyes sparkling with fire—rather like she looked when he spanked her. "You had a seat you refused," he said quietly. "A voice, if you'd cared to use it."

"I can still use my vote! And don't think it won't cross my mind to recommend they sit you naked in the sunshine!"

His palms itched to feel the smooth, soft flesh of her bottom. He wondered how quickly he could strip her of the clothing they'd been provided for the summons. "You want me naked?" he drawled.

Her eyebrows snapped together. "I don't want you at all!" When he straightened from the door, she retreated a step, then stopped, her expression growing even more mulish. "Don't you come near me!"

"It's an awfully small room. Do you really think you can escape?"

Her gaze slid to the bathroom door, and she darted toward it, clearing the doorframe before his arm encircled her waist and drew her back.

"Seems I'm always pulling you back from disaster," he said, shifting his arm upward to clasp her breasts.

The tips beaded against his forearm. "How's going to the bathroom a disaster?" she said, jerking against his hold.

"You'd miss what comes next."

"I've seen what comes next, and, buster, it ain't so great!"

"Liar," he whispered into her ear.

The shiver that shook her shoulders had him smiling in triumph. Her anger was so easy to deflect. Did she even know that when it came to him, she was all bluster? She wanted to be conquered, wanted him to overpower her and remove any choices.

Because he knew exactly what was best for her. He told her so.

"You're so fucking arrogant. You think you know what's best for me?"

"Of course," he said cheerfully, dragging her toward the bed. "I've made a study of you. Chessa 101. Want to know how the lesson starts?"

She dug in her heels, but skidded as he pulled harder. "Hell no. I just want you to let me go and stick to your side of the room."

"No you don't. You want me to rip off your clothes. One piece at a time."

"No, I don't. I won't have anything left to wear."

"Then you want me to place the manacles at the end of the bed around your wrists and your ankles."

"Wrong again. I'm fine with clamping one tight around your cock to make sure it never comes anywhere near me again."

"Then you want me to lick and suck every inch of your body, until your arousal forms a puddle under your ass."

She huffed. "That just sounds nasty."

His palm cupped her breast, his thumb sliding over the thin material of her blouse to tease the nipple into a tight point. "But that's how you like it, don't you?" he purred.

Her head fell back against his chest. "I really wish you wouldn't ask."

"So you can pretend you're not agreeing?" He tongued the bottom of her ear lobe, conveniently offered when her head leaned to the side.

"It's embarrassing—the things I want you to do to me."

"Then fight me."

"I already did, and see where I am?"

He slowly unwound his arms. "Anywhere but the bathroom," he said with a quick kiss on her cheek. "I really don't want to splinter the door."

Chessa giggled and darted away again, leaping onto the bed and then to the other side, to stand with her legs braced apart, her hands fisted in front of her.

Nicolas grinned. "Think you can take me?"

"I know I can. I'm Born, remember?"

He unbuttoned his borrowed shirt and shrugged it off his shoulders. Then he unzipped his pants, toed off his boots, and pushed away all his clothing.

"Afraid I'll shred your clothes?"

"No, I'm getting ready for you to take me."

"Dammit, Nic, you're making me mad all over again," she said, dropping her arms and stomping over to him. When she was within arm's length from him, he clamped a hand on her shoulder, spun her backward and tossed her onto the mattress.

Faster than she could spit out a curse, he'd pinned her with a knee in the middle of her back and clamped first one, then the other cuff around her wrist.

"I don't believe I fell for that."

"What can I say? You couldn't resist me once you saw how hard I am."

"That was it, all right," she said, her tone dry. "You know, we're not going to have nearly as much fun with me facedown on the mattress."

"Maybe you won't," he said, skimming her rump with his hand, "but I will."

Her short gasp was followed by the steady increase in her heartbeat. The scent of her womanly musk deepened, tugging at his cock.

"You know, smart ass, you really should have done something about these clothes before you locked my arms in the cuffs."

He grabbed the neck of her blouse and ripped it, tugging

the fabric from beneath her and dangling it in front of her face. Then he pulled at the waistband of her pants until the button popped and drew them down her legs.

She kicked at him, cursing and twisting, making a great show of how much she didn't want what would happen next. He straddled her naked bottom, pressing his cock into the crease, and then leaned slowly over her back to snag the pillows that had bunched at the top of the mattress.

He dragged them slowly over her head and down her back, then moved to the side to snake an arm around her waist and lift her.

The pillows under her belly were a nice touch. Her bottom was raised, and with her attempt for leverage forcing her knees wider to dig into the mattress, he had an excellent view of all the places he intended to plunder.

Question was did he want to start with his tongue and fingers or go with his cock? He decided to ask her preference.

When she'd finished cursing him and telling him exactly where he could "stick his dick," he pulled back his hand and swatted her square on her glistening cunt.

"Oh God, I really, really hate you."

"Of course, you don't." He slapped her pussy again, gratified when his palm came away coated with her juices.

Chessa moaned and buried her face in the bedding, murmuring curses.

"I didn't hear that."

Her response was to slowly inch her knees up and outward, widening her stance and lifting her bottom higher.

An invitation he wasn't about to refuse. He bent close and

buried face against her moist flesh, swirling the whiskers sprouting in his cheeks and chin into her sensitive folds.

"Oh God, Nic," she gasped.

When his lips and tongue found the little kernel peeking from beneath its pink hood, he suckled her, earning a deep groan and a tremble that shook her frame.

He palmed her cheeks and squeezed, parting her and licking her clit to asshole again and again, until she dipped and lifted to follow the motion.

"Fuck me, please," she whispered. "Just fuck me."

His tongue stroked into her center, lapping at her inner walls, taking the cream she spilled from her depths. His erection was painful, rigid as steel, and he couldn't hold back a moment longer before feeling her moist channel close around him.

He came up on his knees, gasping as he closed his fist around his cock and fitted it snug at her opening. Gripping her cheeks hard he slammed forward, entering her in one steady, strong stroke, burying himself to his balls before he relented and pulled away, then stroking just as deep and hard again.

Over and over he thrust into her, reveling in the wet heat that surrounded him, clasped around him, finally convulsing and squeezing him until he couldn't hold back his release a moment longer.

Cum jetted toward her womb, bathing her in sticky, liquid pleasure while they both gasped and moaned and moved against each other, milking the moment for every last pulse of pleasure.

When he could breathe again, he pulled out of her, came

down on the mattress beside her, leaning close to capture her lips in a deep, stroking kiss.

She pulled back her head. "You know, I could hug you if you unlocked these cuffs."

He shrugged his shoulders. "I don't have a key."

A pout plumped her lips. "Well, now we're really in a pickle. Kinda limits our options."

"Think so?" He swept an arm underneath her and scooted sideways, pushing aside the pillows and slipping beneath her body. When he'd settled directly beneath her, he gave her a crooked smile. He liked the way her breasts flattened against his chest with her arms pulled up and out. His cock was smashed between her thigh and his belly, and the pressure was quickly growing uncomfortable as he filled again. "This position offers all kinds of interesting possibilities, don't you think?"

She wrinkled her nose. "When I get free, I really am going to kill you."

"Think you can wiggle a little to the left," he said, ignoring her comment.

She frowned, but did as he said until his cock slipped between her legs, the head cramming against her folds. "So, now what are you going to do? We're both trapped," she said, slipping her knees to his sides and squeezing tight.

"I'm exactly where I want to be," he said softly. He brought up his hands cupping the back of her head to force her down for a kiss. With her lips hovering over his, he said, "I do love you."

A blush stole over her cheeks, but her soft smile said how

pleased she was with his words. She wiggled her hips and the tip of his cock slipped inside her. "I could stay like this forever," she whispered, then dipped her head to seal their lips together.

Surrounded by her scent and her slim form, Nicolas breathed deeply. Whatever challenges the future brought, he'd make damn sure Chessa stayed safe and never again had reason to doubt him. He'd saved her for himself long ago, and he'd never let her go.

"Is it over?" Byron asked, glancing beneath the tarp in the back of the pickup Alex had parked in the station house's garage. Bernie's cold, waxy body lay beside the wheel well.

"Well, he's not in the city anymore." And now, they were the only ones who knew The Devourer had jumped hosts. Alex had secreted the body away from the compound while the security force had closed in on Nicolas's band of *Revenants*. He'd have to let Simon know to warn the occupants at the compound.

Byron blew out a breath. "At least it's one less problem we have to deal with here. I'll get someone down here to pick him up. Damn shame. He was a good officer." His gaze swung back to Alex. "What about Chessa? She not come back with you?"

Alex let the tarp drop and headed toward the station house entrance, Byron's footsteps treading heavily behind him. "She's not going to be back for a while. I'm sure she'll give you a call once she's able."

Byron drew alongside him and gave him a searching look. "That's all you're gonna tell me?"

Alex gave him a tight-lipped smile and opened the door into the busy station house. The din of life—voices calling out to each other, laughter, heated conversations, curses—welcomed Alex as he headed up the steps to the second floor offices and his cubicle. He hesitated when he passed a soldier in camouflage.

"Yeah, get used to it," Byron said. "We need all the help we can get. Those mean streets are gettin' meaner by the minute."

"That's why I'm here," Alex muttered, dropping the truck keys on his desk and reaching into a drawer for the Beamer's keys. Unbidden, he drew a deep breath, inhaling Chessa's scent, which permeated the cubicle. He was going to miss her, but he'd known all along she wasn't for him.

Natalie had wanted Chessa's grief redirected—he'd accomplished that—and so much more. Now if he could only stay alive long enough to take care of one or two more loose ends.

He picked up a report from the desk, idly scanning the contents—a pack of large, wild dogs had been seen roaming the alleyways. Wolves, one witness has said. The cop taking the report had indeed found large paw prints in the muck.

"You've got cases stackin' up," Byron drawled behind him. "Reba's been busy."

Alex snorted and laid the paper on top of the rising stack. Perhaps he'd check it out himself. If the visual wasn't helpful, his sense of smell might unravel one more tangle in the web of intrigue deepening around New Orleans.

He touched the medallion at his throat. Chessa and the baby weren't safe—and for once, Inanna was the least of his worries. The wily bitch was probably trying to figure out a way to make it all work out to her advantage.

Now, they had to worry about the *sabat* descending upon them and finding the Hell-beast her machinations had unleashed.

"Cuttin' it kinda close aren't you?" Byron asked, his hands stuffed deep into his pockets. "S'posed to be a sunny day."

"About damn time," Alex said, suppressing a grin. Byron thought he had it all figured out. "I'll get right on this," he said tapping the stack of paperwork, "as soon as I get some shut-eye."

With a determined step, he strode back the way he'd come.

"You sure you don't want one of my guys to take you home?" Byron called after him. "Drive you out of the garage?"

Alex shot him a grin over his shoulder. "I'll be fine," he said, lifting a hand to wave.

Moments later, he stepped out onto the pavement. Dawn crept slowly along the sidewalk, drawing the moisture clinging to the ground into the heated air in a swirl of steaming, glistening mist.

One storm had passed, but another, far more dangerous one, followed in its wake. With Nicolas and Chessa on the inside and Simon riding shotgun, maybe they had chance.

The Devourer gloated. Things couldn't have worked out any better. The van load of bodies he'd stolen from the morgue while Chessa fought the dead already raised, had been a stroke of genius.

A little powder, a rising moon, and he'd created another diversion tonight.

Leaving Bernie's body slumped over an iron spike on the compound fence had been an inspired touch. In the morning, when they gathered the bodies to dispose of them, perhaps he'd be recognized. Then Inanna would know he'd reached the estate. She'd quiver in fear at the thought he could be anyone.

He could be anywhere.

Even so close he could smell her growing arousal.

She turned and slowly drew open the ties at the front of her robe, letting it puddle on the floor at her feet. Her glorious body, tawny and lithe as a cat's, glowed in the lamplight. She glanced at him over her shoulder, biting her lip.

"How can I please you, mistress," he asked, although . . . he knew.

"I would have you take me," she whispered.

As he closed in on her, he suppressed the glee tugging at his lips, tamped down the excitement that even now filled his borrowed cock.

He'd make love to her, punishing her sweet form, wallowing in her tight cunt until he'd had his fill, renewing their old acquaintance— while he plotted her death and the destruction of all those who shared her lineage.

His hands reached around to palm and squeeze her breasts, then slid lower over the bottom of her rib cage. There, where it was softest, where bone didn't deflect a powerful thrust. Soon . . . he'd feast on her heart.

For now, he'd enjoy the widening of her eyes as he showed her how well he remembered her peculiar tastes. How well he knew the dark lusts that ruled her.

DELILAH DEVLIN resides in South Texas at the intersection of two dry creeks, surrounded by sexy cowboys in Wranglers—she likes living dangerously! To Delilah, the greatest sin is driving between the lines because it's comfortable and safe. Her personal journey has taken her through one war, many countries, cultures, jobs, and relationships to bring her to the place she travels now—writing sexy adventures that hold more than a kernel of autobiography and often share a common thread of self-discovery and transformation. To learn more about Delilah Devlin, visit *www.delilahdevlin*.com.